THE PAINTER OF SOULS

We can reasonably expect that the secrets we have held close – the skeletons in our cupboard, so to speak - will die with us. Secrets that could destroy our reputation. Condemn us after our passing when we can no longer explain or justify ourselves. But why would anyone begin to dust down the handles, oil the lock and turn the key to open up that cupboard when we have gone?

But what should happen if that cupboard broke open unexpectedly and the contents spilled for all to see? If you were a child genius, one of the greatest painters of your generation, an artist who had sought and found the very essence of his human subjects, what secrets could possibly tumble out?

Perhaps all it takes is an earth tremor to loosen the cupboard door.

THE PAINTER OF SOULS

By Neil Fieldhouse

Neil Fieldhouse is an award winning journalist. His previous book Silent Night was highly acclaimed. He also contributed to short story collection Grit featuring the work of Northern writers.

Copyright Neil Fieldhouse 2019

FOR JACOB AND SAMUEL

For over two hundred years the phrase 'skeletons in the cupboard' has been used to describe someone's secrets which, if revealed, would harm and perhaps destroy their reputation.

Apparently, we all have them.

CHAPTER 1

THE first tremor shook Scotland's icy south west coastal area of Dumfries and Galloway in the silent, moonlit early hours of winter. Bone-chilling winter. An area of outstanding natural beauty jutting out across the Irish Sea towards its Gaelic brother Ireland. Rugged sea cliffs towered over storm-swept beaches. Dark forests lay still and silent beneath brooding hills, snow-capped this shivering winter. A narrow, twisting path, silver in the faint moonlight, snaked across forlorn uplands to the Devil's Beef Tub - a vast bowl scooped deep into the brown landscape, overlooked by the massive, frozen Annandale and its neighbouring hills. River valleys, heavy with skeletal black trees that would be lush again in the far off spring, gripped iced-over streams.

To be precise: 2.18am, January 22 and registering 4.2 on the Richter scale. A gentle tremor, according to scientists later quoted extensively in the media, but strong enough to wake some residents in ancient Kirkcudbright on the banks of the River Dee which ebbed and flowed through the town before swelling into the broad Solway Firth and from there dissolving into the Irish Sea.

Puzzled and befuddled by sleep, people groped in the cold darkness for bedside lights, shook partners awake. "What was that?"

Over the next half hour, the part-timers from the local fire brigade - shopkeepers, plumbers, electricians - called in to their central control. Was it an explosion? Were they needed? No. Apparently there had been a small and highly unusual earthquake. No need to panic. No immediate reports of damage, but they should remain on stand-by at home. Just in case.

One, John Mahoney, who had left the warmth of his marital bed to quieten their dog in the chilled kitchen, decided, as a precaution he told his wife, to walk down to the fire station; a squat, unremarkable brick building on St Mary Street, with a single fire engine, and at the rear a training tower that would later collapse. The night time street, flanked by grey stone Victorian houses and shops, part of the A711 scenic tourist route winding out from Dumfries along the Dee, was deserted and lit only by the shadowy orange glow of street lights and fleeting appearances of a half moon. To be expected at such an early winter hour. For the moment.

Twenty minutes later, with silver edged clouds now shrouding the moon and as many men, women and children settled into a deeper sleep, a second quake measuring 5.2 and centred out in the velvet dark waters of the Firth struck the area. A shock wave rumbled out, north across the inky darkness and hit the coast. Seconds later a large wave followed, a metre high, pushing back the Dee where it entered the Firth, sending the swollen river crashing over its banks through gardens and fields.

Kirkcudbright fishing boats, moored by the river bridge, slammed into each other, wood splintered. Some were lifted high enough to come to rest on their sides in the adjacent car park. Smaller dinghies capsized. Two white vans parked overnight floated away into a nearby field.

In the Firth, night fisherman John Douglas, father of three, unsteady as rocks moved beneath him, his head torch flashing wildly into the darkness, struggled to re-gain his balance, fell and was swept off into the freezing waters where he succumbed to the numbing cold and drowned. The only fatality, he was later found washed up on mud flats, remarkably his head torch still working, though faded.

Those in Kirkcudbright still awake screamed, the few bedroom lights still on flickered, windows cracked like a gun firing and ornaments and televisions toppled. People clung to their beds.

Fireman Mahoney, who had been marvelling at the absolute thick silence as he strolled to the station, taking in the brilliant stars and cold half-moon that appeared now and then amid fleeting clouds, almost fell over as the ground swelled and shifted. He grabbed at a lamppost and would later swear he had seen the spire on the nearby church lean so far it should have toppled. This was like being drunk.

Earlier in the fading evening light, and heavily wrapped against the clinging cold, he had taken his Border Collie Whisky for a walk, before the first tremor, and had been startled when a sudden mass of screaming seagulls had powered out of the darkening sky, a blinding white mass of noise. His dog had barked furiously and refused to quiet. He thought he could hear other smaller birds all heading out to sea, but the dog was spooked and going mad. Odd. He had wondered why. Once back home the dog had refused to settle, but prowled from kitchen to sitting room and back again. And again.

In nearby Hornel Street, a neat line of colour-washed terraced houses, alternating white, blue, pink, whose back gardens ran down to the river bank and whose lawns and flower beds were now swamped by the swirling water and its cargo of junk, people jumped from their beds, grabbed dressing gowns and hurried out into the hushed, freezing night. Clouds clearing. Stars brilliant. Moon a hard silver. Some barefoot. All numbed, stunned. Pulling thin clothes close.

They stood, shivering arms crossed tight, on the pavement, orange street lights jabbing on, off, calling to neighbours: "Did you feel that?"

The ominous silence suddenly broken by dogs howling. A car alarm started some way off. Suddenly, a thunderous crash like a bomb exploding. A burglar alarm joined the dogs. Two miles beneath their feet the earth was shifting. A mild 2.3. The ground like rubber. A shout 'get into the road' and the residents of Hornel Street ran to the centre of their narrow street. Children pushed. Hands held. Couples embraced. Children, sobbing, gathered close. Feet spread, braced, ready. Street lights failed. Only the moonlight, shifting beyond thin clouds. Freezing people frozen into the thick night.

A young man ran from the far end of the street, mobile phone to his face, shouting:

The Painter Of Souls

"There's been a collapse. House down."

People turned to him. Alarmed. Braced for more, not moving. But that was it. The earth had settled. Six miles away at the epicentre in the Firth it was as though nothing had happened. The swell of waves had sunk to a gentle sluggishness. The surge which minutes ago had pushed remorselessly up the River Dee, petered out and the water settled, sluggish with the cold, dropped away from the gardens, leaving a debris of toppled trees, silt and a weather beaten settee in Mrs MacLeod's garden. Mr Colquhoun's shed was found a mile up river from Hornel Street, intact: forks, spade, lawnmower, compost bags, tools, all undisturbed. His wife said it was neater than when he'd left it.

The young man had raced past them and into the darkened side street towards the fire station. For long minutes they stood, not daring, not able, to move. Confused.

Suddenly an emergency siren cut through the barking dogs and jarring alarms, startling the residents to their senses. A fire engine, blue lights strobing the darkness, still picking up speed heaved round the corner, headlights sweeping yellow across groups of people, young and old, hurrying out of the way. John Mahoney stamped on the brake, held the swaying engine firm as it slewed to a halt only fee from the residents. Orange street lights flared, failed again and the only light came from the cold moon and the fire engine's blue emergency lights strobing the street and buildings and its headlights yellow beams. A fireman leaned from the cab. Someone else killed the siren.

"We've reports of a house down." His breath clouded grey in the blue light.

"Further along, at the end." People pointed, some began to move that way.

The fire engine edged slowly forward, people parted, fell in behind. The silent procession inched along the street and finally arrived at the last of the long terraces. The fire engine, although crawling, hissed and bounced to a halt. The crew, some struggling into their uniforms, jumped down. Doors slammed. Powerful torches sliced the night and showed the ruined end of the last house. The chimney stack had toppled, tearing away parts of the roof and the gable wall. Joists stuck out like broken bones. An elderly woman, silver hair, pink nightdress, stood barefoot by her front door, trembling, hand to her mouth.

John Mahoney hurried to her. "Are you alone?" She nodded.

"No-one else in the house?" She shook her head.

"Its Mrs Johnson, isn't it?" She nodded.

Widow. "Can someone take Mrs Johnson into the cab while we sort this out?" He took of his coat and wrapped it round her thin shoulders. "Meanwhile no-one go back to their houses until we find out what the hell has gone on. Stay by the fire engine." They gathered, about twenty shivering men, women and children, by the driver's open door. Yellow light and a little warmth. Children, numb and dumb, pushed to the front.

A fireman, his uniform still unbuttoned, hurried with a blanket for Mrs Johnson. Led her to the closed group of silent people which opened and swallowed her. Someone helped her up into the warmth of the cab where a radio crackled with static. She sat in the driver's seat, gripped the steering wheel and stared through the windscreen, beyond the headlights and into the far darkness.

Attention returned to her broken home, lit now by patchy moonlight and firemen's torches. The damage clear to see. Dust danced in the beams. A heavy, pressing silence, with only the hum of the fire engine.

Next door to Mrs Johnson's home, with only a narrow gap between them, stood a large, imposing Georgian house, slightly back from the road. It appeared intact as the beams played over its blank brick face, white shutters closed across the windows. Its narrow front yard of cobbles and planters was strewn with its neighbour's rubble, a shattered chimney pot and what to an expert eye, of which there were none there at that moment, was a human shin bone. Yellow.

CHAPTER 2

AS coincidence would have it, on this very same date, 100 years ago to the day, January 22, 1902, a bedraggled, small group of passengers, wrapped and muffled against the cold wind, waited in silence in the wet darkness on a rain-sodden railway platform in Carlisle for the 7.20pm onwards north to Dumfries. All hardy travellers. Twenty bloody minutes late. A large, once white, but now soot-grey faced clock, hanging over the gloomy platform, ticked the achingly slow seconds with a dull thud whenever its large, black minute hand moved.

Not one of the group had risked re-crossing the wooden bridge over the rail lines to the waiting rooms and café by the station entrance on the opposite platform, where gas lights spread yellow into the darkness and fires burned and tea and buns were on offer until 8pm. It was too touch-and-go. Regular travellers knew only too well, sometimes from bitter personal experience, that there was not always time to hurry back to the north-bound platform to board a late train before it lumbered out of the station, wheels spinning and squealing, in a thickening cloud of white steam and smoke, stationary only for seconds, desperate to make its timetable.

Unusually, this cold evening no trains at all, north nor south, had passed through for some time. An express had been due to thunder north on the through line ten minutes ago, not stopping, or even slowing, bound for Glasgow, just over an hour away. The only sound was the wind, the rain slanting just beyond the filthy glass canopy, and the hiss of the few gas lamps.

One gentleman, heavy tan leather holdall at his side, his face almost obscured by a thick scarf and pulled down fedora hat, removed his watch from deep inside his bulky overcoat and, leaning towards the yellow light, cursed at the time. He shuffled closer to the dull glow from the lamp to read his newspaper, folded it down in a struggle with the icy wind to a story noting one year since the death of Queen Victoria – Our Longest Serving Monarch.

Finally, finally some action. He glanced up from his newspaper to see a man he took to be the station-master struggling towards them

The Painter Of Souls

through the gloom, umbrella bucking in the wind. He removed his top hat, coughed to attract their attention. "Please." They gathered round, his face sombre in the weak light. "I'm afraid there's been an accident down the line. A derailment."

He was cursed by one of the group.

"I'm sorry. It's not my doing. I'm told the line could be blocked for some time. The porters are coming to help you across to the waiting rooms and I'm sending word to the George Hotel that people may have to stay overnight. They have a telegraph service there should you wish to send a message onward. I'm sorry."

He turned to two porters who hurried towards the group, muffled bodies bent against the winter, hands holding their hats firm.

They approached the man with the holdall, but he irritably waved them on to help the women in the group and bent to lift his own bag. He often made this tedious journey to and from Manchester or London and rarely did it go without problems. But this would be the first time he had been delayed overnight. Thankfully there was no one waiting at the other end, his sister away with friends in Glasgow and their housekeeper given a couple of days off. No one to worry. He climbed the steps to the passenger bridge, a slight twinge in one leg, following the straggling line of grumbling fellow passengers.

That's where he first heard it. Became aware. High up on the bridge. The clatter of horse-drawn wagons driven furiously on the rain-slicked cobbled street outside the station. And then shouts from men and women, muffled by the biting wind. His brain, numb with cold, began to warm with excitement. From the bridge he looked down the line into the darkness and could see an orange glow towards the horizon, as though the sun was rising, though not at this hour,

He hurried forward, down the steps onto the south platform, leg pain forgotten, and, lugging his bag, ran to the station master's office where lamps burned yellow in the window. Without a pause he grabbed the door handle and pushed. Stumbled inside. Two men, in railway uniform, warming their backsides by a fire, turned. Surprised. One held up his hand, to stop the intruder mid stride.

"I'm sorry...but you can't barge in..."

"Are people injured?" He gushed the words, garbled, pulled away his scarf to make himself clearer. "Injured?"

"It could be very bad sir. Often is. But you cannot come in here. You should be in the waiting room. Accommodation has been arranged."

"My bag, here." He dropped it the floor. "Keep it safe."

He turned and dashed from the office, in his haste slamming the door so hard it pulled a choking cloud of smoke from the fire into the room. Ran along the platform, hand to his hat, out past the ticket office window, jumped down four stone steps to the dark street, oblivious to the stabs of pain in his leg, and almost collided with a horse-drawn flat wagon. The animal reared and the driver, on a high bench seat at the front, cursed, struggled with the horse and pushed hard at the brake. "Bloody fool!" The driver's breath clouded in the glow from the gas street lamps.

"Sorry." Out of breath. Breathing hard. Heart pumping. "Are you heading to the accident?" He held out his hands by way of apology, looked up at the driver wrapped in a black rain slicker, his face largely hidden beneath a broad flat cap. Darkness and rain.

"Yes," the man pulled at the reins, shouted at the horse. The night wind pulled at them.

"Then let's go." Without asking he jumped onto the flat bed wagon and the horse heaved forward, slipped, hooves hammered for purchase on the wet cobbles. The driver urging on.

He clung to the edge of the wagon, fearful of falling, passed others rushing along the street. Men, women, children, shouting. Then, above the noise, the dull sound of a muffled explosion rolled over them, a belch of heat with it, and in the near distance they could see a shower of orange sparks flare into the darkness.

This could be the chance he had been waiting for. He felt at the sketch book in his coat pocket, pencils held in its closing band. If there were flames, and now he could see clearer the red glow and hear the crack and hiss of a fire, then he would probably have enough light to work. The rain seemed to be easing. This was all in his favour. If nothing else he would have sketches from the scene to sell to the London illustrated newspapers and the Manchester Guardian. Not that he needed the money. His work was always in great demand. But perhaps the greater prize, the one he desperately wanted, was in his grasp.

They careered through the clamour of horses, carts and people for a mile, leaving the last of the terraced houses and yellow gas street lamps behind, entering the night only briefly, before rounding a corner where the road turned sharply to the right and dipped to go in a tunnel beneath the line. He nearly fell from the cart as it skidded round the corner, throwing him half way across its flat body. It jolted to a halt. Thankfully he was cushioned by thick clothing.

The railway ran on an embankment, a good twenty feet above them. A scene from hell. Fierce red fire licked into the night sky. He could feel the heat. He jumped from the wagon and was immediately amid a mad dash of people. Some going. Some coming. Some helping people hurry away. Some carrying. A man, children in each arm. He suddenly felt his senses acutely aware of everything around him. A deafening chaos of noise: shouts, screams, explosions, the roar of fire. The stench of burning wood and thick smoke.

He pushed through. In control. He could see wooden carriages of the mainline express which had jack knifed down the embankment, crash-landing on their sides in the road, throwing out people and luggage. Gas pipes, which fed the coach lights, had ruptured and the gas ignited by coals spilled from the firebox of a huge steam engine that hung down the embankment on its side. Screeching steam and smoke escaped into the blistering air. Flames were spreading to nearby undergrowth. He only needed to find one, one on the very brink, to catch that moment. He pulled out his sketchbook, felt the pencils secure, and ran forward, the heat burning his face.

Someone grabbed his arm. "Get back you fool. There's nothing. Nothing. You can't do owt."

"But I have to see." He struggled to free himself. Screams feet away to his right.

The man let him go. "You must be bloody mad. The whole lot's going to blow."

"I have to see."

He turned to the screams and felt a sudden blow in his back as another victim fled, clothes on fire. He fell, a screaming woman under him, the roar of the growing fire pressed down. He was momentarily winded, confused, the heat, the vast plains of southern Africa where he sketched furiously as the farmsteads were burned to the ground. British troops out to destroy the Boers. Burn them. Starve them. Crush them. Children reduced to skeletons. The smell of roasting flesh. He rolled away from the woman, scrambled to his feet, could smell his own clothes scorching, his hat had gone and his hair was burning, and, afterwards when he thought about it, he realised he had panicked, because, damn it, he bent to the woman, freed her leg from under a broken carriage door, and dragged her away. The heat seared his lungs and for days afterwards he would cough up smoke-black spit. He knew she would have been the one but, foolishly, he had saved her life. Whoever she was. Damn her!

Edward Broughton had helped the injured woman, whoever she was, to a waiting cart. It could have been the one he had ridden to the accident scene, but damn her, he did not care. Others had hurried to help lift her on. He pushed his scorched hands deep into his pockets, scowled at the night and the idiots rushing and shoving. Damned her further if she had damaged his precious hands. He trudged back to recover his luggage from the station and there eased his foul mood by angrily demanding a decent room at the George Hotel. Created a stink. Made them feel small. To hell with sketches for the newspapers. To hell with the lot of them.

A subsequent inquiry found that the north bound passenger express, running twenty three minutes late, had powered through a stop signal for reasons unknown. Inexplicable because the driver was a veteran of the route. The speeding train had smashed into a heavy freighter hauling itself out of a branch line just south of Carlisle station. The driver and fireman on the express were killed along with sixty two passengers and many more seriously injured, some with horrific burns. Rescuers had also died in the inferno.

The official report cleared the signalman

who was initially thought to have failed to stop the express and instead put the blame squarely on the driver whose haste to make up time had blinded him to the stop signal. He either saw it and ignored it, or never saw it. No one would ever know.

The freight train driver, spine broken and paralysed, and his fireman were also cleared.

A number of people were named for their bravery in rescuing the dying and the injured. The list did not include acclaimed artist Edward Broughton, the man with sunlight in his paint pot, wealth in his pocket, shrapnel in his leg, founder of the Kirkcudbright School of Artists, chronicler of the Boer War, art teacher to Winston Churchill, and, perhaps surprisingly, friend of the disgraced Emily Hobhouse.

CHAPTER 3

SCOTLAND'S historic Globe Inn, proudly trading for almost 400 years with little change since opening in 1610 on Dumfries High Street had been Robert Burns' favourite watering hole. Here he happily and enthusiastically bedded and impregnated with her first child the blonde barmaid who was the niece of landlady Mrs Hyslop. No-one, despite fevered research and many claims of ancestry, would ever know where that child numbered in his long list of off-spring, certainly not the first, nor last. At the same time Scotland's famed poet and incorrigible womaniser had his wife Jean in a similar situation after boasting to a friend taking her in a 'thundering scalade'. Proudly displayed on the pub wall is a handwritten letter to long-suffering Jean among framed memorabilia of one of Scotland's most famous sons, variously thought of as a poet of genius, national hero, but also an absolute scoundrel who would take any woman if there was, at a minimum, dry straw convenient to bed her on.

It was also the pub of choice of Detective Inspector John Armstrong, who had no immediate desire to bed anyone. Happily married for the last five years and utterly content until the last two seconds when 'that bloody thing leapt into life'. He stared malevolently at his mobile phone as it whirred, flashed and burred on the table in the dark wood panelled snug. This was where Burns the seducer had sat by the fireplace and scribbled away. Armstrong was not seeking inspiration, just peace and quiet and the enjoyment of a pint of Deuchars IPA, his current drink of choice, the creamy head still thick and heavy on his last remaining third of a pint. Liquid solid gold.

"Sod it!" He grabbed for the vibrating phone as it moved across the table, catching it just before it fell to the floor. He had been sorely tempted to let it drop. The number displayed his own station. Duty called and he pressed to answer the call.

"Armstrong." He glanced across at the pub clock: 6.20pm.

This unwanted invasion of his quiet moments would soon be a thing of the past. Bugger it. Three working days to go before retirement and freedom. A holiday and house search in France with Jane. They had already sold their Dumfries house and planned to move from cold and damp south-west Scotland to Provence. Language lessons had taken up their Monday nights for the last eighteen months. Before leaving they also wanted to complete the research of their family history back to the feared reivers, bands of ruthless raiders who had plundered the English and Scottish borders for hundreds of years, way back into the thirteenth century.

John Armstrong believed he was related to first-man-on-the-moon Neil Armstrong, which would, he thought, explain one of his many interests, astronomy. Jane suspected that centuries ago her family, the Nixons, had been very close allies of the Armstrongs, sharing their isolated stronghold in Liddesdale, a hard wild place that bred hard wild people on the southern fringes of Scotland. She had joked: "You never know we could be related. Cousins." On a more serious note she realised it also meant she was probably related, though hopefully distantly, to Richard Nixon, the disgraced president of America. She found that distasteful, no matter how far removed.

"Ringo? Mike. We have a situation down in Kirkcudbright. Hornel Street. "

"And?"

"There's a team down there. Steve Harrison.

The earthquake last night, remember?"

"How could I forget?"

"Well, it brought down the gable end of a house and the lads making it safe have found a body."

"Christ. I'm packing in Mike. Clearing up. I don't need this. Kirkcudbright is nothing to do with me."

"I know. I know. But it's an old body it seems, a pile of dusty old bones. Skeleton in the cupboard job, literally."

"A skeleton? You are kidding?" He realised a couple standing at the bar had turned to the conversation and so he turned away in his seat. Spoke lower. "Bones spells trouble, Mike. Three days and I'm out of here, come what may."

"Sorry, Ringo, I know that, but I'm going to have to ship it your way."

"Can't Steve handle this? It's not even my patch. I'm sure he doesn't want me holding his hand."

"They've all hell on with the royal visit next week, Queenie Liz and her entourage, and he needs to get back for a briefing because they've altered their schedule to take in a visit to Kirkcudbright."

"A briefing? At this time? Are that bloody lot still coming?" He took a drink of his beloved

The Painter Of Souls

pint. "Though I suppose they'll look good visiting the scene of the disaster. Not want to miss that opportunity."

"Precisely, you've always been hot on the royals, Ringo. Maybe you'll get a long service medal for being so, err, what, so enthusiastic about our ruling family?"

"Bollocks."

"The briefing's rescheduled because of the quake. Super said you're to take over and see it through. An easy one and a nice gesture to our Galloway colleagues. Steve's waiting for you. They need all the help they can get, as you can imagine."

"An easy one? Famous last words."

Mike was an inspector running the station control room, a desk job assignment after he was badly beaten six months previously during a drugs raid. Years before he and Armstrong had been probationary constables together and Mike was one of the few at the station daring to call him 'Ringo'. At least to his face. Armstrong today had no wish to add to his friend's problems.

"Ok Mike, ok. I'll go down there. Have they had the boffins in?"

"Not fully. They only found the bones late this afternoon, in the roof or loft, or some such when it was already getting dark. They want to work when it's light. You know how they are, scared of the dark."

"Ok. I'm on my way. How's things with you?"

"Me? Fine. Out there? Relatively quiet considering last night. Your road down to Kirkcudbright should be clear now, but take care because there have been trees down and some are still being cleared."

Armstrong drained his glass. Recalled Hornel Street was near the river where the National Trust owned a large Georgian house, belonged to some artist or other. God, what was his name? He had investigated an attempted break-in at the house, five, no, probably six years ago. Could be seven. Kirkcudbright was too far west of Dumfries to be in his area, but he had been on a regional squad set up to catch a gang stealing art to order from large houses across the south of Scotland.

Who was the artist? The name hung there, but was gone. He pulled on his coat, took his empty glass back to the bar, wished the barmaid goodnight and pushed out into the dark, narrow alley at the side of the pub.

He remembered the house had some fine paintings, one he could picture clearly of children picking bluebells on the edge of a wood, the sunlight dappled on their backs. Victorian stuff. They had nicked the thieves red handed at another country house. None would name the man at the top, he suspected out of fear rather than any code of honour. They had all served time, except Mr Big, as per usual.

What was the artist's name? Getting old. He shivered against the cold. Unlocked his car. Looked like a frost was coming on. Threw his coat into the back.

Armstrong drove out over the River Nith to the A75, the fastest and, after the wreckage of the earthquake, the most reliable road to Kirkcudbright. It was deserted and he booted the car to 80mph-plus. Should make it in half an hour. On his passenger seat the evening newspaper slid into the footwell as the car slewed round a tight left curve. Headline: 'The Galloway Groaner'. Bloody hell! Friends had telephoned from America to ask if he and Jane were OK. Never felt a thing. Well, Jane had woken, she was a light sleeper and it was unlikely to be the earthquake which had barely registered in Dumfries, but he had slumbered on, no doubt dreaming of retirement and France.

Street lights were back on and their orange glow made it appear warm outside. Deceptive. He glanced at the car digital thermometer 0c and alongside the ice warning light glowed an ominous red. He eased up. There was no rush. A load of bones suggested the murderer, if there was one, had escaped a long time ago. Though never assume. Probably the skeleton of a dog.

He dropped to the A711 south. Far off he could see the twinkling lights on the English side of the Solway Firth, north of the Lake District. Never been over to that part of the world - Maryport, Workington and someone he knew had been to a beer festival in Silloth, or some such place. Might be worth a future visit.

As he turned into Hornel Street he could see the usual gathering of locals, plus police officers, a fire crew and assorted others at the far end under an intense white light provided by a generator. Someone had brought a garden brazier for warmth. A fire engine, white vans, an ambulance – some bloody use – and a police car lined the road. Blue lights strobing the darkness. Scaffolding framed the ruined end of a terrace house.

The arc light was so bright he feared planes would try to land down the street. He parked, climbed from the car and shouted at the uniformed policewoman who was walking towards him to turn around and find Steve Harrison. "Oh and tell them to turn off those bloody blue lights." He wanted them to know he had arrived and was in no mood to be messed with. It was bitterly cold after the false warmth and comfort of his car. He ducked back inside to grab his coat. Seconds later, a figure swollen by a padded jacket, hurried up, opened the passenger door and climbed inside.

"Evening, sir." His teeth were chattering.

"Mmm. Good evening, Steve. Make yourself at home. What have we got?" He sat back into the driver's seat.

"The earthquake brought down the gable end of the house there." They both peered into the blinding white light. "Builders working to secure the place found a pile of bones and called us in."

"A pile?"

"Well, looks like a full skeleton, though it seems some fell with the wall into the place next door."

"When was this?"

"The earthquake last night, well to be more accurate, this morning."

"I bloody know that. No, no. When did they find the bones?"

"Around four o'clock. It was already dark and they were working under that spotlight. I think they saw the skull and threw a bit of a wobbly. Anyway, uniform was already here making sure no-one helped themselves to the house jewels and they called us. I've had a shufty and the boys and girls in their fancy white overalls have been down to take what photographs they can then cleared off until tomorrow. The place has been secured and is ready to be covered with a tarp. But I've run out of time 'cos I've this briefing on the royals."

"Lucky you. Do we know who lived there?"

"Neighbours say it was a widow. In her 80's. A Mrs Johnson. A bit shaken. She's in the local hospital, just round the back of High Street. Know it?"

"No, but I'll find it. Was she hurt?"

"More precaution than anything. She was skipping around in just her nightie last night, in the street. Freezing."

"Must have been a sight. Anyone spoken to her?"

"No, no. Want a look?"

"At the house? If we must."

They left the warm car. Armstrong waited, stamping his feet, as a uniformed constable approached Steve Harrison. The sky was black and the stars brilliant white. He picked out Orion high in the south east.

The constable reported: "The fire lads are ready for the off, sir."

"Fine, we'll only be a few minutes. Have them wait while we take a nosey. Then I'm off as well. DI Armstrong is taking over."

"From Dumfries? Ringo? Bloody hell."

"From Dumfries. And I wouldn't call him Ringo." He glanced across at Armstrong who pretended to be looking away, deaf to the conversation. Together the two men hurried to the ruined house.

"We're around the corner, it's a bit tight, and up the scaffolding. The house isn't safe to go in. We can see all we need up there. We had the newspapers here earlier and they took photos of the damage, but we hadn't found the bones by then so that's a question to come."

"And no doubt they'll find out."

"No doubt. Somebody will say something. Probably the fire crew. They're a gabby lot. I thought we'd pass it off as one of those things artists used for their drawings. Tell them it's plastic or whatever."

"Nice thought. I'll bear that in mind. Though I'll look a right pillock if they find out it's a con."

A metal ladder had been roped to the scaffolding. The rungs freezing cold and the harsh light from the spots was blinding.

"I'll follow you." John Armstrong stood to the side, searched his coat pockets and pulled out his gloves. "At my bloody age!"

Dark green tarpaulins had been hauled between the scaffold and the house to cover the gaping void opened by the collapse of the gable. For the moment, nylon rope had been used to tie it back. A large part of the rear wall of the house had also fallen into the garden. Armstrong could see where a window ran along the entire rear upper storey of the house. The only support at the corner was a stone pillar which had fractured, shattering the wooden window frame and sending the wall tumbling. Armstrong, a DIY enthusiast who had renovated a 17th century cottage successfully claimed by his first wife, was not surprised that the walls around such an obvious structural weak point had collapsed. Who would have been daft enough to put a huge window there?

He paused on the ladder to take it in, realising the window would have given panoramic views north over the Dee to the hills. A bedroom full of light. How the hell did you sleep in that? He hauled himself up the final rungs to where scaffolders had built a temporary wooden platform alongside the gable end's broken chimney stack. Here both men knelt, shuffling to move their own deep black shadows off the scene.

"What do you make of this place? That window? The other houses aren't like that from what I could see."

"I asked the same and no-one seems to know. The neighbours reckon Mrs Johnson will know because she's lived here like forever. The bones are over there."

"I thought it was an attic?"

"No, not over the top of the bedroom. The house roof sloped down steeply at this end here. A bit continental like. So the bedroom had a false wall at this end where it was too narrow for anything else. Some of the false wall has come away and you can see around into the bedroom. I think the old lady had her bed head against it. My mother had a similar thing in her dormer bungalow and there was a small door into it. Useful for storing suitcases, that sort of thing."

The space, deep in shadow, and about four feet at its highest point, appeared of no use other than for storage, should anyone have wanted to leave their treasured possessions in the filthy darkness.

Steve Harrison picked up a heavy-duty inspection lamp and turned it on. The beam picked out the ends of bones, grey in the intense light, sticking out from the deep dirt and debris between the joists. And to help the first on the scene to recognise them as human – a half-buried skull, devoid of flesh and tilted on its side, stared out at them with an empty eye socket. Imploring.

Armstrong coughed at the cold and the soot in the air. "They look bloody ancient. And hardly plastic. What are we playing at here?"

"They might not be old."

"Not old? You are joking, or you'd better be. I finish in a couple of days, come what may, and I didn't come out in this Arctic bloody weather to start a fresh murder inquiry. Look at them, they've been here since Adam was a lad. Who reckons they aren't old?"

"Might not be old, John. Might. The white suits said they could be any age. They want this tarp tying back down until they can have a proper look see and get them out. And anything else there that might help identify or age them. Wallet, something like that. I'm not telling you how to suck eggs. I have to go if I'm to make this briefing." Steve Harrison stood, a little wary of John Armstrong, an officer he knew well, and who he well knew was, at this point in time, seriously brassed off. He had a reputation for being calm and controlled, but there was always a first time. He turned off the lamp.

"Aye, piss off then. I'll go and see Mrs Johnson, see what happened to her husband, if you get my drift. This could be dumped back on your desk tomorrow."

"I'm off the rota. Royal duties from now."

Steve Harrison was already half way down the ladder and called: "All yours, John. The firemen are waiting. They'll get the tarp tied down and secure." He was gone.

Armstrong's knees popped as he stood, a sure sign of age, and he felt slightly unbalanced, reaching for the scaffolding to steady himself before descending. As he climbed down he thought back to Mike in the control room. 'An easy one'. Not bloody likely. A skeleton could throw up problems that could take weeks, months to solve. He'd dealt with many a death, but a skeleton? He could not immediately remember, but he had read about the difficulties.

Murder? If it had been sixty or seventy years ago, he doubted anyone alive would know much about it. More recent than that? Also unlikely considering the amount of grot and other filth all over it. He guessed the house was around hundred and fifty years old. Perhaps a builder had died there, bricked up, forgotten. Hum, ridiculous. But why would anyone put a body in there? How would it get there?

The house was so close to the river, why not just weigh down the corpse and throw it in? But he had tackled a few suicides where people had gone to lonely places to die. A void in a roof? Well, no, but there was always a first time. And there was that one case in Dumfries some years ago, strictly not a suicide, where the victim, in his 40's, had built himself a secret sex chamber in the attic and died while strangling himself to get a hard on. Now that had been something for the man's wife to find when she returned from her weekly shop at Tesco. The inquest and subsequent publicity a torment for the family.

He reached terra firma, kicked angrily at the ladder and stood aside as two firemen moved in. 7.50pm. Not too late to see Mrs Johnson. A Black Widow? Husband butchered and hidden in the attic. He doubted it, though most murder victims did know their killer and it took only one blow to the wrong part of the head. A rolling pin when he staggered in drunk.

He waited for the firemen to come back down to ask for directions to the hospital thinking of ancient traditions where a cat, a dog, even a donkey he had once heard, had been bricked up alive in new buildings as a sacrifice to keep evil spirits away. Immurement had been in the Daily Telegraph crossword only last week. He'd had to look it up. A strange coincidence? And when he and Jane had been away in Riga last year they had visited St John's Church where two priests had volunteered to be bricked up in the walls, hoping for sainthood when they died. They did die, but martyred? Ridiculed, yes. Martyred, no. But here, in Kirkcudbright? Dark arts, religious mania, sex kicks, murder?

CHAPTER 4

EDWARD Broughton RA, shy, fresh and flushed from the success of his first major London exhibition - "A Sensation" roared the London Times, adding: "Child Genius Comes Of Age"- nervously boarded the Nubia, a passenger steam ship turned troop carrier, at Southampton port, bound for the long voyage to Cape Town, in the British Cape Colony, southern Africa. The quayside crammed with people in their Victorian finery. Thankfully he pushed through unrecognised, head down, hat pulled low, the collar of his heavy black coat turned up and his face almost obscured under a thick red scarf knitted by his sister, Flora. He pushed her from his mind, momentarily.

Friday, October 20, 1899. The morning brought a steel blue sky and crystal clear light with a lazy breeze from the north. He had never set foot outside Britain, and here he was, a 25-year-old Scottish bachelor, acclaimed by the art world, tempted out of his cosy home and studio in Kirkcudbright, away from his admiring followers, destined today for the underside of the world where he had been told it would be summer. Hard to believe on a chill day like this.

The Illustrated London News and the London Times had commissioned him to report and record in pictures the expected glorious victories of a Second Boer War, should it happen, the first having petered out 20 years before. The Boers occupied lands rich in diamonds and gold, which the British had long wanted. And this at a time when some were openly questioning whether the British Empire was on the wane, daring to test the resolve of the Government to finally stand up against the troublesome Boers. Make an example of them. These were dangerous times, with insurgents in India also watching closely for signs of weakness in their colonial masters.

Newspapers had asked would he, Britain's most famous artist, go out to cover the war, if it came to it? Sensing glory, he had agreed.

Since mention of the potential commission Broughton had followed the developing story in his newspapers. Eagerly at first, thoughts of heroically taking to the battlefield, but then as the days progressed and war became more likely, he became more nervous. His sister did not help, constantly urging him to stay at home.

Newspapers, commentators and the Opposition were piling pressure on the Government to act, and act decisively. They rubbished suggestions of negotiations with the intransigent Boers, although by now Broughton was hoping they would come to some peaceful arrangement. Prime Minister, the Marquess of Salisbury was goaded for his reluctance. His critics, at home and abroad, wanted to crush the unruly Boers, who were, after all, only a scruffy rabble of Dutch, German and French drifters who had settled in the country almost 300 years earlier.

Finally it was the Boers who acted. They demanded the British withdraw troops sent out to southern Africa within 48 hours, or else. Broughton's hands trembled a little as he read his Times newspaper the following day which said the whole affair had become 'an extravagant farce'. Flora hurried out to collect a copy of the Daily Telegraph which he rarely read, but was eager to see how far they would go. His mouth dried as he read: "The Boers have asked for war and war they must have!"

She pleaded with him. But could he cancel the commission? Hardly. The nation's mood was growing darker. He would be branded a coward.

Within days Boer forces besieged the important towns and garrisons of Mafeking, Kimberley and Ladysmith. It was an outrage. 'A grotesque challenge', according to his Telegraph.

Broughton sought immediate comfort in stories that the war would be little more than a skirmish with a bunch of backward, stubborn farmers. Over and done within weeks, certainly before Christmas only three months away. Then Britain would control the region, its trade routes and its rich assets. What the Empire wanted, it got. History clearly demonstrated this. No question.

His dear younger sister, who largely organised his life and career, urged him to think again. No one would brand him a coward. Why would they? Yes, his genius was mighty, but not his health. They knew that. He was easily fatigued, could not cope with stress and not only would the assignment be very stressful, he would, on his return, also face pressure to complete the many commissions waiting at home, some from very wealthy and important clients. He should be working at home, building on the success of his sell-out exhibition. They should concentrate on the conversion of the large house they had bought next door to their terraced house overlooking the River Dee. There they could properly accommodate a studio and exhibition space, permanently establish an artist colony and receive their aristocratic patrons. He was needed at home.

She had pleaded with him, urged him to see that of all the things he should do, setting sail into the unknown, into the darkest reaches of some hostile foreign country and the chaos of a war, was certainly not one of them. Africa, of all places!

Yet, at the opening of his exhibition, among the thousands of people who came through the doors, he had met Bruce Ingram, the new, young and vibrant editor of the Illustrated London News and George Earle Buckle, editor of The Times. They in turn were enthralled to be introduced to the young artist whose genius, "a golden dawn" wrote one critic, had eclipsed such established figures as Lord Frederick Leighton, William Morris, John Evert Millais and William Holman Hunt. Buckle assured him his war work would feature in newspapers read by hundreds of thousands of people, no millions. Surely, an opportunity he could not pass. Ingram had raved about his painting 'Glencoe Massacre 1692', which it was rumoured Queen Victoria wanted as a gift for the Royal collection, and told him he needed to get out and experience a real war, draw from the battlefield, feel the

The Painter Of Souls

blood of it, the cut and the thrust. Imagine, then, the pictures you could paint. He genius would capture something, a certain something, the new-fangled camera never could.

He had been flattered and finally persuaded. It would only be a matter of weeks. And he had been assured of accommodation in the officer's first class cabins for the three-week voyage. A civilised lot with good food and good manners. Indeed, he would probably know some of them and certainly their families. And he would be well cared for in the field. He would be better served abroad, than staying at home amidst builders rubble, dust and noise.

The troops sailing out this autumnal Friday were the First Battalion of the Scots Guards, so he hoped for talk of home. But as he stepped onto the gangway he could not help doubting yet again, in the cold light of day, the wisdom of what he was doing. It looked a steep and long climb up to the deck. The ship was enormous, over 400 feet long, an unfriendly grey-white hulk. By Christ, he wished he was taking the train north to Scotland. Flora had been right. Could he turn back?

He was half way up the gangway. His baggage was already on board, taken along with piles of other equipment and belongings from the railway station by a convoy of horse drawn wagons that had met the troop train. He could ask for it to be off-loaded. There were men behind him, pressure on his back. Men who had claimed a last farewell from a lover, a wife, crowded on the noisy quayside below. No-one had travelled down with him to see him off. Flora at home, seething, nursing their ailing mother.

A bearded man in a dark uniform and hat approached him at the top of the gangway, held out his hand.

"Mr Broughton?"

He nodded. Mouth too dry to speak. Lowered his scarf.

"A great pleasure to both meet you and welcome you aboard the Nubia. I'm Captain White and if you would please follow me I will show you to your cabin." Edward Broughton, legs unsteady, mind unfocussed, stepped onto the scrubbed deck and knew there was no going back.

The Nubia was a steady, six-year-old, veteran of the ocean whose single tall funnel left a fading trail of grey-black steam over the still water as they prepared to leave Southampton. Broughton, at the upper-deck rail, sketched furiously as they cast off, concentrating on the page, not his doubts. Soldiers crammed against the lower rails. Below, families, sweethearts and supporters threw caps in the air, blew kisses, tossed posies of flowers into the water. Dock workers struggled through the swarming mass to clear mooring ropes. Beside him Broughton heard Guards officers calling they would soon return. Home for Christmas.

He wished they would stop jostling him as he tried to sketch the seething mass of folk.

Finally the docks receded as the Nubia slipped away. Broughton stayed at the rail, surprised how long it took to clear land, the grey slab he was told was the Isle of Wight inched by, and then they were on the open sea. Steel grey and increasingly rough.

Men moved from the decks. The Nubia rose and fell with the swell and immediately Broughton felt sick. An officer beside him advised he should look to the front of the ship, not stare at the foaming wake. "Or you'll see your breakfast again." It was too late. He leaned over the rail and vomited. And again. An officer who had been watching him sketch hurried forward as Broughton's knees gave way and he slumped, grasping at the rail for support. His sketchbook fell to the deck. As he slid down, he remembered that train journey the previous year, the stuffy carriage rocked by a gale-force wind, when, to his shame, he had fainted in front of his sister.

Now he heard something about a doctor, a rush of intense heat that had him perspiring, then darkness when as his head struck the wooden deck with a sickening thud.

It was the smell of cold dampness that lingered at the edge of Broughton's delirium. The chill of the classroom in the old cattle shed at Home Farm, converted to a school room for families on the Scottish estate of the Kennedys. Twenty three children of all ages, in that one room with Mr Armitage, their teacher, tall, thin, angular. His voice deep and strong for such a gaunt man.

Friday, winter rain beating at the window. Outside a harsh wind strained the black naked oak and had it scraping across the stonework and glass. Witches nails digging deep. Screeching.

"This weekend I want you to draw a picture and write about it. There's pencils and paper here for those of you without them. I suspect that's most of you. Collect them as you go. One sheet each 'cos its costly stuff. No more. Bring them in Monday. And no excuses."

On Monday six-year-old Edward Broughton, one of the youngest, handed in his picture and retreated toward his place only to be immediately called back. He froze. Had he done something wrong?

"What's this?" Mr Armitage waved his drawing at him.

"My sister, sir. Flora. It says under."

"Aye, the new bairn. I know. And who has drawn this?"

"Me, sir."

"You? You? Aye I'm sure. I'll be seeing your da to night at the parish meeting and you can expect to be in for it. Sit down"

He had often wondered what was said between his father, head gamekeeper on the estate, and the teacher. Neither long on words. He had drawn his sister and put down some words his mother had helped him with, that Flora was the first girl after seven boys. As he had been asked to do. He was good at drawing. Paper was scarce but his mother had saved food wrappers for him, ironed them flat. She had found a discarded roll of wallpaper at the castle. Taken the blank pages out of the few books in their croft, a low white building on the edge of thin woodland below Black Fell. He had drawn all his family, farm animals, the dead stags his father had brought down from the hills slung across the backs of ponies. He did chalk drawings on the cold stone flagged floor that were soon scuffed and then washed away. His father had warned him to leave the walls alone.

The following day, as a pale yellow sun struggled to show through filthy cloud racing before a bitterly cold wind, the children arrived at school, chapped and churlish, only to be told at the end of prayers to remain standing. Be quiet. Spruce up. Stop snivelling. Surprisingly the stove, which was normally iron dull and dead cold on such an icy day as this, was lit and throwing out heat. Mr Armitage stood with his back to it. Jacket tails raised. On each desk was a pencil and another piece of the precious blank paper. This was not the routine start to the day.

Mr Armitage told them Lady Kennedy was on her way and they would wait in silence. Minutes passed, tension mounted, no-one dared speak, nor move. Lady Kennedy had never before been near the schoolroom, never been seen by most of the children. And then the door creaked open.

She entered, alone, wearing a thick, red coat that came to the floor and a matching broad hat tied against the wind with a white scarf. The boys bowed and the girls curtsied. Everyone nervous. Very nervous. What was going on? Silence. Young Edward had only seen her from a distance - she looked very old, at least 30, he reckoned. She stood by a chair at the side of the teacher's desk while Mr Armitage, quick to move from the stove, repeated that day's prayers. Lady Kennedy sat, smiled at the class and at Mr Armitage who then ordered

The Painter Of Souls

everyone to sit. Chairs scraped into the heavy silence.

Their teacher, also clearly nervous, cleared his throat. "We will start with a bit of art today. Lady Kennedy has come to see what you can do. Agnes Elliott come to the front of the class."

The youngest child, no more than four, hair matted and held from her face by a blue ribbon pushed back her chair, which toppled over banging the desk behind. She froze, half standing. "Never mind, leave it" Mr Armitage beckoned her forward. One of the bigger boys stepped from behind his desk and righted the chair. Slowly she came, scrawny, grimy face flushed. Pushing through the silence. Mr Armitage reached out and roughly pulled her the final few feet.

"You'll all be drawing Agnes. Look up girl, they can't draw the top of your head." He spun her round to face the class. "Here, stand on this chair, they'll never see you." He lifted her. Titters. "Aye and there'd better be no nonsense. Extra number work for any foolishness. So heads down, pencils up and tongues still and get your brains working. Twenty minutes and for those that don't know, that's when the big hand here is on the five there." He pointed to the large clock on the wall behind his desk, the clock that ticked away the long, long slow days of school.

Agnes Elliott, despite her best efforts, began to sob, matching the slow tick of the clock. The twenty minutes seemed an eternity to every child, bar one.

"Time's up! Bring you work with you and form a line down that side, oldest first. When I tell you, step forward and show your work to Lady Kennedy. Thompson you first."

Some had managed only a stick figure with a triangle skirt. The youngest of the children produced no more than a scribble.

Young Edward was next to last and when he stepped forward, gripped hard by fear, Lady Kennedy took his picture and gasped, hand to mouth. This was a disaster and he desperately needed to wee. Stomach cramped. He had only drawn what he had seen. It was Agnes. She had been sobbing and he had included a tear as it rolled down her cheek. His mother had shown him how to draw water drops when he'd been painting a vase of daisies in a jam jar last summer. He had done nothing wrong. Had he? He turned round at his classmates, they all looked away. He was on his own. On fire. Burning.

She looked up from the picture. "I'm astounded".

Young Broughton tearful, the class all looked

at him now, sensing blood. He was in for a beating. He felt his own tears welling, snivelled, wiped his nose on his sleeve and, despite gripping all he could, holding as tight as he could, to his eternal shame his hot wee stained down the front of his grey short trousers and puddled, steaming slightly, on the schoolroom stone floor.

Lady Kennedy led him from the classroom there and then. Out through the stunned silence of everyone. His drawing, rolled, in one of her hands, her other holding, almost dragging, him along.

Warm wee quickly turned cold in the winter wind and chaffed on his legs turning them red raw above the knees as he hurried, struggling not to fall. They marched across the frozen ruts in the farm yard and onto the short lane, bordered by frosted grass, and along the tree-lined drive, breaking ice on puddles, to the white castle. Men working in a small group by one of the trees turned, doffed their caps and looked to the earth. Their breath fogging.

The castle stood massive white against the grey day, the black hills beyond lost in a gathering mist. Edward stared hard at the ground as he stumbled along, dared not look up to the castle, nor at Lady Kennedy. This was forbidden territory. No words were spoken. Then into the castle. Servants hurried to them, Lady Kennedy dismissed them. Asking just one, a man in red uniform, where Mr McTaggart was. The library.

"Please take young Broughton to clean him up and then bring him to the library."

He was led, mute, down stone steps to a laundry room where he was stripped, lifted into a sink of warm water, washed down and eventually handed a pair of clean, but too long trousers. He had never worn long trousers. He knew some of the people here, they rubbed his hair. One turned up his trousers. Mrs Spencer, who often came to their cottage to talk with his mother, asked what he was doing in the castle. He shrugged. "You'd better be on your best." She gave him a hard look, left with a heavy pile of white bed sheets.

He was then led back up the stone steps, along a dark and wide corridor, lined with marble busts of men. Large men. It seemed to run for miles. Finally they came to a huge pair of dark wood doors with polished brass handles. They halted, knocked, the doors were opened and a red liveried footman appeared and beckoned them into a library. Walls lined with books. At the centre, a large round table and settees and easy chairs.

His mother was there holding his baby sister and behind her in shadow, his father. He pulled away and ran to her, buried his face in

The Painter Of Souls

her black frock. Some of his drawings from home were spread across the table. A fire burned in a grate and he could smell cigar smoke. But that was it, the heat, the smell, the rest lost in his blind confusion. He felt sick. Other people were in the room.

One, a heavily bearded, balding giant, approached. He was dressed like the undertaker who had come when his grandma had died in their cottage and been laid out on a door borrowed from down the lane. The man bent and asked to shake his hand. He refused, buried deeper into his mother's skirt. She reached down, tried to push him away. "Go on," she said.

"Hello. I'm William McTaggart and you are?"

Silence. Hands firmly gripped on his mother's skirt. She pushing at him.

His mother answered for him. "Edward, Edward Broughton, sir. He's shy, very shy."

His father stepped forward. "Edward, your no in trouble. Find your tongue. Let go of your Ma and shake Mr McTaggart's hand. He's a famous artist."

The big man stood, hand on Edward's head, steered him to the table. "And these are yours?"

"Sir.

"Remarkable. And how old are you?"

"Six."

"Just a little boy. Incredible."

"No sir. I'm a big boy." The room was incredibly hot and he felt the sick rising in him. He swallowed against it. Trying to hold down the acid taste.

"And a clever one. These really are, really quite remarkable. Six? Lady Kennedy, I have to say, I have never seen anything like this."

Edward could remember little else of the meeting, though that was when his life had changed.

He had returned to school late in the day and everyone had stared at him. Mr Armitage told them to get back to their work. He expected to be mobbed by the other children at the end of school, eager for news, but he was treated as if he had a deadly disease and walked home alone.

Yes, now he remembered how a few days later, it would have been the Thursday, a footman had arrived at school in the afternoon, asked for young Broughton, never spoke another word and escorted him to the castle.

After that, most afternoons Edward Broughton walked, alone, to the castle, in through a door at the side, through the servant's quarters where he was often teased, and up the back stairs to the Kennedy children's rooms where art was a regular event with their tutor Miss Scott and sometimes Mr McTaggart.

The Kennedy's three children, Patrick, 12, Robert, ten, and Mary, eight, were friendly from the start.

Within two years he had almost moved to the castle full time, with his own room in the attic and often his sister Flora at his side. He had also become quite a local celebrity, sitting in at balls and dinners, sketching the people, first from a high desk and chair in a candle-lit corner and, as he grew, from an easel where guests would gather round to watch the young master at work. "He's how old? Eight? Remarkable. Couldn't draw a thing at that age."

His drawings, all signed by their subjects, including Queen Victoria and her children, were carefully placed by Lady Kennedy in a series of folders whose value would later save the estate from ruin.

CHAPTER 5

DI ARMSTRONG drove Kirkcudbright's quiet streets to the hospital. The policeman guarding Mrs Johnson's house had advised: "Follow up the High Street from here and it's on Mary's Place. You canna miss it." He pulled into St Mary's Place, suggesting an open green area, but to his disappointment a narrow road squeezed between a jumble of mismatched buildings that apparently made up the hospital and a sullen slab of terrace houses slap bang opposite. Too late he realised there was no roadside parking, slammed the brake and reversed out. "Bloody place."

He left the car on a side road and, pulling on his coat, strode purposefully up a ramp past what looked more like an exhibition of dilapidated garages from history in various stages of decline than a modern hospital. Like those art instillations Jane had dragged him to see at galleries that left him shaking his head at how gullible people could be. "No, not you," he would hastily say to his wife as she turned to him, frowning. "But look at that, a load of crashed cars wrapped in barbed wire. Come on."

The ramp led to the main door under a flimsy flat porch. Locked. "Damn it." He pulled harder. It did not budge. He checked his watch. 7.55pm. Then he saw it. A simple sign, white letters on green, PUSH. He pushed and entered the over hot, over-lit silent world of the health service. Hospitals held bad memories for him. Very bad. He would always pause on entering, gather himself, focus, move on. He had telephoned home to say he would be late and Jane assured him there was no rush. "Nothing spoiling". His first wife would have thrown a wobbly. Years ago she had thrown her lot in with someone else, someone with a real job who she saw during evenings and weekends. Good riddance.

A middle-aged female nurse, crisp and efficient, was walking towards him. "I'm sorry, but visiting is almost over." She held her hand out to block his passage and usher him back through the door. He glanced at the clock above a pale wood reception desk. She continued: "In fact, it's 8pm and it is over. Tomorrow?" Hand on his arm, gentle, but firm.

"Police. Armstrong." Abrupt. Tense. He needed to relax. Was she rude? Or was it him? "I've come to see Mrs Johnson." He forced a smile.

"Oh, right. Just a second. Her house? How terrible. Her daughter was here, but I think she's away. I'll just check. If you'll wait." She smiled. She wasn't rude. It was him. He took a chair in the corridor opposite an information poster about Alzheimer's. "Five signs you need to know to help a loved one." He stopped reading half way down.

She returned and beckoned Armstrong along the hot, stifling corridor. "She's awake and quite happy to see you, but please remember she's 92 and somewhat frail and hard of hearing."

"Oh, I was told she was in her 80's, though I don't suppose it makes a great deal of difference."

"She's got all her marbles. Just speak clearly and a little louder than normal. Can I bring you a tea?" She held open the door onto a small ward of four beds. Only one was occupied.

"And a biscuit? Any chance? Great. Thanks."

Mrs Johnson was sitting on top of the bedding, propped up by pillows. She watched him enter. "It's too hot in here, I'll never sleep. Can you get them to turn it down?" Despite that, she had a pink dressing gown tight around her. He studied the small woman. A murderess? He would not jump to conclusions. Go where the evidence took him.

He introduced himself, apologised for the hour and asked: "How are you?" He meant it.

"I'm fine, thank you. But too hot. Dear boy, I've lived through war, I've given birth to children, I've had open heart surgery, I've watched my husband die slowly and painfully. It was just a house. It was a shock, but I'm over it now. It's nice of you to come, though."

"Well, it's a little more than a social call. I need to explain why I'm here. And I'll get straight there. Can I ask: have you always lived there?"

"More or less. Mother and father took it over when the artist Mr Broughton, you'll have heard of him, died. I was very young. So I've never really known any other house, though I suppose I'll have to now. My daughter says the end's fallen off. She'll take me in. Provide me with a home for the time being. We all go full circle."

Speaking slowly. "Indeed. Well, to be blunt, and I'm sorry to say this, but we found a skeleton, a human one, in your house." Mrs Johnson's hand covered her mouth. The nurse paused at the door, tea and biscuits on a small tray. Armstrong turned to the nurse. "Sorry, I didn't realise you were there. Thanks for the tea." He held her gaze and then shifted it to the corridor beyond. She departed no further than the other side of the self-closing door. She held it part open with her foot.

"As I say. In the attic, well the space behind the bedroom wall."

Mrs Johnson puzzled, more than shocked. "You mean behind my bed? But there isn't anything there. It's just a wall. A wall. That's all it's ever been. It's a solid wall. That's for sure. A body, you say? Behind my bed? Oh God, excuse me, but what a thought? Who?"

"Well, we have specialists coming tomorrow and hopefully they can tell us more. But yes, a skeleton."

"Well, who is it?"

"That we don't know."

"At all?"

"No, at the moment we haven't a clue. Obviously, and I don't mean this to be offensive, we wondered if you might know anything about it." He took a sip of tea to hide his embarrassment. That, he thought, was a little too blunt. But he carefully studied her face to see her reaction.

"Me? Hardly." She laughed, coughed. Held his eye. "Hardly. And you have no idea? A skeleton? Well, it must have been there some time, don't you think? Behind my bed. Well, that's a horrible thought. I can't imagine."

"Do you know how old the house is? Anything about its history? It would be useful." He wished more of the people half her age were as lucid and straightforward during interviews. Most left him despairing of modern education.

"Well it's older than me. So that's old. I think it was one of those Victorian things. My mother and father moved in there when I was only a bairn."

"About?"

"It was just after the artist had died. Father used to tune their piano, well his sister's, and after Mr Broughton died his sister, that's Miss Flora Broughton, she never married, oh, she was awfully kind. It was so sad when she died, and she asked my parents if they wanted to move in to their old house. They'd lived there before moving into the big house next door. Mr Broughton had kept what became our house as a store and a bit of a studio. It suited my parents because I was the youngest of six and their own house was too small. It was a very poky thing they had alongside the school where my father taught music so Miss Broughton's offer of a house was, my mother always said, a godsend."

"Can I ask the names of your parents?"

"Of course. Mother was Mary and father was Joseph. How about that? But their surname was Alexander. Father was a piano tuner and teacher as I've said and a Methodist, very staunch Methodist. No alcohol. No gambling. I was the youngest of six and mother in her 40's when she had me. Too late to be carrying. So it was a long time ago. Before that, as far as I know, Mr Broughton had it as a studio, that's why there was all those windows around the bedroom. They looked out north because the light was good for an artist. I painted a bit myself. He would paint up there."

"Were you any good?"

"No, no, no. Not like Mr Broughton. You've seen his work?" He nodded. She continued:" I hadn't an ounce of his talent. Not an ounce. He kept his finished paintings downstairs, in our sitting room as it became. Like a shop. We always had heavy curtains in the bedroom to keep out the light or you couldn't have slept. Red velvet, though I suppose they are ruined now. He was very successful. Very talented. The family did a lot to help the people here. They came to own many houses here and let them out at low rents. Well, I think that was Miss Broughton. He had a studio at the back of next door down to the Dee, it's still there. Lovely house. It's National Trust so you can go in. He died quite young. But his sister, I used to help her in the garden, when I was a girl. There was only her after Mr Broughton died, and her housekeeper and her family. She had a funny name." She paused, deep in thought.

"Do you remember her name?" He was always amazed at how little people knew about others. Their neighbours – "never met them". Their friends – "I just knew him as Paul, I know thirty years, but that was it." But when he thought of himself, he had to admit he was perhaps no better.

"Puddle, that's it."

"Puddle as in water? Very unusual. But no-one ever accessed that space in the bedroom?"

"No. No-one. Well, none that I knew of. Father often said he wanted the windows taken out of the bedroom because it was too bright. Or boarded over. But it never happened. And I'm glad it didn't, in a way.""

"And before it was used by Mr Broughton. Was it lived in? Used?"

"I suspect it must have been, wouldn't you think? It was a house. But I don't know who lived there."

"So, the Broughton's lived in the house before moving next door. Mr Broughton kept it on as a studio and store, even though he had another studio in the big house, and you and your parents moved in after he died and have lived there ever since? That would be about the history of the place in the last 100 years or so?"

"Yes it would. Before that I'm afraid I cannot help you. I know the Broughtons weren't from Kirkcudbright. I think they had connections with the Kennedy family further north. You know, THE Kennedys. But who lived in the house before them, I just don't know? Now, you're a detective, I'm sure you can find out."

Back in the comfort of his car, Armstrong pulled out his notebook. "Broughton – Mr and Miss". "Alexander, Mary and Joseph." "Puddle." "Age of house and who'd lived there." He'd start with the electoral register in the morning.

There was a tap on his window. The nurse. He lowered the glass, a cold blast. Her breath fogged. "Mrs Johnson says I have to catch the young man and tell him the house could have been newly built when the Broughtons had it. He would have asked for the windows to be put in then. Hope that helps."

"Thank you. It all helps." He believed the house to be older.

He gave a cheery wave, pulled away, heading back to the cottage to check out the attic. He would not sleep if he didn't know for sure whether there was a door of some kind.

A lone policeman strolled the street, clapped his hands against the cold. And another figure, gazing up at the ruined end of the house, in what looked like a fireman's uniform, but with no helmet. Armstrong walked across to him.

The fireman turned to him. Held out his hand. "John Mahoney. That's going to be difficult to put back. Quite a mess."

"DI Armstrong." They shook hands. "Were you with the fire crew on the night?"

"I was."

"Ah, good. I need to have another quick peek up there. Any chance of a bit of help?"

"Sure. I'm not on duty, I was just calling on my way back to the station and on home. Have you seen Mrs Johnson? How is she?"

"I have and she's fine. Tough as old boots."

"Good news. Though she'll be some while before coming back here."

"I just want to check out the roof space. I have a torch here."

"Where they found the skeleton?"

Di Armstrong did not answer. The two men scaled the ice cold scaffolding and scrambled onto the makeshift platform. The torch, though not strong, cast a yellow light into the roof space.

"Can you see a door or anything hinting at one that could have been one?"

"Not a thing. Most of the gable has gone. It would be easier from inside, though why not wait until morning when we can better see? It should be safe enough."

"No time like the moment."

The policeman had a set of keys to the house, and stood aside for the two men. Carpeted stairs ran up from a short hallway immediately behind the front door where Mrs Johnson's coat, hat and umbrella hung, waiting. They tried a light switch. No joy. Their torch beam was blurred by a mass of bitter tasting dust particles. The stairs creaked, he guessed more from age than damage, and they climbed to the main bedroom, its far wall wrecked, a large part of the ceiling down on the floor and bed. Fortunately Mrs Johnson had moved downstairs to sleep some months ago. They used the torch to pan along the remaining broken, bedroom wall and found no obvious door. The house was perishing cold.

"You didn't see anything in the rubble that fell next door that could have been a door?"

"Can't say I did. But it wasn't something I would notice. Why a door?"

"Just a thought. Has the rubble been cleared away?"

"I don't know." They exited into the bleak night and looked over the wall next door. A large tarpaulin had been spread across the yard. Too heavy to move and too dark to make out much it was covering, even if they could lift it.

"Best tomorrow. Must get home." John Mahoney headed into the night as DI Armstrong walked to the policeman guarding the house.

"Lock it," said Armstrong. "Hang on," he held the policeman's arm. "Are the people still in next door?"

"No, sir. They have moved off to relatives, at least for tonight. They will want to be sure it's safe. More could come down. I don't have keys for them. I've been asked to tell you that the Press have been on to our station asking what's going on here. They said you should call them back. Some reporter called Jewson or some such."

"I'll bet they bloody did." To hell with them. He was going home.

CHAPTER 6

THE voyage south had been a grim succession of tedious days on a grey, heaving, empty sea. Troops had grumbled continually about the poor food aboard the SS Nubia, an unrelenting diet of brick-hard biscuits and foul tasting, pickled pork. The officers, including celebrity artist Edward Broughton RA, now fully seaworthy after his initial bout of sickness and delirium, had fared little better. There had been a crisis as they crossed the equator when the men, bored to the brink of mutiny, staged a drunken celebration which threatened to get out of hand.

Their arrival in Cape Town on November 13, 1899, after day upon day as dull as the diet, brought relief all round, only Broughton among them disappointed because low, white, drifting cloud obscured the incredible view he had been promised of a bustling harbour overshadowed by the bulk of a mighty table top mountain. Drifting, wet fog also hid much of the view of the quayside.

The Painter Of Souls

Fortunately Edward had known one of the officers, Gordon a cousin of the Kennedys, and so had an immediate and affectionate welcome into their small group. He doubted he would have managed it on his own. Much to Broughton's astonishment, Gordon Kennedy had brought along his scruffy looking Jack Russell called Smith. A fine ratter and his good luck charm. There had been talk among the lower ranks of kidnapping Smith and using him to supplement the diet, but it would have been a brave man to have challenged the owner and an even braver one to challenge his dog.

The officers were a friendly bunch, astonished at Broughton's skill in drawing cartoons of them all, but their chief pastimes of drinking, gossiping and gambling soon drove him down to the lower decks with his sketch books and finally down deeper into the suffocating heat and deafening noise of the boiler and engine rooms. Here, in the bowels of the ship, was a world all of its own, populated by a race of men, smeared with grease and coal dust, set well apart from the remainder of the crew.

But, here, he was fascinated by the thunderous noise, the intense heat and the relentless toil of the stokers, stripped to the waist, muscular and slick with sweat, as they fed the huge boilers with ton upon ton of coal, seemingly unaware of life beyond the dense steel walls surrounding them. Prisoners in their own inferno.

Broughton wondered how they would escape their iron prison should the Nubia sink, but it was not a thought he wanted to hold on to. He had never learned to swim and feared he would perish anyway in a scramble among these tough men to get into one of the few lifeboats should the worse come to the worse.

An engineer tried to explain the triple expansion steam engine that propelled the ship to 14.5 knots. Graduated cylinders, condensers, balanced beams. Edward believed he feigned understanding quite well. In reality it was all above his comprehension, never mind that he could hardly hear above the thundering noise. The chief engineer, a fellow Scot, "Mac", took him into the heart of the engine room, took his hand and put it to the warm brass and steel where he could feel the vibrations, the pulse of the mechanical beast. A living monster.

Broughton fully understood how you had to get deep into the heart of a subject to accurately portray it; the sinews and bones of a body, the geology of the landscape, the nuts and bolts of a machine like this one. You simply had to know what was underneath. It was as though the engine had a life and with it a soul all its own. Yes, he had done some dissection of animals, starting with small ones with William McTaggart. But McTaggart had talked about these things - mice, frogs, a rabbit - in a dispassionate way during the art lessons at the castle. He had dissected a red deer stag brought down from the mountains by his father and that had proved very useful, even though his father had been furious at the waste. He had studied the human skeleton in books. But here in this blistering hot, thunderous engine room he felt he was in touch with more than that, something he did not yet fully understand. He could feel the soul of this iron monster. It was all about finding the spirit of the subject, whether it was a person or a stag, or a mountain. Without it a painting would be sterile. You had to find its soul. Mac spoke of the engine as though it were a woman, a woman he was passionately in love with. Always 'she', not 'it' and once 'my love'. Broughton could understand that.

He disembarked into a chaotic dockside crowded with soldiers, workers, horses, carts and machinery. The fog was thick and damp, every surface slick and dripping. People, trolleys, horses and cranes loomed grey, faded again. He heard them before seeing them. It was mild, but the Cape weather was more like a London pea souper and it was difficult to grasp that summer, here, was just around the corner. He was assured the fog would soon burn off. Christmas only weeks away and he was promised it would be hot, unlike the stinging cold and rain back home. The men were in high spirits, ready for the fight, pitying the Boers for putting themselves into conflict with the pride of the Empire. Fame and glory beckoned. But first the Nubia had to be unloaded.

Meanwhile Broughton, caught in a mass of organised confusion, was keen to locate his luggage, especially his chest of artist materials. He carefully avoided tripping on the thick ropes coiling out from the Nubia. Her own lifting gear was off-loading crates and bulging sacks to carters lined up waiting to haul them away. Once or twice men eased him out of the way. He had to jump to avoid a horse and stoop as heavy cargo nets swung above his head. Gordon Kennedy rescued him, gave assurances that his possessions would be safely unloaded and transported to their camp, wherever that would be.

"I have to go, Edward. We have a meeting where we expect to receive orders. We might even meet General Buller who's going to give the Boers a good kicking. If I were you I'd hang around here until we return. I'll search you out. At least the fog's lifting. Smith, come on." His Jack Russell ran out from a tumble-down shed, reluctant to leave the sharp stink of rat.

The sun was gaining strength, fog melting away. Broughton found a large bale of cloth against a warehouse wall, climbed on top, safe from the cart wheels and horse hooves, and raised his face to the yellowing sun. He had a small sketch book and pencils in his pocket and took them out.

He watched as the troops in their khaki uniforms, who might have expected some refreshment and relief from the locals, particularly the women, were called to order to help with the prompt unloading of the cargo of war onto the dockside. Broughton, stomach tight with apprehension and again wondering why on earth he had embarked on this mad journey, could not imagine where they would sleep and eat that night. Bed down with rats on a warehouse floor? He shuddered.

Gordon Kennedy found Broughton still sitting on his bale, shielding his eyes as he sketched the dockside scene.

"Edward. Stick fast. As soon as this lot is finished we are marching out to join our train north. The Orange River. Sounds exotic, eh?"

"Truly orange? Is it far?"

"That remains to be seen. Come on, we're

meeting up at the old Custom House."

They threaded through the jumble of horses, carts and men out onto Cape Town's city streets. The sun now brilliant in a blue sky. He was stunned. It was like being back in London or Edinburgh, even Glasgow; handsome, stately, colonnade buildings lining wide, wide streets, with tram lines and fine horse drawn carriages. People dressed as though they had just stepped from the finest London theatre. A skyline of steeples and domes. Broughton had not expected this. Books at home had shown straw huts, camp fires, natives with spears. Not Glasgow with sunshine.

The troops, done at the docks, were marched along Adderley Street - it could have been London's Oxford Street – where groups of town's folk gathered to cheer them on. The sun shone warm. Not a breeze. Broughton ahead of them with the officers, walking past gardens, trees, fine architecture. The air fresh and clean. He was told they were making direct for the rail head where a train had already hauled in and was waiting. The word was spreading down the ranks that they were moving straight to the fight. Some 650 miles away the renegades had laid siege to the diamond town of Kimberley. The British were trapped and urgently needed help. Gordon looked across at Broughton. "If you were expecting death and disaster then I'm sorry you might well be disappointed. Treat it as a holiday, Edward. Enjoy the sun."

For the next day and a half their train steamed through a never-ending landscape of wide-open, boulder strewn, dung-coloured plain; dotted with large tussocks of grass and scrub, and only relieved here and there by scabby hills hardly more than a hump, some in small groups, like islands in a flat sea. The occasional, very occasional, twisted tree.

The journey was urgent, but monotonous, broken by stops for fuel and water, and for legs to be stretched, bladders and bowels emptied, a hasty brew and biscuit. Broughton was thankful he was in a carriage, many of the troops were in open wagons, like the coal wagons at home. He slept most of the way.

They finally arrived at a large army camp on the border of the Boer-controlled Orange Free State. White bell tents, equally spaced in neat lines covered the barren, brown landscape. Here troops were gathering under the command of legendary Lieutenant-General Lord Methuen ready for the final seventy-seven mile push to Kimberley.

Tuesday, 4am, November 21, 1899, Lord Methuen and 8,000 men, left their base on the Orange River, breaking out into the freezing cold, silent night. Edward Broughton, allocated a horse, among them. He had been shocked by the sudden departure. A quick brew, a slab of biscuit and off. A sliver of intense moon cast a silver light and overhead a canopy of thousands of stars glittered in the hard sky. To Broughton's dismay the river had not been orange. Someone explained it had been named by Dutch explorers in honour of their Royal House of Orange. A long, noisy, steaming column of marching men and horses, wagons and canons followed the railway line out into the vast, listening darkness. Later in the day the column had been joined at the rear by a steam train edging along, heavy with freight and armour plate, occasional piercing screams from its wheels filling the empty landscape.

Lord Methuen, at 54-years-old a veteran officer with wide experience in South Africa and a reputation as a fearless leader, confidently expected to enter Kimberley well within a fortnight. Today's early start would give them a full day in fine, warm weather for a march over easy terrain northwards. Boer terrorists had sabotaged the railway line in places, but they would carry out repairs as they progressed, opening an easy transport line to Kimberley. Spirits were high.

Edward Broughton RA, re-united with his

crate of artist materials, had re-supplied his sketch bag and now, with a pencil line of yellow sun along the horizon spilling a little daylight, moved to ride alongside Gordon Kennedy in a group of officers behind Lord Methuen.

Gordon turned to him: "A fine day, Edward. And it should get a little warmer."

"Indeed, but I never expected it could get so cold in Africa at night. My hands are freezing. I've known warmer winter days in Scotland. I expected more green than this. It's all very, well, very brown. When you can see it."

"Not good for drawing?"

"No. I tried a little drawing in the camp for my diary, but that man, Beck isn't it, he told me to stop. Said my book would be useful information to the Boers if I were captured."

"Beck's a tedious chap. But he has the ear of Lord Methuen. Best to go along with him at the moment. Nothing lost."

"I was talking to some men from the North Lancashires. Apparently some of their lot are stuck in Kimberley."

"Yes, but not for long. A few days and we'll be there and the Boers will be on the run. You'll see."

Daylight was growing fast as the sun spread red along the deep blue horizon. Stars fading.

A group of horsemen riding at the head of the column, slowed and reined in alongside. Edward Broughton recognised the long, heavily moustached face, of the very same Lord Methuen, next to him, squinting into the rising sun. He made out Beck next to him.

Their breath plumed gold. "Our artist, eh? I hear good things of you Broughton. Stay close to young Kennedy here and you should do fine. Hope we can give you some action to get at. But these Boers are likely to turn and run." Lord Methuen dropped further back to talk to another group of officers.

Camp was made that night, most of the men sleeping rough without tents, and the following day the column re-assembled in the half-light of a growing dawn, and moved on, completing eight miles, arriving, Broughton was told, at Thomas' Farm, just south of Belmont Railway Station. It all sounded strangely rustic to Broughton, who stood by the white, low farmhouse, staring out across brown grass and a rubble of rock to the far horizon, becoming purple in the evening light. What on earth could you farm in this stony, barren place? Dreamy thoughts of the green hills of home.

He moved forward to saunter across the open ground thinking he could at least sketch the house in the last of the days light. "Get down, you bloody fool." A blow to the back sent him sprawling into the dust.

CHAPTER 7

DI ARMSTRONG had telephoned journalist Tony Jewson when he arrived home from Kirkcudbright. No point pissing him off by failing to return the call, especially as he knew him of old and would be asking a favour. He also gambled that the impending royal visit was pre-occupying the Press as much as the police.

They small talked football. Armstrong was completely disinterested in the pampered cheats who took to the pitch in the modern game, but kept abreast of events because it was the only topic of conversation among so many of his colleagues and others he met through the job. Such as Jewson. Common ground. Otherwise it was music, and he did not want to go there.

Yes, he confirmed, a skeleton had been found when the gable end of the house on Hornel Street collapsed, but ....

"Murder," interrupted Jewson, immediately a

sense of excitement.

"No, no. We're not looking at it like that, Tony. I wouldn't be on it if it were because, as you know, in a couple of days I pack this in."

"So, what then? It must have been a shock."

"Are you writing this down?"

"Not every day a body, sorry a skeleton is found in a roof. A cupboard, maybe, but a roof?" A small laugh.

"It wasn't a shock as such. The occupant didn't know about it. The thing was found when the lads moved in to carry out some emergency work on the house. No, no. It looks like it was one of those things doctors and artists use for their training."

"Oh, what, so it was a false thing? A toy. Well, artificial?"

Armstrong paused, wondered whether he should let that assumption go unchallenged. Decided he would.

"People shove all sorts of stuff into their attic and forget about it. Look have you missed your deadline for tomorrow morning?"

"Not quite, but there's a bigger problem."

"OK, well we are taking a look at it tomorrow. I don't think there's anything in it at all. It could be plastic. Nothing to it."

"Famous last words."

"Well, agreed, but until tomorrow I can't say

much else. If you're prepared to wait on it I'll let you know what we find. Otherwise I think we could both end up looking bloody stupid. What's your 'bigger problem'?"

"Mmmmm."

"Pardon?"

"I was just considering what you said. Are you going to release this generally?"

"No. If there's anything in it, I'll keep it to you. I presume it was your brother-in-law in the fire service who tipped you off, so it's unlikely any other reporters will be onto it."

Tony Jewson let that pass. "Shit. Problem is, I'm off from tomorrow. I was hoping to leave them a bloody good story to go at."

"Somewhere nice?"

"Hopefully. It's a freebie cruise to New York, two days in a luxury hotel and a jet home."

"That must be costing a bomb. It'd be the end of my job if I took a freebie of any kind, even a turkey for Christmas."

"Thankfully the Press are not so honourable. So I'll be writing them a nice travel feature."

"For your own paper?" Keep him distracted.

"No, since that award last year I get into the nationals and syndicated through the group here. Fame has its rewards."

"What sort of time are you leaving?"

"I'll be leaving home about six in the morning. Too early?"

"Certainly, yes. There's a lot to sort. I imagine it will be afternoon before we start."

"Look, I'll leave a message with the news desk and they can get someone to ring you tomorrow afternoon. Is that okay?"

"Fine." Hopefully that 'someone' would forget. "Enjoy your holiday."

John Armitage drove through mid-morning murk and rain to the mortuary at Dumfries Hospital. A forensic team had carefully removed the skeleton and also filled bags of debris from around it. All to be sifted for clues.

Trouble reared its ugly head within minutes of walking into the hospital. He hoped to learn something about the skeleton, perhaps an idea about the person it had been and how he or she had died. No such luck. He was greeted at the doors to the lab with news that the pathologist was on holiday, his stand-in had not taken a look at the bones because he was ill but they had called in someone from Newcastle University who should be arriving early afternoon, about 2pm, traffic permitting. This was pushing his retirement to the limit.

Two days to go.

He had spent the early morning in his office shouting 'come in' to colleagues whose shifts and duties would mean they would not see him again before the Big Day. Between visits he sorted files for the archives, boxed personal items and prepared his initial report on the skeleton find, which he hoped to complete by the evening. A mountain of things to do. Would any one bother if he just closed his door and walked out? He suspected not.

He strolled to the hospital cafeteria and on his way tried to telephone home. He would have a grumble to his wife. He'd feel better for that. She was out. It would be one of those days.

DI Armstrong had not heard of Newcastle University's Professor Francis Cuthbertson, forensic anthropologist. Why would he? Professor, he mused, imagining some stooped, grey haired, arthritic, has-been who'd ducked out of real pathology to preach and boast to students. In the café he'd shared a table with an assistant in the mortuary who explained that Cuthbertson was an expert on bones. His work on digs at Roman forts along Hadrian's Wall was celebrated. Armstrong grumpily replied it was unlikely to be 'bloody Caesar' who'd accidently been bricked up in the house.

The Painter Of Souls

Professor Francis Cuthbertson was, well, Armstrong had to admit, a shock. They met at the door to the laboratory. If it wasn't to be a doddery chap nearing retirement, he had hoped Francis would be one of those leggy, attractive blonds who crop up on television, seduce the hardened detective on the case – inevitably old enough to be her father – before racing away in her open top sports car leaving behind a cloud of dust, the faintest smell of expensive perfume and viewers, certainly in Armstrong's case, who switch off because it was a complete load of bollocks.

He was less than 5 feet tall. Armstrong estimated four feet ten inches. Did he shave? Was this someone's son, the call too sudden to find a child minder, although it wasn't school holidays?

"John?"

"Yes. Err, I'm looking for Professor Francis Cuthbertson?"

"Spot on. You've found him. Frank. Just Frank." He reached out his hand and they shook. "Shall we go in? Follow me. I've had a quick looksee. Most interesting."

Armstrong helped him push open the door, felt a lump grow in his stomach. Interesting? Sounded ominous. The sweet chemical stench of the room hit him, burning his nostrils as it always did. It would weave into his clothing and he would stink of the stuff all day. They walked across to the stainless steel table where the bones had been assembled into a grey, grinning skeleton. Minus the right shin bone.

Frank hauled himself onto a stool and reached across to two metal contraptions propped against the wall and dragged them to him. Armstrong was puzzled then recognized them as builder's stilts like the ones worn by a plasterer who repaired his ceiling after a bath had overflowed. Frank strapped them on and stood, balanced himself. "Right. On with the gloves and the face visors. Then, lights, please, John. The switch is behind you. And action."

Overhead tubes flickered on, blinding white from all directions. No shadows.

"Now John, I only had chance for a quick poke around before you came. A minute or so. Mainly photos of today's subject and the problem is that you see what the camera wants you to see. Anyway. By the way, you're not the John Armstrong who was drummer in Teal? Fave music."

"Right. Can we just…." He nodded down at the skeleton.

"Sorry. So we at least can say it's a human." Frank pulled an overhead bank of lights closer and angled them onto the bones.

The Painter Of Souls

Armstrong's hopes sank. What kind of expert was this? Talk about stating the bloody obvious. His face must have betrayed his thoughts.

"You'd be surprised. About a third of all cases like this turn out not to be human at all. Usually we don't have the full skeleton just a few bones. Horses, dogs, cattle. There's all sorts buried out there which people find and believe there's been a grisly murder. Next thing is they're crying 'Help!' because they believe they've found another victim of Jack the Ripper or Dr Crippen, when in fact it's his pet poodle."

"Oh, really, Crippen had a poodle?" He felt an idiot as he said it. "No, no forget what I just said. Sorry. Really. Look we thought this may have been one of those skeletons artists use for drawing thing. Any chance of that?" He hoped it would be a simple yes, but feared - and received - the worst.

"No. Nothing like that. It would show evidence of bones drilled to take the wires to hold the thing together. Perhaps a nice hole in the top of the skull for a hook to hold it all up." He leant over the skull and Armstrong feared he would topple on his stilts. "Nope. Anyway, they tend to be plastic these days for the artists, though years ago they did have the real thing. They used all sorts of stuff –

real skulls, bits of animals. You name it. Talented people are often a little odd."

"Indeed." A straight face. "But it could have been used to just help an artist? Bought in bones, so to speak."

"I suppose. Apparently the bones were in a bit of a jumble and there's one or two pieces missing. A rib. And the right shin. Might turn up. So, are we looking at a man or woman? Well, I would say it's female. Let's move down." They shuffled. He pointed to the groin. "You can see the width? The pubic bone. Have you done this before?"

"Not with a skeleton."

"Oh right. Well, the female pubic bone tends to be wider to allow for the child's head to pass through at birth. Not 100 per cent. Not certain. But here."

They moved back to the head.

"The supraorbital ridge…"

Armstrong looked blank.

"Ah, yes, one of those technical phrases we use to make us look particularly special and clever. Beloved of crime writers who think it makes them credible. It's that there." His finger pointed to the top of the skull. "The brow. All around this part of the skull here." He turned and now jabbed at Armstrong, more or less between the eyes. Armstrong recoiled.

Frank smiled at him. "You see, the brow tends to be more pronounced in a male. Like yours. Feel it. Go on. And this bit here, between the brow and the nose, the glabella, is bony on our specimen here. We men don't have that. So female. Not 100 per cent. Not certain."

"Right. Those marks, on the jaw."

"Could be where rats had a nibble. There's similar marks all over which probably explains why there's no skin, none at all on the skeleton, although there may be some in the debris. Some of the marks could be an indication of syphilis. Anyway, I can't see anything that's an obvious injury to explain death. No crushing hole in the skull, for example. Could you pass me that magnifying glass? Thank you." He peered closely at the bones.

"Could they have been made by a blade, a knife?"

"Well there's so many. You'd expect to see evidence of stabs, a cut in the bone itself. Like a gouge. But there's none of that. If these were made by a blade then it would have been death by a thousand cuts. Possible. If I could have one of the bones to study I could be definitive."

He gave an enquiring look, which Armstrong ignored.

"Anyway, as mentioned, no great hole in the skull. Once had a skull out of a medieval battlefield and you could see where a sword blow had sliced away the side. Clean off. The brains would have spilled hot and steaming and death a certainty. But 400 years on and who knows who the culprit was or even the victim. But back to our companion here."

"It would help me if you could estimate how long she had been there. Just a rough idea?"

"Of course. I'll come to that. I'd say some years because we have no hair and that can last a long, long time. Years. But first the age when she died - or was murdered." He gave Armstrong a wide smile. "There's extensive decay in her teeth, must have been painful, and that could be an indication that our skeleton had a sweet tooth and poor hygiene. But that didn't kill her."

"So she's old?"

"Not too old, I don't believe. Now, John, when we are born we have all sorts of bits and pieces that are not yet joined up. This happens over the years. Ossification, we call it. Around 800 bits and pieces have to glue together. I looked earlier and it's completed. So she, if it is a she, not 100 per cent certain, then she must be into her mid-twenties at the least."

"Right."

"Look here." A quick shuffle down the table. "The head of the femur and the hip are complete. Usually happens by 24. And then here." They shuffled back to the skull. "Bad teeth and the third molars are well through. So mid 20's again. And the teeth are quite rotten. Probably had very bad breath. There's no sign of dentistry, none at all, which would be unusual if she was living in this country in our, shall we call them, modern times. So again suggesting she died some years ago, and was probably into her 30's, not 40's. Depends on diet and nerves."

"Nerves?"

"Do you grind your teeth, John? You do. Don't. Back to the groin. The pubic symphysis, that's the joint between the right and left pubic bones, it's quite rough and tends to wear smooth with age. Feel that."

"I'd rather not."

"Ok, well it's rough. So probably not old, old. Not certain, not 100 per cent. And back again." He shifted to the skull. "She has all the characteristics of being Caucasian."

"So we have a white woman in her late 20's, 30's at the most? Died some years ago."

"Most likely. Not certain. Not 100 per cent. 162."

"Pardon?"

"She was approximately 5ft 4 tall. Just a quick measurement. 162 centimetres."

"She looks shorter."

"Add a little for flesh."

"Right. I have the picture. But what would really help here, Professor…"

"Frank, John." He smiled.

"Sorry, Frank. Any idea of how long she's been there and how she got there."

"Well, as I explained, no obvious cause of death, well, no obvious major trauma. The hyoid bone is unfortunately not with us. It could have fallen out or still be at the scene. Worth a look."

Armstrong was on a little more familiar ground.

"Ah, yes, the hyoid. It breaks on strangulation."

"Indeed, John, yes. Worth checking to see if it can be found."

"But how long ago? Recent? It looks old."

"Well, John, that is an interesting observation. Not many realise how quickly a corpse is skeletonised. Just because we have a pile of bones does not necessarily mean we have an ancient crime on our hands, if a crime at all."

"Right, I understand that."

"So, clearly we are beyond the normal stages of decomposition. The fresh, the putrefaction, the fermentation and the dry. You know, decomposition starts moments after the final breath is drawn? The body starts to eat itself. Then maggots and beetles move in to help out. So at least a year. Conditions are important. We have no adiopocere – that's grave wax to mere mortals – which needs cold and humidity. But I understand this was by a chimney stack, so warm and perhaps quite cosy. I believe our skeleton was against the chimney, perhaps propped against it originally. Cosy also for rats and insects and they can work very quickly on a corpse. We can have complete skeletonisation within eight or nine months."

"Shit. So this could be quite recent?" Armstrong had a vision of a long and drawn out murder inquiry, wrecking his plans for a peaceful wind down to retirement.

"Unlikely. Remember the condition of the teeth. But, if this was a desert."

"Which it is not."

"Indeed it is not. But we could have arrived at skeletonisation within a week. Time since death is very difficult. But, we do have help."

"All is not lost?" Armstrong was finding it difficult to keep hold of the salient facts.

"All is not. The lack of hair suggest some years. Hair can last a long time. Think of those lockets with the last remnants of loved ones who lived centuries ago. Lockets and locks. Carbon dating would tell us if this was the remains of a young lady who walked this earth many, many years ago. It would take weeks and I doubt very much that it is."

"OK, so not Neanderthal man?

"Woman."

"Sorry. Woman."

"No. We can test for radiation. Over the last 60 years we've been absorbing increasing amounts of radiocarbons thanks to the nuclear age. From 1955 to the mid 60's, the amount of radiocarbon in the atmosphere almost doubled and we humans soak it up like a sponge. We can examine the enamel on teeth to find out how much has been absorbed and fairly accurately give the year of birth. That's if it was since we started exploding nuclear bombs. So if she was born, say, 1974 I could tell you that, given time and a bone."

"The lady of the house has lived there more than 90-odd years and we reckon it must have been there at least that long."

"OK. When was the house built? Refresh me."

"It's still being checked but, I'd guess 150 years, perhaps a little more."

"Mmm. Well I've found nothing which suggests that this young woman, if young woman it is, died outside that time frame. Of course this is all preliminary. Not certain.

Not 100 per cent."

"Not certain, but I'm looking here at a young woman, white?"

"Most likely."

"Has she had children?"

"Not conclusive, but I'd say perhaps not looking at the pelvic indents."

"The pelvic what? Never mind. So a young woman, late 20's early 30's, most likely 30's, probably no children, white, about five feet four inches, no obvious cause of death, bad and bloody painful teeth, perhaps syphilitic and death occurring, what at least 100 years ago. About it?"

"On the face of it. Nothing certain. Relieved?"

"Too early to say. Any clues how she got in there?"

"Not obvious. Not from the skeletal remains. Could have died there. Could have been hidden there. Could have been a skeleton bought in and used for study. Any one of a number of explanations."

"But, if it was murder then the culprit will be long dead themselves. Long dead. Probably look no better than this."

"Indeed. Not certain. Not 100 per cent. But most likely."

Armstrong thought of the costs of further testing. Budgets were tight. He would have to follow the recent guidelines and recommend that at this stage there would be little point continuing. He had nagging doubts, but it would please his budget-obsessed boss.

They removed their protective gear, dropped rubber gloves into a bin marked 'Gloves' and pushed out into the clearer air of the corridor.

"Thank you very much for your time and advise, Frank. Can I offer you a coffee in the café here? It's not half bad. Well it is, but."

"Isn't there a pub near here? Surely a decent ale house is never far from a building with so many doctors in it. I'd like a bone for my own testing. Out of interest. There are so many bite or cut marks on the bones. Intriguing. I'll buy the beer. You can vouch for my age. Always a problem. Oh, I came by taxi. Don't worry."

Bloody taxi from Newcastle to Dumfries. John Armstrong gagged. Who the hell would get billed for that? Hopefully the pathologist and health service. They zipped up anoraks, pulled up hoods. It was dreary dark and raining hard as they emerged onto the car park, eyes blinking to adjust to the sudden change from bright light.

Armstrong's mobile burred, just as his new friend launched into another subject. Bumblebees, metamorphosis and some such.

"Hang on, I'll have to answer this. " They hurried to a plastic shelter half full of bicycles.

It was Mike in the control room. Officers at the scene had found the remains of a small door inset into the bedroom wall – boarded over and plastered and papered over. The covering looked very old, invisible from the bedroom side under wallpaper yellowed and crumbling with age. "Looks like it's been there years."

"Thanks, Mike." He slipped the mobile back into his coat pocket. "Sorry, Frank. You were saying?" Heads down against the rain, holding their hoods, they hurried through the fuzzy blue cast by the car park's lights.

"Yes. Bumblebees. Most people think that wonderful process called metamorphosis applies to butterflies and moths. But bumblebees, well, they are just as remarkable. They start out as maggots, pupate, all their innards dissolve and then reform and you have, as if by magic, a bumblebee. Now…….."

A car reversing from a space on the car park lurched backwards and caught Frank a glancing blow.

"Fuck!" He staggered and fell into a shallow puddle.

"Are you OK?" John Armstrong had reached to stop Frank falling and now almost stumbled onto him.

"My leg's gone. I felt it crack."

A young man unfolded from the car, face contorted by rage. Shouted at them: "Don't you look where you're fuckin going?" He glared at the two men. Frank down and John Armstrong staggering to remain upright. "You old fucker."

"Us? You're joking? And you?" John Armstrong regained his balance and turned to confront the youth. "What the hell were you playing at?"

"Don't swear at me you old bastard or I'll drop you as well, grandad. So you, fuck off. You should look were you're going. Twat." Fists clenched, he advanced at John Armstrong.

DI Armstrong stood his ground. Pushed down his hood. "One more step, son, and I'll drop you." He took out his wallet and showed him his warrant card. "Now, you little shit, get against the car. Now. Hands on top and don't move." John Armstrong walked past him, bent into the car and took out the ignition keys.

"See these?" He held the keys up to the youth. "You are going to have a nice fine to pay the car park folk cos your car's going to be here some time." He made to thrown the keys into a distant shrubbery and the youth followed the arc to where he expected them to land, marking the spot by a waste bin in his memory. Meanwhile DI Armstrong slipped the keys into his coat pocket, never having let go of them. He would dump them roadside miles away.

"Now, this gentleman you have hit is in need of help and you, you little shit, in need of a conversation with my colleagues. Don't try and get up Frank." He took out his mobile phone. "Here's my coat."

CHAPTER 8

THE temperature was falling rapidly as Africa swiftly moved to evening. Thomas' Farm, a square, squat, low white building amid dry trees, dry dirt and dry air, looked out over a boulder strewn landscape towards Belmont, a scrum of stone and prefabricated buildings thrown up to accommodate a railway stopover on the line to Kimberley about fifty five miles away. A couple of hours by train. Beyond, distant hills smudged the horizon and rapidly turned to darker shades of purple as the night closed in.

Broughton stood by the farmhouse porch, picking at the peeling whitewash, looking out to the failing horizon. He shivered as the warmth of the day was sucked away by the dying sun. What on earth could you farm here? He had met the farmers, brothers John and Alexander Thomas, and was none the wiser. He hardly understood a word they said. Scrappy trees pushed gnarled roots down to find whatever water might lurk in the parched earth, but little else seemed to grow. At least here there was some relief to the monotonous flat landscape. To the north east, hills lifted to what could be mountains, although it was again difficult judging distance and scale as the light faded. He pondered how he would adapt his work to this different perspective. At home there was always landmarks here and there. But the African landscape of flat beige veldt gave little away. He longed for those green hills of home, imagined the brackish smell of heather on a hot August day. He set off to find a vantage point to sketch the farmhouse. He would have to hurry, its white walls already shifting to pink.

"Get down, you bloody fool." He felt a sharp blow in the back and fell, sprawling into the dust. Only then did he hear a sharp crack.

"There are Boers out there. We need to get back to the house." Gordon Kennedy had been standing near to his friend Broughton when the sharpshooters began to range in. "Don't stand! Shuffle."

The two men crawled into a scrubby stand of stunted trees by a pond, which even in the half-light they could see was fed by surprisingly crystal clear water. Silence, and then, without warning, in-coming artillery shells exploded, thankfully some way away to their right. One of the two farming Thomas brothers, John, was already among the trees taking shelter. He was angry.

"You've brought some bloody trouble down on us." They clung to the trees as the deafening explosions shook the earth beneath their feet. One shell sent showers of dirt into the trees.

The bombardment stopped as suddenly as it started, but they waited, in silence, until full darkness before hurrying to the farmhouse.

Lord Methuen and his officers had gathered in the kitchen that also served as the only living room in the house. Windows shuttered. Candles lit. Intelligence officer Lieutenant Colonel Verner had earlier braved gunfire to survey any Boer positions that lay ahead. He spread out a map on the kitchen table. Edward Broughton stood to the back of the room, sketching by candlelight. He had been badly shaken by the earlier shooting and shelling and even now had trouble controlling his hand. But, the men around the table had a confident air. A sense of outrage that the enemy, because that's what they were now, the enemy, had dared to launch an attack. Albeit one that had claimed no casualties.

According to Verner, Boers had occupied a line of broken hills to the north east which crossed the very route they were taking to

The Painter Of Souls

Kimberley. Farmers John and Alex described the area as being like a natural fort, with rocky outcrops providing good cover for anyone on the summit, while the approaching veldt and slopes were barren and provided little cover. John seemed pleased to tell them: "You'll be picked off real easy. Them lads are crack shots."

Verner suggested an advance under cover of darkness, timed to launch a surprise attack at first light, overrunning the Boers before they could react. Methuen agreed. "Let's give those Boers an early breakfast treat."

Broughton had wondered whether he should excuse himself and take his breakfast at the farmhouse, but Methuen announced: "It will be a rout. That rabble of peasant farmers won't know what hit them. We'll show them what the British Army is made of."

Orders went out to the troops to prepare for an early start.

That night, men were handed a biscuit and cup full of brackish water. "Keep you hungry for action. You'll soon be back for a good feed." The officers enjoyed a handsome dinner of beef and brandy.

Later, Broughton, provided with a bed roll on the floor of an outbuilding adjoining the farmhouse, was shaken from a deep sleep by a figure he could hardly make out in the thick night. "You're with us, sir. Grab your stuff." Was this wise? He stood cautiously, aware the roof was low. A candle was lit. Dim yellow light wavering in deep darkness. Other men were moving around him. He was handed a cup. "Coffee, it'll help get you going." The man had loomed out of deep shadow and melted back in to it. His legs were shaking, fear or fatigue? He did not know. Probably both. This was madness. The canvas bag of artist material weighed heavy on his shoulder, seeming to pull him back. An omen? The coffee was only lukewarm, and bitter.

He ducked out through the low door. Men carefully moving about. Hushed voices called them to order. Some moonlight, shifting under clouds, now and then showing soldiers coming together. "Absolute silence, gentlemen, if you please. We want to take them by surprise, so save the chat for the stroll home."

Broughton hitched his bag higher. What on earth was he doing? He could only just make out the white of his hand in front of his face, never mind see to draw. He may as well be wearing a black hood – or stay behind.

Shortly after 2am they began to move out under a star-lit sky black as velvet. Broughton completely unaware who he was with or even precisely where he were going. The soldier in front had a white strap across his back and he focussed on that, stumbling forward as best he could.

The ground underfoot was treacherous, loose rock. He tripped more than once, grabbing at the white strap to steady himself. Finally, with no reaction from the man in front, he held on to the strap for dear life.

Stars and compass guided the way as the groups of soldiers moved on across the silent veldt. Edward Broughton cursed his luck: the first action and he could not see a thing. What was he to sketch? And the luck for all of the men moving around him was also running out because it was becoming obvious that the distance judged hurriedly yesterday was inaccurate. They were taking longer than expected to cover the open ground and then, as the first milky glow of dawn smeared the horizon, they reached barbed wire fencing. Unexpected. It had to be cut. The noise of the wire cutters echoed like gunfire into the approaching morning's silence.

Broughton's party finally arrived at the base of the hill, all hope of a surprise attack long gone. He looked up through the grey light and could see distant figures moving along the ridge. Men, presumably Boers, hurrying to take up position. Then the blood red sun split the bruised horizon and gunfire rained down. His group ran forward, Broughton still clinging to the soldier in front. Suddenly the man fell, breaking his grip. He almost stumbled over the man. Shot or tripped? Broughton, struggling to balance, flung himself behind a boulder to his left. Crack, crack, crack. He saw the soldier who had led him through the night rise again, run, fall again.

Growing daylight. Broughton realised he was some way up the hill. From his position he could see groups of men below and alongside. And his was one of the few large boulders providing any cover. The ground was like a sun-dried lawn back home.

A bugler sounded charge. More gunshot exploded overhead. Bullets thudded into the earth and sparked off his boulder. The sun now heaving its bloody bulk into the pale, early morning sky, the few clouds red with it. He watched in horror as men he now recognised, men he had sketched in camp, ran forward and fell. Others running at the hill, rifles with bayonets, faces contorted with bloodthirsty rage. He pulled out his drawing book and pencils.

As suddenly as it started, it stopped. Silence.

The Boers, later estimated at 2,000 strong, had escaped on ponies as the advancing soldiers neared them. He did not know how long the fighting had lasted. Seconds? Minutes? An hour? A heavy, pressing silence pierced by what he though was birdsong. It lifted his spirits, and then, he realised, it was the screams of the wounded men, some pulling their last breath.

Broughton stood, shaking, tried to brush himself down, felt at his head and studied his trembling hands. No blood. Picked up his canvass bag, then dropped it. Pushed home his sketch book. His pencils. Dazed. Checked his head again. Couldn't remember what he had drawn. If anything. Surveyed the carnage around him. Twisted bodies. Khaki uniforms deeper brown with blood. Helmets scattered like stones. Wiped tears from his eyes. Realised he had peed himself.

They had convinced him he should experience real battle. But surely not this, not this slaughter. Yes, he had seen stags brought down on the hills at home. Clean shots. He turned, took the strap of his bag and walked away, dragging it behind him. Dust rising. Heard someone shouting: "Help me, please." A tug at his leg, but carried on walking. They were not calling to him.

Later that day, as back home in Scotland the first snow of winter softly fell, the heat of early summer warmed the backs of men digging holes in dry dirt for their dead. Now laid out wrapped in blankets. Stiff. Broughton, handed a flask of neat whisky by an officer he knew only by sight, had recovered senses enough to record in a sketch the burial of an officer, a popular man called Burton, who had stood to accept a Boer white flag of surrender, only to be shot through the head. His blood made a rusty brown stain on the white sheet which was already soiled by the orange earth. He was gently lowered into the grave. The men agreed: "The Boers were cowards who deserved, and would be given, no mercy."

Earlier the wounded and dying had been carried on carts to buildings by Thomas's Farm where a makeshift field hospital had been established. Hastily. They had not expected this level of casualties - 75 dead and 243 wounded. Inside frantic activity, blood spurting, screams. Outside, row upon row of stretchers laid out in the shade of feeble trees growing around a pond of clear water.

The officer who had offered Broughton whisky now watched him sketch scenes of the field hospital. "You know, if only we'd set out half an hour earlier this would have never happened. Half an hour. Still, our Boer prisoners say they have more in store for us – so we'll get the chance for revenge." He strode away. Broughton, oblivious to the chaos around him, did not hear and continued to draw. He was finally interrupted by the offer of champagne to toast the first victory over the Boers. The bottles had been stored in the clear pond and the champagne was chilled.

The following day, mid-morning in warming sun in a sky entirely clear of cloud, Broughton, who had slept unusually heavily for him, despite fearing he would not sleep at all, stood on the platform at Belmont Station, waiting alongside a group of officers for the return of their armoured train. It had been sent in advance to test the line of Boer resistance ahead and perhaps push on to Kimberley. Indeed, was there really any resistance ahead after the Boer's had been put to flight yesterday? Their Boer prisoners claimed it was only a tactical retreat and their comrades would re-group. But who could believe such a ragtag band of defeated men? More likely, the Boers had run like beaten dogs. They had taken to their cowardly heels when the first of the troops crested the ridge, bayonets fixed, and had probably carried on running. The British hoped the Boers would make a stand, a last stand, because they could avenge their fallen comrades.

Mounted cavalry of the Loyal North Lancashire had ridden out with the train, with orders to peel away at times and reconnoitre the dry kopjes to assess Boer numbers and locations, if any.

He had sketched their departure, his materials replenished that morning from a supply train which had steamed from the south into Belmont carrying ammunition, food, mail and personal belongings for officers, including Broughton's packing case. He could at last change into some clean clothes.

The previous evening, in the farmhouse, over a good meal and a glass or two of wine, he had listened to Lord Methuen claim the resounding victory. He sketched Methuen, surrounded by admiring officers. Each recognisable. They had applauded his drawing of the assault on the hills, their grim-faced troops emerging from the night to thwart the cowardly Boer. He called it The Battle of Belmont and had sent it back to the Cape on the supply train. Within days it would be splashed across the front of patriotic newspapers back home.

The reconnaissance train had set off early morning, its engine, clad in armoured plate, looked like an enormous steel box with a smoking funnel jutting out of the top. It pushed ahead a similarly armour-clad wagon mounted with a light artillery gun and pulled behind two open goods wagons filled with heavily armed troops and officers. The train and mounted company, horses rearing in excitement, had been sent off by cheering comrades. "Give our love to Kimberley." "Tell them to have supper on the table."

Broughton, on the very edge of the high-spirited group, though he felt very much admired by them all for his artistic skill and bravery, was again questioning his own sanity in agreeing to travel to Africa when he spotted in the far distance a plume of what looked like smoke. He squinted at the horizon made hazy by the sun. Conversation among the officers also halted as they too tried to focus. Men leaned forward, hands shading eyes. Was it the train? He thought he could just make out the dark shape of the armour-plated engine hauling around a curve of the line. As yet silent and somewhat indistinct in the heat haze. It appeared to be pushing the pair of heavy wagons with troops and officers, and as it emerged from the throbbing horizon he could make out they had rifles, bayonets and pistols at the ready. He saw that the engine was in reverse, the armoured tender with its light artillery gun trained on the retreating line ready to engage anyone who tried to chase down the train. He glanced beyond the hurrying train but could see nothing. Men alongside moved to the edge of the platform. Cleary disturbed. The train should have arrived at Kimberley. Some had their own binoculars which they passed among the group.

One with a pair that looked more like opera glasses with its rich blue and white enamel handed them to Broughton. "Take a look." The train was speeding in reverse. Shaking dangerously on the lines. He could see men with one hand on their rifles, the other steadying themselves on the wagon sides. He could now hear the racing beat of the engine.

Eventually, the heavy train slid to a squealing halt, sparks flying from the locked wheels, steam billowing out into the clear African air. Everyone hurried forward. Men jumped from the wagons. What had happened and where were the Lancashires? Breathless.

They had been moving slowly, stopping here and there to check out the lay of the land. Then, as they approached Graspan Station, only eight miles ahead, they had suddenly come under heavy artillery fire and feared being blown off the line. The Lancashires had already ridden into the hills and hadn't been seen since. Lord Methuen's aides pushed through the gathering. The officer in charge of the train was hurried away to the tented field headquarters.

A little after lunch the Royal Lancashire's rode hard back to the British line. Their story was similar. They had ridden out into the hills to find the Boer and had encountered snipers. One officer and two men shot dead.

Attempts had been made to catch the Boer, but they had again escaped on ponies more used to the difficulty terrain of boulders and scrub. They had spotted an enemy force of about 400 occupying a line of kopjes that rose wall-like from the flat veldt just north of the sidings at Graspan. They had at least two artillery guns. They blocked the route to Kimberley.

Surely this was bad news, thought Broughton aloud, but he was immediately corrected. Enemy troops an easy march away and only 400 of them, against their 8,000. It would be a rout. Then on to Kimberley. Job done. Someone slapped him heartily on the back. "Don't worry, Edward. A bit of action to sharpen your pencils."

Excitement spread through the troops. Revenge. It was decided to march out that afternoon, make camp south of Graspan and attack early the following day – if the Boers had not already panicked and fled. Spirits were high.

The armoured engine was re-fuelled with coal and watered. Carriages added. Broughton joined the officers in the second, preferring a ride to a march as the sun rose high and a breeze developed, sucking in a hot afternoon. He again found himself alongside Gordon Kennedy and his Jack Russell.

"Your first taste of action then, Edward. Enjoyable?"

"Yesterday? Hardly enjoyable. It's like the hunt. When the stag is finally brought down I always feel a sense of sadness. Everyone else cheering, but, well."

"I saw you put some sketches onto the return supply train heading back to Cape Town. They'll be on the front pages in no time. Strange to think it can be so fast when it's all that way back home. A matter of days. You know, old chap, you only have to ask and you can have one of me, get Smith on." Gordon Kennedy struck a pose in the limited space, gave him a wide grin. "What do you think? Set the ladies hearts a-racing? Me, not Smith. Can you do dogs?" Other men in the carriage laughed at them. Gordon Kennedy, jaw jutted, and Smith lifted up to sit on his shoulder, barking.

The pair would indeed feature in an illustration drawn the next day that would make front pages around the Empire and the remainder of the world. One that would only enhance further the reputation of Edward Broughton RA.

CHAPTER 9

JOHN Armstrong unfolded from the rear of the taxi, held onto the door to help pull himself upright, stretched his stiff legs, paid the driver and watched him three-point turn before heading to his next customer. A dank and dark winter's evening. He then walked passed the For Sale sign with its SOLD banner, along the neat garden path to the front door of the stone-built house he and Jane had renovated in a quiet street on the edge of the Maxwelltown area of west Dumfries. He fumbled, then dropped his key. "Shit". Fumbled, not because he was drunk, but his whole body was shaking. Thankfully Jane, who had been watching from the front bay window, hurried to open up.

"So, that's it?" Yellow light slanted out into the gloom. And warmth.

"That is it."

"Come here, plain John Armstrong." They embraced in the doorway in the golden light. "I can't believe it. You're earlier than I thought.

Come in. Shut out the night and keep in the warmth. Are you cold? You're shaking."

"Nor me. I can't stop shaking with the nerves of it. I got to the point in the pub where I felt I was an outsider looking in. That was it. I just got up and came home. Rang you. Left them all to it. Crazy?"

"John Armstrong has nerves? Sorry. It was the same when I packed in at school last year. You remember? I warned you. And I've never felt the need to return. No more kids and their grumbles about Robbie Burns. No more bloody late night calls for you. Just the two of us. Freedom."

He disentangled Jane and stripped his coat and scarf.

"So how was your last day at the office?"

"A blur. Honestly, I can hardly remember it."

They moved through to the lounge and he flopped onto the settee. Jane joined him. Silence. Then he turned to her. "Fancy Edinburgh tomorrow?"

"Edinburgh? Well, yes, why not. Of course. Are you sure?"

"There's someone I need to see. Then we can find a good restaurant. Henderson's if you fancy."

She smiled. "Someone? Someone to do with your, err, former job? To be honest I could do with the break. A trip to Edinburgh. It seems ages since we were last there. What with selling the house, both of us retiring – God, that makes us sound old – and finding somewhere to rent here before we can move to France. I assume tomorrow by train?"

"No, I think we should drive. Its time."

Jane reached out to hold his arms, look deep into this complication called a man: "Are you sure? If you are, I'm with you all the way."

He had gone in early on his last day to catch his Chief Superintendent and settle the issue of the skeleton. His last case. Clearly it had been there many years and if there had been foul play then the culprit would also be long dead. There had been no further clues. Frank Cuthbertson had been detained in hospital with a serious break in his leg and other complications. Scenes of crime had come up with nothing new to explain how the bones had got into the void and who they were. Their boss, Tony Foster, whom John had known and respected for years, had repeated long held grumbles about pressure to meet budgets and not waste limited resources satisfying politicians who knew not a damn thing about policing, but arrogantly thought they did.

"John, we are chasing ghosts. If I were you I'd just leave it and enjoy your days gardening, making music, or whatever. I'll miss you."

He had surprised DCI Armstrong by moving forward and hugging him. "Give my love to Jane."

There was no easy way to identify her, if a way at all. But it was a "her". A woman. Someone who had a life, who had probably been missed. There were many un-answered questions and they troubled him. He would have not let them go so easily if he had not been retiring, and under pressure to 'file it away'.

"I think, like you, that we'll draw a line here, John." The chief superintendent was, as usual with John, tilting his chair back, feet on the desk. Loose tie. Informal. No stuffy chain of command. Almost friends. Almost.

"You are certain? You are happy to leave it at that?" John leaned forward.

"To be frank, as you know, we haven't the resources to pursue it further. No bloody money for a bloody thing. The last thing coming down the line was a memo asking to cut back on the number of pens we use. Pens! Fucking hell. I read the note you left last night after the examination. We'd be chasing our own arses all the way down history. Unless, of course, you feel there's a good reason, a really good reason, why we shouldn't close this down. Although, I have to say, I'm not happy about releasing the skeleton and I think we should keep it in store for a time.

The Painter Of Souls

How is that chap who came to look at the bones?"

"Not well. He's detained in hospital. Well, the Standard know about it. They could stir it up."

"They phoned back yesterday. I told them it was an artist's thing and of no interest. They tried to suggest it must have been a shock, but I knew where they were going, and told them not at all. No shock, no interest. It was that old fart of a reporter, I've forgotten his name, Bill whatever, he's always more interested in getting to the pub than into print. Said he was following up for someone else and didn't seem that interested. So, John, the last day. How does it feel? I hope to get back for the do later. Are you still thinking France? Lucky bastard."

His filled the remainder of his day completing paperwork, checking all files were as up to date as possible and compiling a timetable of court cases which he might drag him back to give evidence. Surprisingly few. Otherwise, tying up loose ends from a career stretching back thirty two years. Good God, his life had almost passed him by, and he had not noticed. It all came down to a small cardboard box on the floor containing the few personal possessions he would take: a photograph of Jane, a map of France, citations which he found embarrassing but Jane insisted he keep, an old press cutting describing how he'd accidently handcuffed himself to a shop dummy while trying to arrest a struggling shoplifter. He had been a young PC then. He stood, lifted the cutting, smiled and put it into a waste sack.

By late afternoon he had completed his tasks, dealt with everyone who'd poked their heads around his office door, and so he went down the corridor for a coffee and brought it back to his desk. There was a couple of hours until the do in the pub across the road. Meanwhile, although he had promised himself he would not, because there was little he could do now, but the temptation was too much, he turned on his computer and scanned the internet for details of Edward Broughton. His previous hurried search had revealed little about the man who could have been occupying the house skeleton was sealed into the roof space. Now, with a little time on his hands, he would make a proper search. But the result was the same. Hardly anything on Edward Broughton RA despite being the foremost artist of his day and obviously a very successful one commercially given the size of the house he had lived in that was now owned by National Trust Scotland. Broughton had become another victim of historic amnesia.

The Painter Of Souls

He checked the National Trust site for Broughton House, but other than an alarming picture of the Georgian house painted a livid pink, there was only three scant paragraphs of information about the man. Even Wikipedia had only five paragraphs, outlining Broughton's artistic style and the bare bones of his life and work. Almost nothing about the man himself. An enigma.

He pulled out a foolscap sheet of paper, headed it 'The Bare Bones', realised that was unfortunate to say the least in the circumstances, moved to cross it out but then left it, smiled, and listed what he knew.

Broughton was a child prodigy brought under the protective wing of the aristocratic Kennedy family. He had travelled to Africa to cover the Boer War for national newspapers. Staged numerous very successful exhibitions and worked, attracting great acclaim, until he died in 1912. Unmarried. He owned the large house on Horner Street in Kirkcudbright, where he lived his final years with his sister Flora, also unmarried. When she died almost 20 years later, the house and its contents passed into the care of a local trust which ran a library there and then the National Trust. Meanwhile Edward Broughton, the man and the painter faded into history. But his paintings were in collections world-wide, including the Scottish National Gallery, Edinburgh.

John Armstrong leaned back in his chair. He was very partial to a gallery or two during holidays and was always struck by how many works on display were by artists, obviously famous in their day, whose names were long forgotten. He always read the information cards at the side, resolved to remember the artist, but rarely did. Art was the gateway to eternity. Who'd said that? He couldn't remember. It hardly seemed true. Many great artists of their day, forgotten and their names never mentioned again.

He stood and lifted down the last picture frame from his office wall. It was a poem, the words printed across a background of pink and white cherry blossom, by the Haiku poet Shiki. "Without my journey, And without the spring, I would have missed this dawn." His favourite. He carefully placed it in the cardboard box. Perhaps that one poem had given immortality to Shiki.

He had gone through a phase as a youth when he had been fascinated by Japanese Haiku poetry. They all had. Three lines of tight verse, each with a first line of five syllables, the second with seven and the third, five again. Simple, but when pondered on, so very, very delicate, difficult and profound.

Not all translated well into English, sometimes losing the syllables and the rhythm and with them the meaning. But the poems had given them ideas for a song. All those years ago. The pretentious early 70's. Perhaps more than a song. An album. A concept album built around Haiku poems. The Land of the Rising Sun. The record company had been keen. Art work suggested. Perhaps a double album.

They had all been younger. The band. They had read and discussed at some length one philosophy that believed in three stages of death and which they thought they could work into a theme through the album. First, the actual death, when the body simply stopped functioning. Secondly, when the person was mentioned for the last time by those who knew them. Thirdly, and finally, when the person was last spoken of by anyone. Anyone at all. Art in all its forms could give you that immortality, your name living on forever. Shakespeare, Rembrandt, John Lennon.

He sat down. Tapped at his computer. Edward Broughton, along with many other artists, appeared to be heading with speed towards that third and final stage. Did the act of someone reading an artist's name on the bottom of a painting save that artist from the final death? Maybe. But did it mean little more than Kellogg's on a box of cornflakes.

Immortality had to be more than a label on a box of cereal, a name on a painting, a book, a rose, a record. Surely? We are more than a name. Perhaps not. He was getting maudlin.

It was down to the people who survived to speak of the dead to keep them from that final stage. Perhaps Broughton's sister, Flora, had not kept her brother alive, the memory of him. Why would you do that? She must have been immensely proud of her brother. Perhaps she'd had good reason to let his name fade away.

He brought himself up sharp. John Armstrong silently cursed the emotional turmoil of his last day at work which allowed these buried thoughts to squirm to the surface. He knew he was as guilty as anyone. He had failed his band mates, his friends. And failed miserably, merely because he couldn't face it. He never mentioned them. Fought against it. In the first months and years they had cropped up regularly, but he had refused all requests to allow their music to be used. Mention of them petered out and now, never. He knew they called him Ringo, mostly behind his back, but the younger ones would not have a clue why.

There was no movement from John Armstrong, none at all, as his coffee grew cold. Anyone entering his office would have thought he was in a trance. Turned to stone.

Finally he snapped to. Searched the files stacked in his office for his contacts book. Years ago, when had worked on the art theft case, there had been one chap at the Scottish Art Gallery who had been very useful. A mine of information.

CHAPTER 10

TWO huge naval guns, hauled from Cape Town on the supply train towards Graspan and now under the skilled direction of Lieutenant Dean of the Royal Navy, had been pounding the Boer positions in the low hills 5,000 yards away from 7am with uncanny, deafening, accuracy. The plan was to force the Boers to retreat into the waiting arms of the British troops sent forward in the early hours to outflank them. The shelling marked the start of the Battle of Graspan. Unfortunately for the British, the Boers held fast and responded with similar precision, having prepared in advance by marking out the range of their own guns with stone piles which appeared to be a natural part of the barren landscape. They came within yards of scoring a direct hit on the armoured train sent forward on a sortie. The train, showered in dirt, hastily retreated, four shells bursting close behind.

Artist Edward Broughton, buoyed by the

camaraderie and praise of the officers, and Lord Methuen in particular, was feeling well restored, but utterly bemused that a brigade of Royal Marines, sailors for God's sake, had made their way across miles of dry land to the front line, many, many miles from the ocean. Here in the middle of Africa about as far as you could possibly get from their ships and the sea. Some in naval uniform. And he was with them.

Yesterday evening, at the meeting to discuss tactics, he had been introduced to the Royal Navy's Commander Alfred Ethelston of HMS Powerful and Captain Reginald Prothero of HMS Doris, who together would lead a small brigade of their own men in the attack on the Boer positions. Broughton asked if he could join them and, with much amusement, was welcomed aboard. They spoke as though they were still at sea, astride their fighting ships. Broughton privately thought the seamen, here on dry land, bone dry land, would be kept well out of harm's way. And he would be safe with them.

Gordon sought him out as the meeting broke up and the men took a final brandy. "I was surprised you volunteered yourself to the marines, then realised you'd arrived at the meeting a little late."

Edward gave him a quizzical look.

"They are being given the privilege of leading one of the attacks as a sort of thank you from the rest of us for bringing up their big guns. Their chaps are deadly accurate shooters and we'll be using them to dislodge the Boer from the hills. A sort of reward for them and an honour."

"Oh."

"So, you'll be up there in the thick of it again. Never mind, Edward." He put his arm around his shoulder. "I'm sure you'll be fine. I know you were badly shaken after your experience at Belmont. I confess, it does take some getting used to. Rest well. Early start tomorrow. The Boers are a few miles off."

Edward stifled his horror. Mumbled: "You're right. I do have to harden myself to all this. I really do." Took a deep draught of his brandy, felt it burning at his dry throat, and then excused himself from the room. He had been allocated a tent of his own where he spent a troubled night, finally falling asleep only to be awoken, seeming minutes later, into the pitch dark by a man leaning into his tent.

"Thirty minutes, Sir." It had an all too familiar ring to it and Broughton felt his stomach grip hard. He could hear movement outside. Horses. Men. He held his watch to a candle. 3am. "Hell."

They crossed the bare plain almost to the

foot of the kopjes without incident as the dawn broke orange into a wide, lavender sky. From below he could make out men atop the black hills. Again, he thought this all too familiar.

The marines gathered close, their officers, swords drawn, bravely ready to lead them on. Broughton, sheltered by a towering termite hill, sketched the strange spectacle of sailors preparing to attack. Much later he would be astonished to see the sketch filling the front page of the Illustrated Mail on December 2. But for now, he was equally astonished to see marine officers brandishing swords in the face of the murderous rifle fire he knew would be coming. He could only watch, dumbfounded, as the marines bunched together and moved forward. Then he flinched at the sudden crack of intense rifle fire. Broughton numb, detached, squeezed against the termite hill. Head down. Men fell all around. Scream. Shouts. Then the thud of artillery shells. Rocks and dirt and limbs. Officers were brought down almost immediately, easy targets for the Boer snipers, swords no defence against Mauser rifles. Within seconds Commander Ethelston dead, Captain Prothero horribly wounded. And then the marines, charging forward close together rather than strung out, mown down with ruthless accuracy.

Some of the navy men began to make headway, soldiers now pushing up with them, yelling at them to move apart to lessen the target. Bayonets fixed, but as they crested the summit to engage the enemy, the Boers fell back, mounted ponies and escaped further into the hills, deep in the shadow of early sun. Again.

Broughton moved up with the last of the troops and saw a small party of Boers riding hard away under a hail of fire when one of their ponies stumbled, or was hit, and fell. Two other riders reined hard and rode back, dismounted, hauled the fallen rider over one of their saddles, re-mounted and galloped away. All this under heavy fire. Broughton would never again accept that the Boers were a ragged bunch of cowards.

His group pushed further, running down the slope of a hill to a farmstead flying a white flag. The men approached with extreme caution, the lesson at Belmont hard learned. But there was no gunshot. Inside they found wounded Boers being attended by three nurses who sounded German.

Only now did Broughton realise that many of his group had also suffered bullet wounds. Bloodied arms and legs. One man had a deep furrow across his brow, his blood a curtain across his face that would no doubt leave an ugly, though heroic, scar. If he survived infection. At Belmont he had overheard a surgeon say that many wounds would become infected by dirt and pieces of the men's own uniforms buried deep inside, and the casualties would probably suffer future amputations, and in the worst cases death. It was better to have a bullet through the brain than a slight wound and a lingering death from infection.

Here there were Boer men, and to Broughton's horror, youngsters who could have been no more than twelve-years-old. Not one of them cowered. All looked hard and defiant.

None spoke English, or would admit to it, but it became clear there was an acute shortage of water, a problem also for the advancing British army at their camp the previous night. The farmstead's well had been filled in to stop the advancing British from using it. Now there was not a drop for anyone.

Broughton spoke a little German, thanks to the tutor at the Kennedy household who eschewed the redundant Latin and Greek for the modern European languages. The men with him were impressed. He told them that the nurses appeared to be agreeable to treat their own wounded if they found water and brought it to the farm.

Three Boer ponies were tied outback.

Broughton, happy to be away from the stench of blood and the groans of wounded men and boys, along with a soldier he knew only as Yates, set out north. A pony each and Broughton led the third carrying water skins. Yates had insisted, because he needed his arms free to use his rifle. They travelled in silence through the growing heat of the sun, acutely aware that Boers could descend on them at any time. Or snipers, alerted by any sound, would pick them off with grim ease and accuracy. They followed a wide, deep valley, keeping to the shaded side, green with stunted trees and shrubs, suggesting moisture and after two miles they found a large pool, heavy with slime, but water nonetheless. Here the valley ended and opened out into a wide plain. They halted in the last of the shadow cast by the hills, stared out into the bright, trembling distance. They saw no-one else. It appeared deserted. Away to their right they could see the railway line shimmering in the morning heat.

Yates dismounted and took two leather water bags. He suddenly broke the silence. And his abrupt manner showed little respect for his eminent companion.

"I'll take these back. Some of us haven't had a drop all day. You head down there and then south along the line. You'll meet the lads coming up. You should be safe enough." He didn't seem to care whether he would be safe or not.

Yates bent to fill the water bags, pushing them beneath the slimy surface. He looked up, squinting at the sun. "And I'll say this - and you can gladly tell them buggers back there - if those Boers keep this up, we're going to be a long time to Kimberley. A bloody long time. Our lot don't seem to have a bloody clue how to fight them."

Broughton crouched low in his saddle as he followed the line south, his kit bag full of his artist materials dragging at his shoulder. Any time he expected a bullet to hit. He made good time, and later wished that perhaps he hadn't, because as he skirted the base of the escarpment of hills where the action had been the most intense, where had sheltered by the termite hill, he saw small parties of men struggling under the weight of the dead, wounded and dying as they carried them to covered wagons for the journey back to camp.

He brought his pony to a halt alongside a group of men, stripped to their shirts in the heat of the day. In their midst lay the body of Gordon Kennedy, sprawled on his back, clearly shot through the head. His Jack Russell, Smith, stood on his chest barking and growling at the men.

One turned to Broughton. "Ah, I see artist has come to help. Can you shift that dog? He's been going for us." Broughton called to Smith. The dog paused, calmed. Stepped down. Looked at Broughton. At Kennedy. Broughton crouched on the brown veldt and rubbed Smith's ears. The dog lay down between the two men. Then Broughton took out his sketch book and began an illustration that would make Kennedy a legend when it was published back home. Battle-hardened soldiers watched, silenced by the calm detachment of the artist. Here he was, surrounded by death and the dying, by his own close friend, calmly and confidently drawing. A world of his own. Gordon Kennedy, sword drawn, noble face calling his men onward, forward up the hill, Smith at his heels, bullets ploughing into the veldt, towering white clouds with a heavenly light shining through. Broughton wanted to complete it there and then, with the urgency of the battle in each line he drew, the dull dust gritty on the paper.

Back at the camp he then composed a dramatic account of the battle, highlighting the bravery and fall of Gordon Kennedy. He rolled the illustration, yes he could do dogs and do them well, and his account and put them aside for tomorrow's supply train that would

The Painter Of Souls

travel back to Cape Town.

Broughton then took out his diary and detailed his day, with the usual small sketches. He made a copy of the page, as he did every day, to send to his sister. He did not want to spare her, though he knew she would worry. But she would also know she had been correct. She had yet to reply with any letters, though he was reassured it was not at all unusual for mail to be lost or misplaced, both outgoing and incoming. He was desperate for news of home, and of progress on their new home.

His diary entry for November 25, 1899, began: "Today I lost my great friend Gordon Kennedy and I wonder how I shall survive this Hell Hole without him." But he did not shed a tear.

CHAPTER 11

THE telephone rang on the bedside table and John Armstrong snapped awake. Panic. Grey light seeped around the edge of the closed curtains and the red glow of the clock read 09.10 in those horrible blocky numerals. He threw himself from bed as Jane stirred alongside and then sat bolt upright, sharing his alarm.

"Shit!" He grabbed at the phone, almost dropped it, stabbed the answer button, was about to say: "I'll be there. Running late."

"John? John Armstrong? It's Mike Dearden."

"Mike Dearden?"

Jane collapsed sideways onto the bed, laughing. She'd realised. Her husband still bemused, befuddled by a troubled sleep after last night's talking, and now thrown by her reaction, stood naked, fumbling with the phone.

"John? You OK?"

"Yes, yes, yes." He turned to Jane. What on earth was she laughing at? He gave her a puzzled look. Turned his attention back to the phone. "Mike Dearden? The solicitor? Oh God, I'm sorry, I, well." He finally understood. Rubbed feeling into his scalp.

"Yes, I was telephoning to ask you and Jane to pop into the offices to sign the papers for the house sale. Anytime in the next couple of days. We've also heard from the Freemans confirming they won't be able to move for a couple of months, some delay in coming back from Australia. It's her job. Complicated. But it nicely means you are under no pressure to move out. They suggest a date in late March, just before Easter. Everything's settled otherwise and they have no problem you staying in what's going to be their home. Being cousins helps."

"No problem. I'm sorry about earlier, I thought I'd overslept."

"Well, I thought you'd just retired?"

"Yes, yesterday. Not used to it yet. We're in Edinburgh today but we can call in tomorrow. And we owe you a meal here. Have a word with Sue and see if this Saturday's OK."

"Right. Congratulations on the retirement. You and Jane. Both a life of freedom. We'll bring some bubbly over with us and perhaps an alarm clock as a present? Tomorrow, about eleven would suit."

"Fine. See you. Oh, and forget the clock, I've got one and it's going in the bin." He glared at the dead phone.

"Just look at you. Either get back into bed or go into the bathroom. You'll freeze standing there. In fact bathroom. We need to be off. No, we need to go."

The previous evening he had stunned Jane by saying he wanted to take the car to Edinburgh. It would be the first time in all their years together that he had agreed to travel to the capital city by car. They had always taken the train, a rather messy journey first travelling the wrong way south to change at Carlisle and then north to Edinburgh.

"Are you sure?" She had asked. He was. She had drawn him close and held him. It was time.

A clear, frosty morning, the sun low and dazzling in the iron blue sky. They headed north on the A74, Jane driving the deep red Ford Fiesta, before dropping on to the A702, an old Roman Road that ran north east through fields and thin, bare woodland along the River Clyde valley, and eventually through the Pentland Hills and on to the heart of Edinburgh.

Bars of sunlight flashed at them through the trees. She could feel John tense alongside in the passenger seat as soon as they turned into the A702 and reached across to hold his hand. He was staring ahead. She knew he was trying to keep control and asked: "We are okay? We can turn around."

"We are. It's only a mile or so. Last night I said I would be okay."

"I know, but this is your first time back here."

They passed the Lamington viaduct taking the main west coast railway line over the River Clyde, which could be glimpsed blue-grey and sluggish between the roadside trees. Jane slowed, passed the turn off to the rural village of Wiston and then John pointed to a lay-by across on the right, backed by a heavy, black, bare tree, and just yards beyond it a farmhouse it's peeling white bedroom windows and red roof just visible behind a high unkempt hedge.

"Just there." He said. Jane indicated and turned. The car crunched onto the frozen mud and halted.

Thirty seven years, three months and four days. He looked at his watch. And approximately fifteen hours. The exact time unclear.

The Cartwright family who lived in the farmhouse reckoned they heard the collision, like an explosion, about 5am. "Something like that," the family later told police, adding: "We can't be more certain, it was devastation. It's a blur. Like a bomb going off."

John often wondered what had awoken them because if they had heard the impact – and there was no reason to doubt them - they must have been awake seconds earlier. Was it a car horn? Had someone else been on the road, on the wrong side, forcing the van driver to avoid a collision? Horns blaring.

They waited for a heavy lorry loaded with timber to thunder by, rocking the car, before they moved out of the warmth into the cold, still air. Their breath white plumes. Ears burning. Pulling on coats, hats, scarves. Freezing fingers struggling with zips.

Teal had been in London recording a session for The Old Grey Whistle Test, the BBC's rock music programme, and had then moved on to Edinburgh for a concert at the University. And then it was back on the road again, late at night, a rare chance to crash out at their homes. With family. Crazy days, travelling from one end of the country to another, living in the van. They were at number three in the singles charts, something the four serious musicians were none too proud of believing it put them alongside frothy pop. But their record company insisted on releasing a single to promote their album Blue On Blue which was climbing high and would reach number one for all the wrong reasons in the horrible

The Painter Of Souls

weeks to come.

Two months ago they had been playing gigs in pubs and small halls across southern Scotland. Now they had turned down Top of the Pops – too tacky – and in three weeks would fly to America for a tour and then back to cover Europe before recording a follow up album, already largely written. They had a clear idea for the third. Land of the Rising Sun. All tracks penned together and credited to all four. All for one and one for all. Hardly any money had so far reached the band as it filtered through various managers and promoters and so they continued to use their battered white Ford Transit for moving themselves and their gear. That was the fun of it. Four mates on the road together, making music, smoking weed, meeting girls.

They had formed the band at school in Dumfries – taking the initials of each member to make the name Teal – Thompson (guitar and vocals), Edmondson (bass), Armstrong (drums) and Lacey (guitar and keyboards). There had been a suggestion of using Christian names, but that was ruled out by John, Eric, Rich and Keith.

John, the drummer and so Ringo to some, had no memory of the University gig, or the Whistle Test recording, although some months later he had grudgingly agreed their performance could be broadcast. Just once, the families had asked him. Never watched it. Never again played the drums, nor listened to their music. Refused, point blank.

He and Jane pushed through the scant, brittle blackthorn hedge at the back of the lay by and into the frozen meadow where the large tree stood solid amid the fragile, frosted grass.

She was silent. There was nothing for her to say. Over their years together it had been a subject largely avoided. Last night they had talked at length.

She reached for his gloved hand, her other arm across his shoulder. John spoke, almost to himself.

"You know, they never decided who was driving. Though so what? In a way it was good, because no-one could be blamed. It was all of us. We could have stayed in Edinburgh, but we wanted home. So, it was all of us. A joint decision."

Drummer John, a little worse for wear, asleep among the gear in the back of the van. The other three up front, sharing stints at the wheel as they drove through the night. Police believed the driver had fallen asleep. Or they were trying to swop drivers without slowing down. The Transit had slewed off the road, through the hedge and slammed into

The Painter Of Souls

the tree. Accident investigators estimated a speed "topside of 60mph" and the absence of any skid marks a clear indication that no-one had braked. There was no evidence of a second vehicle being involved.

The van had disintegrated on impact.

When the Cartwrights hurried from the farmhouse into the pitch dark night – father in blue pyjamas and black wellingtons and mother in a red dressing gown pulled tight - they found an empty cab and believed the van occupants had run away.

Their teenage son, jeans and bare chested, climbed into the back through the open doors, found John sandwiched between speakers.

"There's someone here. He's out cold."

Father ran back to the farmhouse and called 999. Then pulled on a coat, grabbed more for his wife and son, and ran back down the road. He opened the gate that led into the field, told his son to stand by and watch for the police. Heavy clouds scudded across the moon.

He joined his son at the gate, struggled to pull a torch from his pocket. Minutes later, it seemed ages, he used it to flag down the police who parked to block the road, blue lights flashing. A fire engine arrived soon after and it was only as it pulled into the meadow that its headlights picked out the bodies on the grass.

Eric and Keith catapulted through the windscreen and into the field many yards away, mutilated by glass and metal. As dawn broke grey, they discovered Rich, in the tree above their heads, torn in half. The farmer's son fainted.

"There's no plaque or anything, John. Nothing."

"No. It was tried at the time. Apparently there was a small shrine, you know, a memorial. People came and put flowers, that sort of thing. Or so I'm told. But the highways authority decided it was too much of a hazard, nowhere to park safely and the traffic moving fast, so they took it all away. No-one remembers now. There's just the graves back home."

"And the music. Would you like to stay a little longer?"

"No. No. I'm done. You know, I broke a leg and cracked two ribs. Mild concussion. Nothing serious. I wasn't even the talent. I just banged the drums. Rich, he was such an incredible musician. An incredible guy. So were the others. And I could have, should have done more to keep their memory alive. Keep them alive. Instead I followed my dad into the police – 'Get a proper job' – and tried to forget. Such a waste. Yes, there was the music, but I never wanted it played. I was wrong."

"As we said last night - yours was an incredible year. You four. Well, okay, I was two years below you lot. I can remember Rich playing - am I alright talking about this?"

"Fine. Fine. I feel fine. Please."

"Well I remember him playing at the school end of year concert, you know when they handed out form prizes?"

"Not to me."

"No. Anyway, we'd suffered that dopey Nixon girl scratching away at her violin, so embarrassing, and then Rich, he was always so quiet, and Eric came on. Eric Lacey. That hair. We all loved him. They sat up there on the stage with just their acoustic guitars and sang Paul Simon's Sound of Silence. Good God. Eric had that long curly hair and the big brown eyes. All the girls were in love with him."

"Really? I remember that. Everyone fancied him. Including……" He raised his eyebrows, gave her that knowing, quizzical look of his. And he smiled. And then he realised she was sobbing.

They held each other close in the icy, silent meadow, the incessant sound of heavy traffic booming on the road yards, but a world away. He eventually pulled slightly back, looked into her eyes. "Hey, this is our first day of retirement together. A day to celebrate. Come on. Edinburgh. You've some serious money to spend."

"What time are we meeting your expert on the man Broughton? At the gallery."

"2pm. We?"

"Oh yes. I want to be there. It's the two of us now. Teamwork, darling. And I always fancied going to his house in Kirkcudbright. The garden is supposed to be wonderful. And Frank – the art teacher at school, do you remember him? So sad – he always used to rave on about the Kirkcudbright Boys and I'm sure Broughton. Knowledge that's lost now."

CHAPTER 12

EDWARD Broughton struggled with the blinding sun slanting down Cape Town's fashionable Adderley Street as he made his way to the railway station. Slowly, he lowered his straw boater until the rim shaded his eyes. He was puzzled. He still could not remember seeing these double deck electric trams which noisily passed him now when he first walked here only a handful of months ago, though it seemed years. They were colossal, the sort of thing he'd seen in London and other cities back home, a world away. Surely he would have noticed them. He was an artist, a man of perception and perspective. He almost collided with people walking towards him, emerging suddenly out of the sun, and decided to cross to the other side of the wide, bustling road where elegant buildings threw a welcome shadow across the pavement.

He was a little early to meet the train and stood for a while in the shade at Cartwright's

Corner, where trams branched off to Darling Street. He had been shocked to find Cape Town so much like London. Grand hotels, theatres, an opera house, banks, a quite magnificent House of Parliament, fashionable clubs, hard surfaced roads, glorious gardens with many flowers and trees he did not recognise, and waterfront promenades which had been particularly important for his recovery. Railways snaked out across the country and the telegraph reached as far as Europe. He walked on to the classical colonnade of the Standard Bank and paused to allow a group of women to pass, raising his hat to them.

He smiled to himself. On the voyage out he had expected something far less. Not mud huts, although that's what the encyclopaedia had suggested back home, but not such a bustling, affluent city which, thankfully, also had a thoroughly professional hospital. The Boer War with its constant stream of troop and supply ships had boosted the economy and many new buildings were being planned. A booming city. Yet, miles north along those railway lines, men were being slaughtered on the battlefield, men, women and children dying in their thousands from disease. Did anyone here realise? Did anyone care?

He checked his watch and realised he must hurry as best he could.

The Painter Of Souls

The wound in his leg had healed. Doctors assured him he had been very fortunate not to lose the limb. It had been a struggle to control the infection, talk of amputation, touch and go. The train evacuating him and other wounded could not travel fast enough. He would always carry the scar on his thigh, perhaps a slight limp. But the stabs of hot, sharp pain and the nagging stiffness had eased, thank God. The regular doses of morphine helped. But he rather liked the effect of his silver-topped walking cane, the head cool, round and heavy, and he kept that with him. He felt it gave him a jaunty air.

The man was coming in on the 2pm train. And had specifically asked to meet him. Broughton felt quite honoured, if not a little perplexed. Winston Spencer Churchill was something of a hero. Why me?

Few had not read of, or could have failed not to hear of, the daring exploits of Churchill, the young war correspondent for the Morning Post, captured by the Boers when his armoured train had been ambushed, who saved the lives of his companions by braving heavy fire to organise the reverse of the train out of the attack before falling himself into the hands of the dreadful enemy. Gallant Churchill had then made a daring escape from a POW camp, journeying 300 miles through hostile territory to safety with a bounty on his head. Dead or alive.

He was very much alive when the train hauled into the station. The large domed roof braced with steel always reminded Broughton of the stations at home. A small reception party, men and women dressed as though attending the theatre, had gathered on the platform to welcome their hero who was stopping off on his return to England. Accounts of his exploits, largely written by himself, had spread like wildfire through newspapers at home and abroad. "How I Escaped. Six Days Of Adventure And Misery" ran the headline in the Daily Mail.

Handshakes done, congratulations warmly received, offers of a glass of cool water declined and then the busy group moved off towards the luxury of The Grand Hotel on Strand Street where a light lunch was ready. Churchill insisted on walking. Ahead.

"I've been cooped up on that train long enough. Stretch my legs. And where's the artist Broughton? Is he here?"

The silver top of the cane flashed in the sunlight as Broughton waved it from the back of the group.

Churchill called to him: "You know where we are heading?" Then pushed through the group and took Broughton's arm.

The Painter Of Souls

"Pardon." Broughton was a little taken aback. The man had a light lisp, he had expected a much firmer voice.

Churchill asked: "You know the way?"

"Yes. The Grand. It's where I'm staying."

"Lead the way." And he was off at a brisk pace.

They walked together, keeping slightly in front of the party. Broughton, hampered by his walking stick, had to lean in close to hear Churchill above the noise of the trams and the horses-drawn carriages. People stopped them to shake Churchill's hand when members of the group pointed out their eminent friend. It was stop and start the length of Adderley Street until they finally arrived at the hotel. The group went ahead to 'organise things' and Churchill and Broughton waited outside in the shadow of a handsome colonnade that ran around the opulent building.

"I have a couple of days here before sailing and wonder if I could trouble you to help with my painting. A little advice. I started with it before I came out here. Inspired by your exhibition in London. Bloody marvellous stuff. Marvellous. Daubs compared to you. But I'll be on that infernal boat for some time and need something to do. Can't just get drunk."

"Of course." Broughton was taken aback.

"You seem a little unsure."

"No, no."

"You are sure?"

"Yes, yes. Tomorrow I'm exploring Table Mountain with Mrs Fraser and her daughters. A Miss Hobhouse will be with us. We have a guide."

"Don't know them. Though Hobhouse rings a bit of a bell. Sounds perfect. A time?"

"From The Grand at nine. You'll find the light is quite superb and the meadows are quite full of flowers. I've already done some preparatory sketches for a painting of the daughters picnicking. Do you have materials?"

"On the train. My luggage is being brought on to the hotel. Hobhouse? Do you know the woman?"

"A little. She's out here on some mission helping families affected by the war."

"What? Boers?"

"I suppose they are, yes. She's asked me to go with her later this week. If I'm up to it. I was wounded."

"Boers. Ah, well." Churchill paused to light a cigar. He carefully blew the smoke away. "I believe we've met in the past, you know."

"Really?"

"Yes. My family know the Kennedy's well, normally we meet up in London, but we came to their place in Scotland a few years ago for a shoot. My late father Lord Randolph, you did a marvellous cartoon of him. Still hanging in the house. Anyhow you're a famous chap and when I read the London Illustrated somebody had brought out here, oh, what did it say, oh yes 'Our Artist Under Fire' I thought I must meet up with you if at all possible. If you were still here in Cape Town. You took a bullet in the leg? I was wounded in the hand during that train business. Men of good fortune, the both of us. Eh?"

"Well. Possibly. I was certainly lucky not to lose my leg."

"Good God. Were you at Magersfontein?"

"No, no. Modder River. I never got as far as Magersfontein."

"An awful business. Our men stuck there for two months. Methuen lost some good men. Henry Northcott, a good friend. Cost Methuen his job and rightly so. Never learned his lesson. Far too rash. Should have done his homework."

"Awful indeed. Indeed. I try not to think too much about it."

A uniformed doorman sought them out to usher them inside. They entered the cool, hushed interior of The Grand. Its intricate mosaic floor emblazoned with the arms of Cape Colony. The staff lined up like a guard of honour. Churchill entered with a wave and a show of modesty. Broughton, feeling a stab of pain, sought out a comfy chair below a potted palm, asked the advancing waiter for a tea and eased his leg straight. The Battle of Modder River had been his downfall. Modder River, damn it!

The railway line ran arrow strait and word had come down from a spotter sitting atop the leading gun carriage of their slow moving, armoured train. Not far to go and no sign of the Boer. It was early morning, dawn having just broken, and they were nearing the Modder River, closing in on the under siege diamond town of Kimberley.

Two officer sitting opposite Broughton discussed the distance to the diamond town and the expected warm welcome.

"About twenty miles or so. The Boers seem to have turned tail. Should be a pleasant jaunt. There's a watering hole at Modder, the next station. Good place for breakfast."

"Actually my sister is married to a chap in Kimberley. She wrote to mother of the pleasures to be had at Modder. A decent hotel or two, boating and the rest. Sounds uncommonly civilised."

Broughton smiled to himself. Just twenty

The Painter Of Souls

miles to go. They should easily make Kimberley, perhaps in time for lunch, and speedily end the siege, perhaps without a single bullet being fired. He hoped so. He was sick of it all. Last night there had been a relaxed, celebratory mood. It was expected that any remaining Boers would scatter in the face of the overwhelming British force. Good riddance to them.

Finally he would find a decent bed to sleep in, a place to wash and a quiet place to complete his daily journal. He looked out at the landscape as brown and dull as a dried cow pat. Soldiers on horses easily keeping pace, occasionally riding off to scout low hills, supply wagons kicking up the dust that hung in the still air. The sluggish army on the move. He wished the train would hurry.

An advance group had marched ahead the previous day, almost everyone now in khaki uniforms, the buttons dulled so as not to attract fire, officer insignia covered or removed. Even the Scots wore dull brown aprons over their bright kilts. Brown, brown and more brown. The men, the grass, the hills. Bloody brown, cursed Broughton whose usual palette was piercing whites, acid greens, golden yellows, scalding reds. Not dung. He was also wearing trousers and a shirt that had once been creamy but were now dulled by dirt and sweat. He knew he stank. Water was rationed. Washing a luxury. When he returned home he pledged he would never paint another brown thing ever again. Well, maybe a stag or two.

"I may as well paint with cow shit."

"Pardon?" One of the officers opposite leaned across.

"Nothing," said Broughton, smiling. "It's the heat. A little crazy."

"Ah, the artistic temperament. A little on the edge?"

"A little." He closed his eyes against any further talk.

The advance party had camped overnight and reports came back of no Boer presence. Broughton, unsure now of believing anything he heard from the so-called intelligence officers, although Lord Methuen himself had been with the scouting group, had declined an invitation to join them, preferring the train. He had tried, but failed, to understand these men he ate, slept, and drank with. This was not his life. They had their friendships, their regiments, their ridiculous ideas of death and glory. They lived a life under orders, under canvas. It seemed, under a hail of bullets.

And the foul water at Graspan had given

him the runs, his backside sore with it. And it stung like hell whenever he peed. He had never felt so miserable and alone. Gordon Kennedy gone. The morning was only just breaking and it was already hot.

He was shaken from drowsiness, almost slid from his seat. Men around shouted. The brakes were full on. The immense weight of the train pushing forward, wheels screaming on the line, struggling to grip. Men leapt from their seats, stumbled, grabbed at rails and each other. Curses. Brougham sat tight, braced, befuddled by lack of sleep. His bag fell to the floor. Then the furious, deafening scream from the engine as the driver slammed in to reverse, smoke and steam gushed by the open window. Finally, after what seemed long, long minutes they halted. Hissing jets of steam. An explosion. Had the boiler blown?

Men jumped down from the train. All was suddenly quiet. Men ran back down the line. Broughton followed. An artillery shell had exploded amid a group of cavalry, the 9th Lancers, men and horses blown apart. A supply wagon overturned. A pistol dispatched two horses, their bellies ripped open and their guts hanging out steaming. Broughton turned and vomited on the veldt. Green bile that stung his throat and burned his mouth.

Men gathered. From where? Eyes shielded as they stared into the haze beyond the river. The group was joined by Lord Methuen and Major General Sir Henry Colville. "Boers?" Someone asked.

Sir Henry stared into the distance. "They're sitting uncommonly tight if they are. Not a sign. Damn them. I suggest a party forward to test the land."

Lord Methuen turned to a man Broughton knew as Robinson who was hoping to return to his home and business in Kimberley. He had recently joined the train, offering advice on the terrain.

"What's that over there?" Lord Metheun pointed to a group of trees and buildings across the river. Broughton stepped aside, moving out of the line of sight.

"Rosemead, sir. It's a very pleasant village. We've spent many a pleasant hour there. Boating on the river. A couple of fine hotels. Its pleasures are a fine relief from Kimberley."

"Pleasures? I doubt it today. And this river? The Modder. I was here yesterday and we saw nothing of the Boer."

"There's the Modder and the Riet. The railway station is just beyond the bridge."

"Any idea where the Boers are skulking. We scouted up there and found nothing."

"No, unless they're in the village. There's a couple of hotels. The Island and Crown and the Royal. Very fine."

Lord Methuen, clearly vexed, turned to his Chief of Staff Henry Northcott, a 43-year-old fine sportsman and finer soldier unaware this was his last day alive. He had unrolled a map, arms stretched. Sir Henry joined them in a close discussion.

They turned to Robinson. Lord Methuen: "Our maps show the rivers are fordable. We can get the cavalry across and outflank them if they are at the river bridge or in the village. Or both."

"I'm sorry, Lord Methuen. I don't know your maps, but I doubt very much that you can cross the rivers. They are a good size and very deep. I wouldn't take a horse into them. Certainly not the wagons."

Lord Methuen looked exasperated. "These damned maps…." He did not finish. Boers, dug into the river bank and hidden by scrub and trees, opened fire. There was no cover on the open veld. Men who were idling through the long grass deep in discussions about bringing up the food wagons and setting out an early breakfast fell. Hard to tell whether shot or taking cover.

The battle of Modder River had begun.

Broughton's group ran to the train, bullets

whining off the armour plate. Artillery shells fell with deadly accuracy, the Boer having again previously marked out the range with old biscuit tins and rocks painted white. Riflemen along the river bank were pouring in lethal fire, their Mauser's accurate for hundreds of yards.

A messenger, his horse foaming and sweating, its eyes bulging wild, was waiting at the train for Lord Methuen.

"Sir. We have a communication from the village. The Boer are there and digging in like rabbits. Hundreds of them."

Lord Methuen turned to his group, "We have to take the bridge, and take in intact, and move across to flush them from the village. And we have to do it quickly. We don't want them firming their position. I imagine it's a small group at the bridge trying to slow us down. We'll meet them head on and give the Boer a bloody nose. Again. Move the men forward."

There was a pause in the gunfire. Men stood up from the grass. Others ran forward to help the wounded, carry away the dead.

Scots Guards were called to make up the right flank to advance on the distant river. It would be a steady, though cautious march in the morning sunshine. Bit of a stroll. Hundreds of men strung out across the veldt ready to move forward. The Guards had urged Broughton to join them and he did, all thought and reason lost to the sense of being part of this hardened group of soldiers. He hurried to the train, reached through the carriage's open window, hauled out his bag, jammed on his straw hat and ran to the line just as the order to advance was given.

They moved as one across the flat veldt, which here was covered with acres of long yellow grass, like over-ripe corn in the fields back home. It barely moved in the still morning. In front, trees and scrub formed a thicket along the river bank. No rifle fire. British artillery shells targeted the river. Broughton could feel the explosions pushing at his chest. Had the Boer pulled out? Run away, again?

They were nearing the river when Broughton heard a shout: "Have at them lads."

And the men, bayonets fixed, suddenly broke into a run, but at the same time the Boers unleashed a firestorm of Mauser bullets. The men were many yards from the river. "Take cover." It hardly needed to be said. Men dropped like stones into the long grass.

Broughton squirmed as low as he could, eating the African dirt. He dare not move. Bullets zipped overhead. Men calling. Cries and screams of wounded. Over the last few days he had listened to men talking of being hit by a bullet, feeling no pain until sometime later. "It's worse having a tooth pulled." Well, men were in pain now. Groans. The shattering explosion of cannon fire followed by brief moments of total, deafening silence.

A raised hand attracted intense fire. "Keep down, for God's sake." Where did that voice come from? Left or right. Broughton did not dare lift his head.

As the morning wore on, the intense sun rose in the sky and beat down. Hot enough to drive a man crazy. Broughton and those around him had not eaten nor had a drop to drink since the previous evening and here they had no water, no food. His group were in a slight hollow, enough to feel safely below rifle fire, but only by inches and certainly too shallow to be able to look up or crawl to the safety of the train.

Earlier there had been various attempts to stand and charge to the river. Including a man on his right, but they were cut down. Now everyone lay flat, sprawled in the grass under the burning sun. Fighting the madness of the heat. Swallowing fear. He knew there were soldiers all around him, some very close. No-one spoke. Talking brought rifle fire. Pinned down. Snipers ruthlessly accurate. He thought of the young Boer boys in the farmstead hospital at Graspan. Were similar youngsters raining down death on them now? Farm boys and peasants. What nonsense.

Artillery shells pounded into the British positions, and ahead fell on what gunners believed were Boer positions around the village of Rosemead. The British would not target the railway bridge, it was too vital to the advance on Kimberley.

Morning dragged into afternoon. Broughton, woke, realised he had dozed. Away to each side shells exploded, and he felt the thuds heaving the hard earth beneath his belly. Had he slept through that? As the afternoon throbbed and hauled on, the sickly smell of death moved across the veld. He prayed for nightfall, the cover of darkness. The only chance of escape. He was so thirsty, his tongue swollen. His straw hat had fallen just in front. His head ached and pulsed. Dare he reach for it? He realised he was laid on his right arm, and shifted as slowly and carefully as he could to release it, the pushed his aching arm through the grass, fingers tingling with pain as the blood rushed back into the deadened limb, fingers now walking to the brim. Grasped and pulled. God he ached. He had an urge to stand, almost did. "Get down you bloody fool," whispered just to his left.

Cramp was seizing his legs.

Slowly, he rolled onto his back, expecting at any moment the heat and agony of a bullet. He stretched his legs. Such a simple thing, yet it could mean death. Above him, in the clear sky, he could see circling birds. They looked large. Could they be angels?

Some had tried to evacuate the wounded on stretchers, but were shot down. A water cart was brought up, and desperate men ran to fill bottles – but were easy targets. Eight of nine who attempted the bowser were shot, along with the driver of the cart and the cask itself was riddled with bullets.

Finally, with Broughton and the rest of the men delirious from the sun and thirst, night came to save them. Suddenly. One moment it was light, the sun sliding down the horizon, the next black velvet night. Broughton, hearing no firing for some time and conscious that some men were moving in the darkness, rolled onto his front and dared to lift his head. Around him, he could just make out men who were moving, crouched. He was disorientated. Which way? He could hardly stand. Someone bumped into him.

"Sorry." He held out his hands hoping to grasp a belt, anything that would help.

A whispered: "Hurry before the moon comes out. Or you'll be done for." Were they talking to him? Then another figure collided with him. A silent curse. Broughton, unable to speak his mouth so swollen, stumbled after the man, his legs and back an agony. He reached into the darkness. Felt nothing. His left leg was dead and wouldn't support him. He shook it, slapped it, stamped. Finally it obeyed, a little. Stars brilliant above. Men all around. He stayed with them. Stumbled, crawled, fell. It seemed miles. Men brushed past in the dark. Finally he saw lanterns spilling yellow light. And came upon a scene of utter carnage. He limped forward. Paused to adjust to the patchy light. To focus.

Outside in the fast cooling night, men on tables being held down, others bent over them. Sawing. The air thick with flies. Rows of canvas tents. Men hurrying, in and out of shadow and yellow light. Screams.

A man ran towards him out of the light, he could barely make him out, or what he said. To his horror, the man pushed him to the ground. He tried to stand. Struggled. Was held firm. Was it a Boer? Had he gone the wrong way? Stumbled into their camp?

"Stay there. I'll get a stretcher."

Broughton, confused, lay in the half light. Stars now silver bright in the black sky. A yellow moon. Would he see a shooting star? He hoped. Then he was lifted. And the sky went black.

"Careful with his leg. That one. Looks bad."

CHAPTER 13

ICE-COLD wind sliced through Edinburgh's bustling Princes Street and anyone who was walking the pavements. Shops and department stores cast a feeble yellow glow into the litter strewn mid-morning. Early shoppers, hoods up, heads down, umbrellas broken, huddled under bus shelters away from stinging spats of rain. Snow was threatened.

"This is bloody ridiculous," John Armstrong, deep in his coat and shallow with his temper, pushed at another window that looked like it could be a door. It did not move. Nose against a heavily tinted window. "There are people inside. How did they get in?"

They had bent into the Arctic wind, struggled through a complete circuit of the National Gallery, tried every door. None opened. Other couples were doing the same. People smiled a "found it?" look as if they were long-time friends. The main doors were locked, though a sign stuck on the inside taunted: "Welcome."

"Fucking ridiculous."

"John language. There are children. Look, there's a man in some kind of security guard uniform over there. I'll ask."

Jane hurried, gloved hand holding her hood in place against the wind, to the man who was emerging from steps which lead down into the extensive parkland that ran in the deep valley through the heart of Edinburgh's city centre. Trees bare and black. Another couple were making their way to him.

Jane reached him first. John close behind. She smiled: "How do we get in?"

The man, all gold braid and solid, pointed at the steps behind him. And moved on. Never looked up. Never uttered a word.

"Thanks for your friendly advice and cheer," John Armstrong deliberately knocked into the man's shoulder as he strode to catch Jane. "He looked like something from the Nazi SS."

They descended the steps below the Gallery, other couples followed. A new entrance had been built, hidden one floor down, all ugly smoked glass sheltering additional security guards.

"You need signs up there." John, brusque. The male attendants, silent, smiled. John did not.

They queued for the bag search. Jane queued for the toilet. They looked into the café saw the long queue for coffee and cake. Decided to join the queue squeezing through yet more security into the gallery proper.

"We have plenty of time." Jane unfolded a floor plan of Scotland's National Art Gallery. "Where are we meeting the professor? John, glowering at that attendant won't make his balls drop off. No matter how much you wish it. Now, where are we heading?"

"Sorry. The Scottish floor. I don't think he's a professor, although he may be. Colin Wallace. It was some years ago, so I hope I recognise him. He said 11.30 in front of A Lady In Grey. Mysterious, eh?"

"Right. We need to follow the signs for rooms B1 to B7, according to this. Over there. Come, dearest." She took his arm.

It was quieter in the Scottish rooms. They asked, hushed, a young female attendant where they would find A Lady In Grey. "Straight there." Blunt. She pointed to a large, long portrait on the opposite wall, almost monochrome of a woman in a grey dress against a black background her pale face shining out, moon-like. An elderly gentleman with a grey beard and grey hair tight in a pony-tail, gold-rimmed glasses in his hand, was off to one side, squinting at the painting.

"Colin? Colin Wallace?" John held out his hand. They shook.

"Indeed. We meet again. And?"

"Jane. My wife. We're a bogof to day."

"A bogof?"

"Buy One Get One Free."

"Ah, yes. I Understand. Good to meet you again, Inspector Armstrong."

"John, please. And now retired. So plain John."

"Well, ditto. Dr Wallace, but now retired although for some reason I get to keep the title. But, plain Colin, please. So, John, how can I help? You were asking about Edward Broughton? You know, I get so bloody annoyed at these places. They spend millions on them and can't even light them so you can see the pictures without an infernal glare. Idiots. Look at her. The spot is straight onto her face. Not good. I was hoping to show you her eyes, but the glare ruins it."

John liked this man.

"Yes, Edward Broughton. He was mentioned in the last case I was working on and I realised that I didn't know much about him, even though he was a local in Dumfries. We found a skeleton and it was suggested it may have been used by the artist as some kind of model, an aid for his paintings. But what do we know about the man himself?"

"Interesting. Interesting. Follow me," He addressed this more to Jane, than John. Took her

The Painter Of Souls

by the arm.

"We pass a portrait on our way, a rather beautiful lady who could be your sister." Jane returned Colin's smile. "Please take note of her eyes."

"Really? Her eyes?" Jane cast a knowing look back at John.

"Indeed. Are you an artist?" Jane shook her head. The day was getting better.

John was used to this. He followed. They paused at the portrait by artist JD Ferguson of Anne Estelle Rice. She wore a rather heavy hat and a somewhat demure look. They studied her eyes, black dots. "Take note of those eyes," said Colin and then escorted Jane into the adjacent Broughton Room. John followed.

"This is a work by your Mr Broughton." The three stood before a life-sized, full length portrait of a woman, clearly Victorian, and which reminded Jane of the romantic Pre-Raphaelite painting she so loved.

Here was an attractive woman, perhaps in her late twenties or early thirties, tall and slender standing in a wood panelled drawing room. Chestnut hair tied in a bun, almost ginger where it was caught by light from a window hinting at the garden beyond. Her pale face appeared sad. She wore a chocolate brown velvet dress embroidered with sky blue morning glory flowers and lip-pink cherry blossom. An easy chair to her right its upholstery heavily patterned with zig zags in muted colours, her delicate hand on its carved back. No rings on her fingers. At its side a small table and on it a pipe with a curl of grey smoke, and empty heavy cut glass tumbler, suggesting a man had been in the chair and had just departed. Her eyes, her intense blue-green eyes, held the viewer.

Colin stood in silence, allowing time for his Jane and John to take in the painting.

Finally he broke the spell. "You can see in her eyes a very special quality. Can you not?"

They nodded. The eyes had a depth that held them. Followed them.

Colin pointed out the other works in the room. "That is the only full-length portrait here. You can see his earlier work was quite different. Children in gardens, in fields, in woodland. Landscapes. Very, very popular in the day and I have to say, very, very accomplished. Broughton had a stunning ability with the use of light. Critics at the time said he must have had a tube of paint labelled Sunlight. They were immensely popular and so was he. Quite remarkable and very commercial in their time, but the later portrait we have come to see sealed his reputation as a very, very skilled artist."

Jane studied a painting of children in a blue

The Painter Of Souls

bell wood. "I can almost smell those bluebells. Like you said, Colin, it's remarkable."

"Thank you. But to return to the portrait." All three moved back to the woman in a chocolate brown dress.

"Strange we'd never heard of him," John stood back to take in the whole of the painting.

"No, really? I'll come to that. This is Woman In A Drawing Room. Now," he looked to Jane. "Study her eyes. They have a depth. Many artists don't get beyond the flat representation of an eye, like a dead fish eye, but when you look at this one of Broughton's it's as though you can see beyond the eye. I don't know what it is. It's a depth. A deeper quality. Almost as though he'd swopped his pot of Sunlight for one that was labelled Soul. There's a soul in her eyes. It's not in his earlier work."

Jane moved closer. "Yes, I see. Mysterious. Almost disturbing. There's sadness. Almost as though you're looking back at yourself."

John stood alongside and turned to Dr Wallace. "Are they all like this? The later ones. I feel she's studying me as much as I'm studying her."

"Well. He gave this quality to his later portrait commissions. People who paid him to paint them. We know who they are and most are head and shoulder portraits and nowadays not that commercial. This is the only one we have like this. An unknown woman. It was found in his Kirkcudbright studio. Could be a one off. Could be more. After all, at that time what would you want hanging on your wall in your dark Victorian lounge - a stunning blond woman, actually his sister, trawling through a field of sunlit corn; a group of children picnicking in a sunlit bluebell wood; or this very dark work, superb as it is, of this woman whose name we don't know, in this dark room. Then everyone wanted the romantic work. Of course it's this one that everyone would want now."

Jane turned to John. "I think this is romantic in its way. Don't you?"

John looked at the picture from all angles. "Romantic? Well, I'd say disturbing." He turned his back to the portrait. "I can feel her behind me. Strange, I know. But I can feel her staring at me. Uncomfortable."

Dr Wallace continued: "Indeed. There's even more to it than that, though. There's a deep symbolism, a sort of story, a message told by the objects in the room. Not unusual for Victorian painters, indeed for painters throughout history, to hide a narrative in their work. But let's look. Her dress with morning glory – a flower that lasts only a day. Cherry blossom is also beautiful but brief. The books behind her – look at the titles. All from the Victorian fascination with the Gothic and the dead. The fire in the grate is ash. Dead. The pipe suggests a sudden abandonment. The chrysanthemums in the vase on the sideboard, notice their petals are falling, they are dying. This is autumn, everything dying back ready for the bleak winter. On the table to the right is a case of mounted, dead butterflies and moths and alongside it a moth waiting to be pinned. I'm told, because I'm no expert on the subject, it's a death's-head hawkmoth, you can just make out the skull on its back. See the stuffed owl in the case? I think it's a long-eared owl. Well, owls may symbolise wisdom to us today, but once they were widely regarded as harbingers of evil and doom. And the landscape painting on the wall over the fireplace – there's a flock of seven magpies in the tree by the cornfield. Can you see them?"

John and Jane both stepped closer, peered deep into the painting. John: "The magpies have a significance?"

"You know the old nursery rhyme? The Magpie. One for sorrow. Two for joy. Three for a girl. Four for a boy. Five for silver. Six for gold. Seven for a secret, never to be told. Eight for a wish. Nine for a kiss. Ten for a bird, you must not miss."

Jane recited the last line with him. "It's a long time since I heard that. A long time. One for sorrow. Yes I can see that. She looks sorrowful. But, seven for a secret never to be told. Any ideas?"

"We all have secrets. Broughton we believe was a troubled man in his later years. He was not old when he died. I've forgotten the dates. Are they on the label? No. Anyway, he never married. Lived with his sister and there were rumours about that. Wordsworth and all that. But no evidence."

"Sorry," said John. "Wordsworth?"

"He was supposed to have, shall we say, enjoyed, a very close relationship with his sister, Dorothy. But who knows? With Broughton we have very little surviving personal information."

"Thank you, Colin. Back to this. How many pictures are like this?" Armstrong looked around the Broughton room. "He wasn't painting this for clients?"

"No. No. His reputation was secure and he wouldn't have needed the money. The fact this was found in his studio suggests he painted it for himself, or certainly for his new home in Kirkcudbright. Very treasured today. It's the only one we know of. There could be more, but."

Jane asked: "Could it be his sister?"

"Unlikely. His sister is in other portraits and

there are some photographs. So, an intelligent suggestion, but no. As far as I know, there's nothing known about her identity. Some have speculated, but no-one knows. And perhaps never will."

John leaned in close to read the gallery's description of Woman In A Drawing Room: "You said 'more'. Do we know if there are?" He felt a foreboding.

"No, no. I believe there was a mention in someone's diary, a fellow artist, of The Broughton Women. But it could refer to anything. It could, on reflection, have been about another series of paintings, or even his circle of friends. I say 'circle of friends' because a number of artists moved to Kirkcudbright to be near him, such was his reputation, but whether any ever got close enough to him to be called a 'friend' is another matter."

They moved from the portrait, Colin and Jane arm-in-arm, to a wide painting in a heavy gilded frame of a summer landscape with nude children bathing in a tumbling stream. Fields of gold, cornflower blue sky, high white clouds, a dark wood on the horizon.

"As I said, his earlier work like this is well regarded, technically very, very accomplished, but seen as a bit chocolate boxy for today's tastes. His nudes, including children, were very popular in Victorian times, but, again, today, people have very different views about such things. If you wanted this you'd probably have to part with, I would think, sixty or seventy thousand pounds. Not much in today's art market. But then it's hard to judge because his work rarely comes up for sale and when it does it's at just one London auction house. It's never clear where it's come from, so there's always some doubt about the provenance. The portrait, however, who knows? Today, a much more acceptable subject, superbly done, and as far as we know it's a one off and therefore could be worth what, half a million? Get a few Broughton collectors against each other, and there are some who still appreciate a truly superb artist, and God knows where the price would go."

"Colin. If I could just interrupt you and Jane, to go back to the skeleton we found. Would an artist normally have one in his studio?"

"Oh yes, definitely. Artists have to get beneath the surface of their subjects. It is very important to have a good knowledge of the structure of a body – the bones, muscles, tendons, how the whole thing works. Anatomy is central to anyone wanting to capture and portray the true form of their subject, man or beast. Central to the craft. There's work in this gallery which is completely hopeless

The Painter Of Souls

in that regard, though strangely it's more regarded than the work of Mr Broughton. I'll show you later."

Dr Wallace was now in full flow. "They have to suggest what lies beneath. Difficult if they don't know. Take George Stubbs, the greatest ever painter of horses. He would personally dissect them, making detailed drawings of every muscle, bone and sinew. A difficult job. Imagine it, a full horse.

"On one well documented occasion he took over an isolated farmhouse and went to work on the horse with the help of his partner, a woman, whose name if I remember correctly, was Mary Spencer. Yes, Mary Spencer. That was 250 years ago. They dissected the animal bit by bit, making meticulous drawings and notes. I think it was high summer. Imagine the smell. The gore. The mess. The pair of them locked away in that room for days on end. But, he captured the very essence of every horse he painted because he knew exactly how they worked, he knew their inner selves. No-one has got near him since. Imagine the rumpus if an artist stripped an animal down to its bare essentials today."

A woman who had been listening, tutted, pulled a face and moved away.

"With Broughton, who knows if he did the same? There is a painting of his in a private collection of a stag, every fibre of its body is there, very much like Stubbs and his horses. Magnificent. So he certainly knew his anatomy in detail. But, his diaries, his notebooks and sketch books were all passed to his sister on his death and she burned the lot. Christ knows why, although it has been argued she was carrying out his dying wish. An odd chap."

Jane frowned at him. "Destroyed it all? How could she?"

"My dear, Ruskin, that Victorian prude who couldn't shag his wife, excuse me, burned a huge amount of Turner's work he was entrusted with because it contained nude women and detailed drawings of women's genitals which he found disgusting. A catalogue of work by one of our greatest artists, lost forever. Reduced to ash. Broughton probably the same."

Jane had moved further down the room, leaving the two men. John took his opportunity. "So we have, what, just his pictures? Not much else?"

"That's correct. Usually there's a wide archive, but not for him. As I said, we learn a little from the diaries of other people who were with him, letters he wrote to people, but it's pretty tame stuff. He didn't give away much of himself, not even to close friends like the artist George Henry. Some of his sisters' stuff has survived. Not much. Perhaps the most we can learn of him is during his war service? From other people."

"War service? He would have been a bit old. If not dead."

"No, not the Great War. Broughton went out to Africa to document the Boer War. The Second Boer War to be precise. Around 1900. There's quite some detail of that from others. He was wounded out there and eventually invalided home."

"I didn't know they had war artists then."

"Oh yes. Many of the newspapers and magazines of the time hired artists, and famous authors, I think Arthur Conan Doyle went out to the Boer War, and sent them out across the globe. It's nothing new. Have a look at old editions of papers like the Daily Mail, The Times, the Illustrated London News and you'll get a good idea of what was going on."

They caught up with Jane. Dr Wallace, again taking her arm, offered a guided tour through the national gallery. John Armstrong presumed he could tag along, if he fancied.

"Look at this. Classic example." They were back in front of the Lady In Grey. "Sir Daniel Macnee, a fine artist. Indeed President of the Royal Scottish Academy in his day. But the eyes. Just look. Dead."

They moved in closer. Black holes. And then were off again. John Armstrong in tow.

"And here, Walton's Bluette, a very well regarded portrait of a young girl. He's concentrated on the face and the hands, quite superb. Her straw hat, clothes and the background almost a sketch because he wants us to focus on her hands and her face. On her. But look at the eyes. Nothing there. The very essence of her is lost."

They walked on through galleries containing work from centuries ago, many of them religious subjects, accompanied by a running commentary from a less-than-impressed Dr Colin Wallace. "That arm couldn't bend there. Pathetic." "The human body does not have muscles there. Never." "That foot – enormous. What was he looking at?" "Whose leg is that? It doesn't appear to belong to anyone. Grotesque."

They made for the café, Colin Wallace remaining indignant. "All of those artists would have used models, some may have had skeleton, yet they couldn't get it right. Broughton did and while some of those artists are revered today, their work worth hundreds of thousands, he's almost forgotten. A crying shame."

In the bustling café, John Armstrong left

his wife and Dr Wallace, who was holding her hand across the table, deep in conversation. They had discovered a shared a passion for Piet Mondrian paintings, which to John looked like a catalogue for wall tiles, but to his wife and her new 'best friend' his paintings provided the building blocks of life and landscape. He commented that Lego was very much the same, before walking to the gallery shop where he bought a postcard of Broughton's 'Woman In A Drawing Room'. Real art.

He searched among the books on sale for a work on Broughton. None. Various reference books mentioned the artist, but told him little he did not already know. He studied the postcard and again looked at the eyes, deep into the eyes. They drew him in. Almost hypnotic. How had he done it?

CHAPTER 14

SHE was a striking woman. Edward Broughton had felt an immediate physical attraction to her on their excursion to Cape Town's Table Mountain and this only increased when they all met over dinner later that evening, perhaps the first time he had experienced such an intense feeling in his lifetime. Obviously she was older by some years, but her erect bearing, her smile, her soft eyes, the wisps of fair hair beneath her straw hat, her voice. Ah, her voice, so full of charm. Her intelligence. She stood out from the other ladies he had regularly seen and talked with in The Grand Hotel. They had such small lives compared to this woman who had lived in America, farmed in Mexico, although she had said little about this and he suspected a man may have been involved in a troublesome way, and she had challenged the British Government, and won. He had never visited Cornwall where she had spent her childhood and where she had, in her own words, 'clumsily and wastefully', taken lessons in art. He could help her. He would visit there on his return. Perhaps capture her likeness, if she would agree to sit for him.

The walk earlier yesterday on Table Mountain with the delightful Miss Hobhouse and also Mrs Foster and her daughters, and that man Churchill had been a disaster. What a show off. The man was unbelievably arrogant. He had flirted with the women. Hardly put pencil to paper because he was so busy bragging and boasting. The women must have found him utterly tiresome, though were noble enough to feign interest. He had departed the drawing party early to prepare for the voyage home to England. Good riddance. He had urged Broughton to accompany him on the journey home. 'Heroes together...we'll make a splash'. The nerve. The cad. Churchill was the last person he'd choose to travel with. Thankfully he had not joined them for dinner later that evening. He had no intention of returning to Scotland, yet. He readily admitted the light of the African summer had seduced him and he wanted to capture more of it. And there was also...... He looked across the lobby from his easy chair where he had been reading the Cape Town News.

She was talking to another lady he did not recognise. They were supposed to be alone together, discussing their itinerary. A stab of jealousy? He felt not. But when he thought about yesterday evening, he really could not remember too much. Not drunk, by no means, but it was a blur. This enchanting lady. Perhaps he was jealous, a little. So confusing.

His leg was fully healed and he had written to his sister urging her not to worry about him. But should he limp a little, just to show his, his what, his sacrifice? It was hardly that. But, perhaps it would help. It did sometimes ache.

She turned to him now. Was that a smile?

"Ha, Mr Broughton." It was a smile. A light across her face. Could he capture that? She seemed pleased to see him. She beckoned him towards them, a gentle and graceful movement. He folded his newspaper and rose from his chair, managing a slight limp, nothing too exaggerated. Miss Hobhouse, glanced at his leg, hurried towards him. "I am just talking with Mrs Joubert. She is asking if we would try to find her sister Mrs Philip Botha on our expedition. I have assured her we will do our best." She held his arm to guide him towards the other lady and introduced him. His arm burned with the pleasure. Please, never let go.

The lady said something to him, but with the strong accent of Afrikaans which he had always found difficult to penetrate, and at the moment he was hardly concentrating. Her touch through his jacket, so gentle.

Yesterday he had drunk deep of all that was said by and about Miss Emily Hobhouse. She was indeed a Miss, a niece of social campaigner Lord Arthur Hobhouse. Never heard of him, though he would never had admitted it. Back home, she had campaigned fiercely on behalf of the Boer families caught up in this bloody war. Stories had circulated in a few closed circles of terrible suffering endured by the Boers. This was being ignored by the Government, the newspapers and almost everyone else. Broughton agreed it was outrageous, though he had not heard these rumours himself. Few dared to speak out, not wanting to criticise during a time of war. But Emily Hobhouse had demanded permission from the Government to travel out to Africa to visit the camps where families had been evacuated away from the fighting. She was scorned, accused of being un-patriotic, abused, but refused to be silenced. Ministers assured her that Boer families were being well cared for. They were housed, fed, watered and safe under the protective arm of Queen and Empire. It was a damnable scandal to suggest otherwise. A damnable impertinence.

Last evening, over dinner, Mrs Foster had vividly described how her friend, the wonderful Miss Hobhouse, who at that precise time had excused herself from their table, had demanded to be allowed to travel to Africa if the Government was so confident it had nothing to hide. Inwardly, he cheered her. Finally, and only after intervention from influential members of her family, a fine and noble family, it was agreed with army commander Lord Kitchener that she could sail to Cape Town.

At this point Miss Hobhouse had returned to the table. Broughton stood and applauded. She had blushed. So had he. Mrs Foster reviewed what she had told the small gathering and asked Miss Hobhouse to please carry on.

Reluctantly, she described how Lord Kitchener had finally conceded she could visit the camp at Bloemfontein, deep in the African interior, but could go no further. No other camps. There was a war and it was no place for a lady. She had heard of many other camps, at places so foreign to her: Johannesburg, Potchefstroom, Norvalspont, Kroonstad and Irene. "I hope I have pronounced them correctly." Lord Kitchener, a man under intense pressure to end this increasingly problematic war against what his army staff described as uncouth farmers acting like bar-

baric terrorists, insisted she travel no farther. His patience clearly at the very limit. The railway line out to Bloemfontein was secure and safe and she could take the train. But that would be the end of the line for her. "Definitely, no farther."

She described her chance meeting with Mr Edward Broughton – she smiled at him across the dinner table – as a stroke of good fortune. The famous artist had agreed to accompany her and record their mission to Bloemfontein. Quite without hesitation. Their train departed in two days and would include a wagon of supplies, both food and medical, which the authorities insisted were superfluous to need, but reluctantly allowed, she suspected, just to silence her. She believed many on the army staff hoped she would be shot.

The two day train journey across the flat, brown veldt passed in a flash. Broughton had Miss Hobhouse almost to himself, and despite their age gap, which he calculated at a mere fifteen years and dismissed as an irrelevance, they found they shared many interests and views. Certainly her views, were also his, he assured her. Repeatedly.

During his recuperation in Cape Town he had heard little of the conditions in Boer camps, as now being described to him. On the contrary, the talk was off families being provided with new accommodation superior to the rough farms they had been living on. Conditions were far better for the Boers than the soldiers who braved death and disease. Canteens provided daily meals, free of charge. Hospitals gave out medical help, again free of charge. He had believed assurances that Boer families were being transported to a better life. But, who would doubt Miss Hobhouse? Called her into question? He was enraged by the very idea of it.

They arrived mid-afternoon in Bloemfontein after an uneventful journey.

"Please, Miss Hobhouse." He stood back to allow her to exit their carriage.

"Indeed, please, Mr Broughton. You go first. You have so much to carry."

He quickly stepped down to the platform, dropped his bags and turned, offering his hand to help Miss Hobhouse. She hitched her skirt and he saw something of her leg just above the ankle. He must not stare.

A small contingent met them at Bloemfontein. To be exact one junior officer two regular soldiers. Broughton felt a flush of anger at this obvious snub of a lady as distinguished as Miss Hobhouse. He had hoped for a familiar face in a crowd, after all he had been on the front line with the troops and wounded. He expected slaps on the back. A warm welcome. Not this shabby showing. It was perfectly clear they were not welcome. Surely they knew who he was?

Apparently not. The officer, who didn't even bother to offer his name never mind the usual courtesies offered to a lady, stepped forward. "I have orders to meet you."

And that was it. He turned to the privates alongside and ordered them to put the luggage on the rough cart waiting on the dusty street. Their cases were thrown on with such a thump that it startled the old mule harnessed at the front and it reared and dumped the load in the dirt. One soldier steadied the mule and the other threw the cases back on.

Their officer, who had not even removed his helmet, added, with a sneer and loud enough for anyone on the platform to hear: "And I must just say that I have no idea why you are here interfering in this war. I can tell you, Miss Hobhouse, if I may, that conditions for the Boer families are far better than we have for our own men. You should, if I may say, concentrate on helping the soldiers who are fighting for you and dying from disease. Dying daily for you. That would win you some friends here. Anyway I am ordered to suggest that you and your companion," at this he gave a look of contempt at Edward Broughton, "stay overnight and take the train back to Cape Town first thing tomorrow. The supplies you have brought can be left at the station and would be best used for your own countrymen. I would have hoped that you Broughton would have known better than to join this shabby exercise. You seem to have forgotten that the Boer tried to kill you."

Emily Hobhouse gave the man a look of cold contempt and walked away. Head held high. Edward Broughton, seethed, and would have demanded an apology but saw that Miss Hobhouse was heading out alone into this hostile place and he hurried to her side.

"Please, Mr Broughton, don't say a word to me at the moment. Not a word, thank you."

A woman approached them. In a thick German accent she said she would show them to their lodgings and, leaning in close to Miss Hobhouse, whispered: "We are glad you are here."

They had expected a hotel of sorts, but were led onto a back street of shabby houses, where their luggage had already been dumped outside on the broken pavement.

The following morning local people brought two wagons hauled by mules and a third by an ox to collect them and their supplies from the station before setting out on the two hour trail to the camp. Miss Hobhouse had not left her room the previous evening and he had not seen her until they met that morning over a meagre breakfast. Edward Broughton wondered what would be said of their treatment. Apparently very little, because nothing was said on any subject.

Soldiers at the station gave no help to locals who loaded the supplies. The small convoy of three open wagons and two guides on ponies left a silent Bloemfontein into the midday heat and dust. The track broken and uneven. Alongside, in the dry veldt, were many small piles of stones. Edward Broughton, sitting alongside the driver, assumed they were way markers. In the far distance he could see a scattering of grey bell tents on the barren side of a low hill alive with heat haze. He assumed it was the camp because his wagon driver appeared to speak no English. He still had a nagging feeling that conditions would not be as bad as feared. The officers would surely not have lied. His spirits were lifting, a little.

Emily Hobhouse rode alongside the driver of the wagon behind. Lost in orange dust. He had tried to insist she take the lead wagon, but her driver was a woman and decorum ruled the day. He was disappointed, but understood.

The stench hit him first, some way from the

huddle of filthy tents. Human sewage and something more sweet and sickly hung thick in the stagnant air. He gipped. Only minutes earlier he had lowered the scarf he had worn to protect against the dust and immediately pushed it back, ensuring a tight fit. In the distance, shaking with heat haze, he saw one or two people moving slowly and hunched. As they neared, he realised there was quite a group, all looking towards their small convoy, eyes shielded with hands.

His wagon halted. Miss Hobhouse drew alongside. He offered his hand to help her down. She hoisted her beige skirt, it was almost white when they had departed that morning, and jumped. Of course, Edward understood, she wanted to show her independence to the men who ran the camp.

"But, thank you anyway, Edward." She surveyed the stinking encampment set out in front of her. "This, if you'll excuse me, looks like Hell on Earth." She moved forward, lowered her scarf, removed her hat. Edward snatched his artist satchel, felt the familiar slap of the artist stool against his side, and hurried after her. She had called him Edward. Dare he be so familiar as to call her Emily? He felt a thrill if intimacy.

A straggle of people emerged from tents and joined the larger group, huddled on what appeared to be a meeting square amid the tents. All gaunt and bent, most coughing, keeping their distance. Emily strode purposefully towards them. A woman in a nurses uniform, looking tired, her eyes black rimmed with fatigue, came forward.

"We were told you were not coming. But, thank God you are here." German.

Edward moved away as the two women embraced. Most unusual, in his mind. He crossed to the nearest tent. There was no one outside, he paused, he could hardly knock on the door, so he called out, heard no reply, lifted the flap and looked in. Recoiled. Dropped the canvas. Wretched. It wasn't just the stench of illness and shit. It was the sight of people he struggled to recognise as humans.

He took a deep breath, lifted the canvas again, and stooped inside. Women and children were huddled on the hard floor, not a bed or a blanket in sight, in the stinking mess and the stifling heat. Rags of clothing. Skin and bone. Bare feet. The air thick with black flies. Large eyes, sunken, stared at him. Unblinking. He must have come to the infirmary tent. He quickly stepped back outside where the sun hit him hard, hammered at his skull and he stumbled down onto the dry dead soil.

He was helped to his feet by a Boer man, one of the few in the camp, who called in a strange language to Miss Hobhouse and the nurse who hurried across. One of the guides, who had accompanied them from the town, brought water. It tasted foul.

Edward Broughton, groggy and struggling to control himself, looked at Emily Hobhouse. "You said it was Hell. It is worse than any Hell. Far, far worse. Far worse." He sat on one of the medical boxes, head in hands. Someone put his canvas bag and collapsible stool by his side.

The sun was fierce and there would have been that complete, heavy pressing silence that accompanies extreme heat, but here it was broken by the incessant buzz of flies and the moans and coughs of families hidden behind thin canvas.

The nurse appeared too frightened to offer information, even if she fully understood the questions. But, with careful prompting and the help of a young girl who seemed to understand both languages, she agreed to help locate Mrs Philp Botha. The small group set off through the stench to a tent higher up the dung brown hillside.

It was occupied by a woman visibly grey and with matted hair but in better condition than many. And she could speak English.

"Mrs Philip Botha?"

"Yes." The woman was sitting on a bare metal

The Painter Of Souls

bed and struggled to her feet.

"Please don't stand. I'm Emily Hobhouse. I'm here, I hope, to help."

"They said you weren't coming." She was shaking on her legs. "I need to get out of here." She offered her hand which Emily Hobhouse took and together they slowly moved to the shade of a nearby veranda outside a wooden hut used by the British troops. She tried to object, to insist this was a place only for the soldiers, who were strangely not to be seen, and there would be reprisals. Emily Hobhouse lowered her into an easy chair and then took the one next to her. The small group drifted away, perhaps fearful that they would suffer if the soldiers spotted them in an area definitely out of bounds to the Boer.

"Your sister spoke to me in Cape Town before were departed and asked me to try to make contact. She wanted assurance that you were still alive."

"Just. For the time being, but not for long. Not in this place."

Emily offered her water from a leather bottle she carried on a shoulder strap.

"We had reports at home of how poor conditions were, but nothing prepared me for this. What on earth has happened? Has disease taken its toll? What has happened here?"

"Nothing has happened. That is our problem. The British have brought typhoid, measles and dysentery, but no food and won't allow us off the camp to get our own. They have soldiers out there who shoot at us if we wonder off, women and children, imagine that, shooting down children like they were wild pigs. They give us rotten meat and flour alive with beetles. Even if it was fit to eat we have no means to cook. There is nothing to burn. You can clearly see that people are starving."

"But we have been assured you are being well treated. I didn't believe it. But…"

"You were right not to. The water is filthy. There is one nurse to help us, but she has no medicines. We cannot even wash. There are two thousand here, nearly all women and children, and we are dying every day. Twenty two yesterday. It is what the British want. They want rid of the Boer. They want us dead."

She took Emily Hobhouse by the arm, for support, and stumbling now and then led her towards a shed-like structure on the outskirts of the camp

"I arrived only a week ago with many others. I'm surprised my sister knew I was here. But she's well connected. Let me show you."

She got to her feet. Unsteady. Held tight to Miss Hobhouse and shuffled to a wooden shed next to the guard house. They stopped by the closed door.

"Our introduction to this place was to show us this. We were forced to line up and wait our turn to look inside. Here."

She pulled opened the door. Inside it was dark and it took some time for Emily's eyes to adjust. And then she saw.

"This is Lizzie. Lizzie Van Zyl. She's seven. Her father is one of our commando leaders and will not surrender. Until he does they will not feed her. It is a lesson to us all."

Laid on a rough wooden, soiled, stinking cot was the skeletal, almost bald and naked figure of Lizzie Van Zyl. Eyes large, staring. Head returned to a skull. Too weak to move. Flies worrying her mouth and nose, eagerly waiting. Her voice weak, a breath. "Are you my mother?" Emily Hobhouse held her hand to a mouth in horror.

"She will not last tomorrow. Then the British will take another child. Bring her here. It will be their turn to starve to death unless we tell our men to give up the fight."

Emily Hobhouse bent to hold the child's cold and bony hand. Her own went to her mouth to help hold back the wretch of acid bile burning her throat. Tears on her cheeks.

Mrs Botha stood in the doorway, against the

light, holding herself up on the door frame. "Miss Hobhouse, we need to leave."

"Someone should be with her. Should be helping."

"I am told her mother came with her, but she died some days ago. People have tried talking to the camp commandant but he refuses to see us, claims he is acting under orders, and spends his time in the town, away from here. No, you won't find him now. No-one will speak to you. If we bring her food they say they will shoot us. Normally there is someone guarding this hut. I don't know where they have all gone. We should leave."

"Then I must get Mr Broughton here now. People have to see this at home. Where is he? Where's the nurse?"

Edward Broughton had finally recovered his senses. He could hear voices chattering away in the background, but could not locate the direction. Just a murmuring. But it was not the drone of flies. Definitely human. Or was it? He removed his hat, wiped his sweating brow, eased the stiffness in his neck. The voices remained, tempting just beyond his grasp. He shouldered his artist bag and stool.

The soil here was black and bare, a startling change to the normal dry-as-dust orange, and he limped across to a tent. Was that him whistling? He was not sure. It was cer-

The Painter Of Souls

tainly no time to whistle a jolly tune. Inside the tent a man, he thought the same man who had helped him to his feet, bent over a young girl, she could have been no more than twelve, gasping for air on the bare earth floor. Body twisting, heaving. Her father, if it was her father, stroked her hair. A woman stood alongside weeping. Broughton knew what to expect. The smell. The heat.

He calmly released his stool from his satchel, snapped it open and sat taking in the scene. Pulled out his sketch book and pencils and began to draw. Emily had wanted him to record such scenes. He studied the girl: filthy blond, her eyes wide and bright blue set in a sunken, yellow face. Eyes wide with fear.

Suddenly, as he watched, she convulsed, sat upright, the light went from her eyes, it had seemed to momentarily burn bright, so bright, and then it was out. Like the flare of a candle, but brighter. Broughton, pencil in mouth, was startled by the sudden flare. For that brief moment the girl's spirit, her soul, had been there. He had seen it. At first he thought the tent flap had opened, letting sun into the hot, grey light, but no. He had seen something else.

The weeping woman turned away and howled. He had seen a soul, he was sure. If he could capture that, capture the light, as it left the child. He stood, the man held the girl close to his body, obscuring Broughton's view, so he peered over the shoulder of the man. Her eyes were dead now. They had been so brilliantly alive. For that brief moment. A jumble of voices. Louder. Very confusing.

Someone entered the tent, tapped his shoulder. "Please follow me."

Emily Hobhouse and Mrs Botha left Edward Broughton at the hut to record for posterity the horrific plight of Lizzie Van Zyl. They returned to the shaded veranda.

"Why don't you leave with us? We could take you on one of the wagons. We could get you to Cape Town. They need to know."

"No. I cannot. My friends are here. I cannot leave them."

"But, your own family?"

"My husband and two sons are fighting. They are risking their lives. My place is here."

"To die?"

"To be with my friends. My nieces. You can take my message back with you. Cape Town will believe you more than they would me. I'm Boer. You have seen. I will tell you what happened to me. It is the same story for all the people here and I'm told at other camps. Our homes and farms have been plundered and burned. Our men hunted down and shot. Women and children, and our older men, are being forced into these camps where if the disease does not take us, then starvation will. All because the British want our land."

They were silent on the return to Bloemfontein. Edward Broughton puzzling over the light he had seen in the dying girl's eyes and the voices which he had failed to track down. He would not write of the camp to his sister. He composed in his mind a letter recounting a pleasant jaunt into the countryside, now made safe from the Boer, perhaps he would mention Emily, who had chosen to sit alongside him on the lead wagon. Out of the dust. A fine woman. At each violent shake of the wagon their legs touched, a shot of electricity jolting his thigh.

Emily Hobhouse was in a cold, silent fury determined to confront the British officers in charge. Oblivious to the artist alongside her. This wagon was too damned slow. She shouted to the driver: "Hurry on, man. Hurry." The occasional British soldier rode past them, going in the same direction. Urgent.

At Bloemfontein she jumped from the wagon before it had halted, hat fell to the ground, stormed up the wooden steps to the army headquarters in a fine town house commandeered for the purpose and through the open doors into a reception room. A man at a desk in the corner of the cool interior said there was no-one to see her. They had obviously been well informed of her imminent arrival because armed guards were stationed at the door leading further into the building, bayonets on their rifles, Blocking her way.

"You are cowards. Not soldiers. Cowards." She began to push against them. The soldier, who had been sitting at a desk just inside the building and had spoken to her moments before, hurried to her and took her by the arms. Dragged her away.

"Get your hands off me. Off me. Now." She wrestled free and in a blind fury turned to slap him. One of the men guarding the door shouted: "Watch out, Mac, she's a wild thing." In the struggle she fell to the floor, banged her head. Blood dripped from her nose and tears stung her eyes.

A man reached down to help her. He was carrying what looked like a medical bag. With his other, he helped her stand.

He turned to the soldiers. "What on earth is going on here?"

"She's not allowed in, sir. We have orders."

"What, to man-handle her to the floor and beat her?" He carefully helped support Miss

Hobhouse with his free hand. Put his bag on the floor. "My handkerchief. It looks to be a simple nose bleed. Shame on you men. I will have your names."

"Thank you. Are you an officer here?"

He stood back, opened his arms to show his shabby brown coat. Something of a uniform beneath. A walrus moustache below a straw hat which had seen better days.

"Not really. Dr Doyle, physician. Arthur Conan Doyle." He doffed his hat. Smiled." I'm a doctor at the Langman Field Hospital just outside town. Can I help?"

"Hobhouse. Emily Hobhouse. The niece of Lord Hobhouse. I have just been to your Boer camp. Have you visited? Surely, you cannot have witnessed what I have witnessed."

Dr Doyle looked puzzled.

"I don't understand."

"The women, the children, they are starving. They are dying. You are killing them. The British. And now these here won't let me in to speak to the officers who are, who are, well, murdering women and children."

"I have not been. I, I suspect like yourself, have only recently arrived. But, Miss Hobhouse, our own troops are dropping like flies. The diseases in this country are killing some of our finest officers and men. Thousands of them. I'm sorry, but it is difficult enough helping our own. We too are short of food. Please, excuse me."

"Will you not help?"

"Please, excuse me."

He moved away and the guards opened the door, making it clear to Emily Hobhouse that she should not even try to push her way in. The door closed on laughter. She was sure she heard her name and then the laughter.

She walked to the door. The guards on alert.

She shouted: "I have in here," she pointed to her head, "I have in here the story of one of those women you are killing. I shall write it down and I shall send it to The Times of London. My friend Mr Broughton has the pictures to prove it all. Will you be laughing then? Will you think it funny when the world knows you are nothing but cowards, butchers and murderers?"

CHAPTER 15

MRS BOTHA turned to Emily Hobhouse. The two women sat in the shade of a veranda outside a guard house in the Bloemfontein camp.

"Please let me tell you, this is a million miles from my home town in North Yorkshire. My father was a preacher who thought it a good idea to uproot his family – I was eleven – and bring us out here to spread the word of God. We could do with some of his help right now – God, that is, not my father.

"My story is the same for all the people here and, I understand, at other camps. Our homes and farms have been plundered and burned. Our men hunted down and shot. Women and children, some of our older, weaker men, are being brought to these camps on the promise of a new home. It's a lie. All lies. The British, and I'm ashamed to say I'm British, was British, have delivered us to a hell hole where if disease does not kill us, then we are starved to death. All because they want rid of us so they can take our land."

She faltered, halted. Wiped tears from her eyes. Emily Hobhouse reached to take her hand and held it firmly between hers. "Your story is important. I promise I will take it home with me. Your voice will be heard. Please take your time."

"The Boer rider came mid-morning. I was alone in the farmhouse, my husband and two sons were away fighting for our homes. Our two helpers, Elsa and John, had taken the ox wagon into town and had not returned. I was very worried for them.

"I didn't know the rider. He hammered on the door and when I opened it, there he stood, covered in red dust and sweat. His pony looked exhausted. He told me the British were coming and he was telling all the farmers and their families to be ready. He asked if I had a spare pony, but I had nothing."

"I asked him 'ready', ready for what? Though I'd heard the stories. He said they were looting and burning. He told me to get everyone out of the house. Save what you can. I told him I'm alone here. My husband and sons are fighting. He was half-turned to his pony, and he looked back and warned me not to tell that to the British or I'd probably be shot. Then he was on his pony, asked me the way to the next farm and rode off. I hope he survived, but his pony looked done for. It can't have taken him far and the British were close.

"For a moment I thought I should take a rifle from the farmhouse, but what use would I have been against the soldiers? So I walked across to our barn where we kept our old mule Pieter. There was all sorts of stuff in there and I dragged out a flat cart I knew Pieter would just about manage. You know, I can remember quite clearly looking across to the far horizon and seeing our cattle moving in the rising heat. I was looking for signs of Elsa and John returning, but nothing. And I can still smell the sweet straw and wood inside the barn. Our hens were in there, enjoying the shade.

"Pieter moved to the front of his stall to meet me. I rubbed his soft warm ears. 'In a moment', I said. 'In a moment.'

"The old cart was propped up against the wall. We hadn't used it for quite some time. Years ago my sons would harness Pieter to the cart and race across the farm whooping and throwing up clouds of dust. Pieter would take us out to the river on the cart where we'd picnic and bath on summer evenings. They were good days. Good days.

"I just hoped the cart would hold together when I pulled it down. A harness was looped around one of the shafts and although it was stiff it would have to do. I could hear Pieter in his stall. Excited. The cart was light enough for me to pull outside and it moved freely. At least the wheels stayed on. I went back to bring Pieter. Led him to the cart, gazing hard at the horizon. No sign. I know Elsa and John would have done everything they could to return and I was desperately worried.

"I hitched Pieter and led him across to the farmhouse, tied him to the rail by the front door and went inside to get some essentials. Thankfully I put on my hat. Within minutes I'd loaded blankets, bedding, our family chest, some dried meat, flour, eggs, water bottles, fresh loaves baked that morning, a drawer of cutlery. But then I stood back, assessed the cart, and Pieter. It was too much. I had to pull off the chest, the cutlery, all the bedding other than a blanket, leave it in the dirt, and even then I knew I would have to walk alongside Pieter into town.

"Then I heard horses. You know, that drumming of their hooves. And sharp gunshots. I reckon a dozen riders, led by a man I presumed was an officer. They reined hard right in front of me. As close as they could. I thought they were going to ride me down. But I wasn't going to show them I was frightened. I stood my ground. Foolish, I suppose. He was brusque, the officer, and shouted to get everyone out of the house. I told him there was no-one else.

"Then he said 'So, your husband is fighting. Right.' Then he turned in his saddle to the men behind him. 'Search it. Burn it. You,' he pointed at me with a pistol in his hand 'stay right there. Shut up. Don't interfere.' Just like that. I knew if I moved he'd shoot. How brave, eh, all those men against one woman and an old mule.

"They ran to my home, kicked open the door, and across to the barn. I could hear them shouting and laughing. I dared move to Pieter, he was getting restless and I thought they would shoot him, and took his head and tried to sooth him, all the time my stomach was heavy with fear. I could hear glass breaking. Things crashing. I knew they were ransacking my home. My home.

"And that officer just sat there, he still had his gun. I asked him what he wanted. He didn't answer. Arrogant.

"He finally got off his horse and he told one of the men, some Johnson or some such, to set a torch. When it flared he walked across, took it, looked at me and smiled, and then went into the barn. He was only in there seconds then he ran out to the house. I went to stop him but one of the soldiers knocked me to the ground and stood with his foot on my head pushing my face into the dirt. There was a tremendous roar. The man who had me pinned turned to look and I managed to sit up. Flames were shooting out of the barn and I shouted at them 'what have you done?' And then my home. I cannot tell you. It was a place we built when we married, where our children were born, where my husband's mother died. Our home. Our everything.

"I just couldn't believe what I was seeing. Couldn't believe it. Then that officer told two of the men to ride back to where they'd shot our cattle and to wait for the cart to come for them. I knew whose cart that would be and I knew what men like that had done to my friends. To John and Elsa. They were my family.

"Then he wanted to know where the next farm was. I shook my head at him. So he told one of the men to shoot Pieter. They put a rifle to his head. I pleaded with them not to. I'm ashamed to say I pointed to the Kotzee's place. They were our close friends and I betrayed them. Though I'm sure they knew where they were anyway. He told one of his men to take me and the mule cart back to town. Then they all rode off.

"I couldn't look behind. I could hear roaring and cracking like explosions. I could hear it. I could smell it. I still can. Sparks were falling in front of us and I knew it would spread to

The Painter Of Souls

the land. It would all burn. But I never looked back.

"The soldier with me was called Carey and he was not a bad man. He walked his horse with me. He said their officer was, and these are his words, not mine, he said he was a bastard. God forgive me. He wanted revenge because his brother had been shot by the Boer. He reckoned they got the wrong one.

"I asked him why my home? Our farm? They had orders to burn all the farms, take the cattle, shoot any Boer terrorists hiding out and take women and children to town. I asked where to then. And he didn't know. Just that special camps had been built, just temporary ones, and we'd be starting a new life with new farms. I never believed that. I was right not to.

"We smelled the town before we could see it. As we neared I could see orange flames and great clouds of black smoke drifting towards us. I feared they were not only burning the houses and shops, but the people in them. We saw British soldiers in our fields butchering our cattle.

"I can tell you it was a long, long five miles to town in the intense heat. Carey allowed a little time for rest and he said I should save as much water as I could because I would need it. By now the smoke was stinging our eyes and we could hear explosions coming from the town. You know, through it all Pieter just kept on going. Head down. Plodding along.

"Carey said they were burning out the houses and shops used by the Boer in the fighting. Another order from on high. He said he'd been in the army twelve years and it was not the way to do things.

"Soldiers were everywhere. They made us walk down to the railway warehouse on the edge of town. Thankfully the fire was blowing the other way. There were sidings there and a long line of open wagons. You know, those open, filthy ones normally used for coal and rock. There were many soldiers, and women and children. Babies in arms. And one or two very old men. And very old women. Some had a few belongings with them, but most had nothing. Nothing at all, perhaps a nightshirt and that was it. They had been dragged from their homes, from the street. From their beds. You might think it was a noisy group standing there alongside the wagons, but no, everyone was silent and still. Afraid.

"We stopped a little way off. Carey told me to take whatever food I could carry and to hide it under my skirts. Bread and some dried beef. He said he'd take care of the cart and Pieter. I had to trust him. You know, as I walked away, towards the soldiers, I heard Pieter start to follow. Heard the harness. Heard Carey hush him. Then two soldiers with their bayonets ran to me and pushed me to the group. People I knew, I'd known for years, but no-one spoke. I watched Carey walk Pieter and the cart away. It broke my heart.

"We were forced to stand for hours in that baking sun. If anyone sat or fell they were kicked by the soldiers. People helped them up. Helped support. Mrs Burgh, whose family ran the store, was at least 80. Poor woman. Some had no hats against the heat, others without shoes, one woman almost naked but for a blouse

"Then we were pushed into lines. They shouted at us to put everything we were carrying into a pile. We were then forced into the open wagons, crammed in, hardly room to move, never mind sit. Soldiers with their bayonets on guard. There was no engine to haul us and rightly I feared we were in for a long wait in the heat.

"Any talking brought an angry response from the guards. So we stood in silence, through the

evening and into the night. It never really got dark because the town was still burning. Babies were crying. Children sobbing. No-one was allowed to leave the wagons and people had to toilet where they stood. There was no water. No food. All the time we all looked down the line hoping an engine would come.

"The night was cold. We were given nothing. We knew the day would break to a hot one. And it did. Not a breeze. We asked the soldiers guarding us for water, for shade but they ignored us. I'd already passed round my water and food. Nothing left. Two women who jumped from their wagon and tried to grab a sheet to use as shelter were knocked to the ground. I thought they would be shot, but they were thrown back into the wagon.

"You know, some of the soldiers stood on the platform drinking water in front of us all. Tipping it out of their cups. Tormenting us. Women and children.

"In our wagon we squeezed closer together to create a little space for the children to lay down. It was in a terrible mess, but at least their heads were shaded under skirt hems.

By mid-morning, under the relentless sun, people began to faint. We were packed so close some didn't drop to the floor. Children and babies became quiet, ominously quiet. Still we had no water, no food, no shade.

"At last we heard an engine coming down the line. No-one cheered. They turned, if they could, and watched the trail of steam as the engine inched towards us. It seemed so slow.

Deliberately slow.

"No one rushed. But, finally we were hauled away and felt a welcoming breeze. We had no idea where to or how long it would take. Surely they couldn't keep us like this for many miles. And without the guards we could talk, although what could we say because the children would hear us?

"Whenever the train stopped to fill with water and coal, guards appeared and ordered us all to stay put. Or else. And we knew what that meant.

"We knew were travelling towards Bloemfontein. It took two days. Thankfully, at the overnight halts we were allowed down from the wagons and handed some foul water and rotten food. But by then many could not walk. Some crawled. And, God save their souls, for some it was too late. We had two die in our wagon. Soldiers dumped their bodies into a heap alongside the railway line whenever we stopped. I dread to think what happened to those poor souls.

"At the second overnight halt we found a large sheet which we took back to our wagon and no one stopped us. The soldiers weren't suddenly friendly, oh no, they just didn't care. They would have been quite happy if we'd all died.

"Finally, finally we arrived in Bloemfontein

and we thought we would get some rest. Some help. Perhaps somewhere to stay. To bathe. To eat. No, only soldiers were waiting for us and we were ordered from the wagons. Those who couldn't were man-handled to the ground. A lot were elderly. Mrs Burgh had made it that far, but I last saw her laid in the dirt. We had to leave them. We don't know what happened. At best we thought they would put them on a wagon and bring them here, but there's none here.

"We were then forced to march two miles, it felt like two hundred, to here. Women, old men and children died along the way, but there was no stopping, no help. Those of us who could, managed to cover their bodies with piles of stone. Keep the animals away. At least for a time. But we were quickly moved on, forced with bayonets back into line. And now here we are, the survivors all dying."

CHAPTER 16

JANE Armstrong, nee Nixon, sat in the car, squinted into the winter sun levelled along Kirkcudbright's High Street and watched her husband as he walked towards her from the newsagents. They had parked close to the home of Edward Broughton and he had gone in search of his newspaper. A crossword to mull over if we find a decent pub. She truly loved this man of hers, although she often wondered how well she would have coped with any further years in the police force. Perhaps, not well. Friends had warned her against marrying a policeman, not John in particular, but any policeman because they all 'shag anything, dead or alive'. There was a chorus of: "He'll hurt you when you have just recovered. When we have just got our old Jane back." That was after her first marriage, when the bastard had just buggered off with the tart from next door.

She was tense and, yes, angry now. Today. She blamed his former job – late night call outs, holidays shortened - or at least tried to, but deep down she knew it wasn't the reason. She had been so foolish, so damned foolish. She watched him now, he waved the newspaper, he would be smiling but he was far off and the sun was too glaring to see.

It happened after her birthday. John had promised to be home, the restaurant table booked, wine chilling in the fridge. And then he telephoned, a case, another bloody case, and he would be late. Late! He arrived home at 4am, full of apologies. But he had also been drinking, stank of beer. The following day had been the end of school term. No one had spoken over breakfast and he left in silence immediately after. She had gone to school angry and had been unusually brusque with her classes. Forcing them to work hard on the final day, it was not like her.

Colleagues gathered in the staff room discussing plans for the break - hiking, decorating, gardening, sleeping – and wishing a temporary farewell to Sue, French teacher, who was starting her maternity leave. Jane, on the edge of the discussion and still seething, envied her. She, thankfully, had never had children in her first marriage which ended in bitter acrimony and now she and John were too old. Too sodding old. Jane herself would soon be stepping down from her job. Stepping down. Not retiring. Do not dare mention retirement and pensions.

People had drifted away and she had been left with Tony French, the head of English. They had always been a little flirty with each other. And suddenly they we were passionately kissing. Mouths open, tongues searching. Out of control. Bodies pressed hard against each other. She felt him harden against her. His hand on her breast, the left one. Her nipple ached. Suddenly she felt something like a hard slap to the back of her head and she pulled apart. Panting. She grabbed her bag, struggled to straighten her blouse, and hurried from the room. And that would have been it. Stupid, but it had gone no further. Then.

Three times she had seen him walk by their house during the half term holiday. Each time he had paused and looked across. Moved on. Normally she would have waved, but something held her back. Not embarrassment.

School re-started and Tony had brushed against her in the staff room, and once in the corridor. Finally she had said sorry, but she didn't want to go any further. He agreed. Apologies. Said he hadn't realised. And he stopped. Pointedly ignored her at school. Fine. She relaxed.

She had resigned from school some weeks

ago, her headteacher asked her to re-consider and promised there would always be a job for her. She was flattered, but she and John had plans. Jane had hoped she'd also left Tony French behind, far behind, a grim and very embarrassing memory. What had she been thinking?

But twice in the weeks running up to John's retirement she had seen him outside their home. He didn't live nearby and had no reason to be in the area. She was not sure, but thought he had taken a photograph of the house on his mobile phone. Certainly he had held a phone up towards the house. A stab of panic. She had been behind the curtain, dusting, and was positive he had not seen her. Could not. Or could he? How long had he been there?

That was the first occasion. Days later she had walked into the front room and saw him again on the pavement opposite. Hands in coat pocket. Staring across. She had edged around to the window, pushing awkwardly past the back of the settee. A minute. Two minutes. Then he had turned and walked away. When she later checked outside and looked back to the house she realised the front room was raised a little above the garden and appeared dark and the view in was restricted. He couldn't have seen her. Could he?

Had he been there before and she hadn't realised? How many times?

For days she had not dared go into the front room, or use the front door. Enough was enough. She convinced herself she was being stupid. Then she would sneak into the room, push by the settee and twitch the curtain.

On John's final day at work, when he came home earlier than expected, and she had been standing by the front window, hidden by the curtain, and then answered the door to welcome him, she had not been looking out for him. Not him. Yes, she had felt pleasure at the end of John's last day of work but that was not her main feeling - it was utter relief which must have seemed like pleasure to John. She had been at the window since breakfast. Why had Tony French taken a photograph of their house? What was he planning?

If this continued she would have to tell John. But, should she tell him everything, everything down to the kissing, or just that she was being pestered? Least said, soonest mended. John, amiable and polite, was also not a man to avoid confrontation and she doubted Tony French would get the chance to say much at all. No, he would not come to physical harm, or would he? At the least, and no doubt the best, he would be left in no doubt that he should disappear never to return. Or, would

John put on his official face and go straight to the head teacher and then…..well, details, details. Why hurt John with her stupid behaviour? And what was Tony French thinking of? One word to the headteacher and his career would be in ruins.

The car door opened, breaking her thoughts. He climbed in behind the wheel. Brought a cloud of cold air with him.

"House doesn't open until twelve, the gardens at eleven. Should have checked. Sorry. There's a very nice looking coffee house back there where we could grab an early elevenses. Fancy it? What's wrong?"

"With me?"

"You looked troubled."

"No, no, it's the sun. I was squinting." She blushed.

The previous day they had driven across to Hexham, supposedly the centre of mainland Britain, but of more importance to them, the location of the Border Reivers Museum.

John was proud of his Armstrong surname, supposedly created centuries ago when a servant hauled his king to safety during a battle, using his one good arm to pick up his majesty and haul him onto his horse. John had flexed his right arm. Feel it, he said to Jane. Real muscle, a real Armstrong. Yes, she thought, it

The Painter Of Souls

could easily deliver a knock-out punch.

His ancestors had been among the leading Reivers families, bringing terror to the lawless border region during the sixteenth century from their stronghold in Liddesdale on the south eastern border of Scotland and England. They would have to make a visit. Explore the ruins of an old fortification, Mangerton Tower, which John reckoned could belong to him. He liked to call it 'my family home'. She just hoped he wasn't thinking of a renovation project.

For centuries, Scotland and England had bloodily disputed the borders, leaving the region wide open to families like the Armstrongs to run protection rackets, to murder, to steal cattle and to violently resist anyone who stood in their way. Almost all of John's ancestors had killed and thieved their way to the gallows. His great, great, great whatevers had felt the hangman's noose and Jane knew that John, strangely, felt a sense of injustice about the whole thing.

She had to admit that her own family, the Nixons, were also brutal Reivers, and operated largely under the protection of the more powerful Armstrongs. John had turned to Jane and told her he would always be there to protect her. Just as his forefathers had protected hers. How willing to protect her if he knew about French? She had to get things in perspective. Nothing had happened. Just a kiss.

In Hexham they had stood together in the old gaol house where the museum was based. The oldest purpose built gaol in England. Dark and sinister and smelling of damp.

"I wonder if they had Armstrongs and Nixons in here, together, 500 years ago?" John held Jane close. "Then off to the hangman."

Today they had driven to Kirkcudbright to visit Edward Broughton's, now in the care of the National Trust. They had parked some distance away on the High Street, the council having banned parking anywhere near the neighbouring house because of the earthquake damage. Its gable remained framed with scaffolding and blue tarpaulins. Yellow bollards haphazard on the road edge. Pavement Closed signs and a gusting trail of red and blue tape.

Bright sun, but a biting wind blew down the High Street as they hurried to the café, warm and golden inside.

Over toasted fruit loaf and coffee John confessed to Jane he was still wrestling with thoughts of the skeleton. His brief investigation had failed to get to the truth of the matter, hardly scratched the surface. The case had been prematurely concluded, buried under budget cuts, the Royal visit, and the chief's conviction that it was all too old to yield the identity of victim or culprit. Tittle tattle for the newspapers. A waste of time and money for the police.

"He kept saying 'move on, John'. Laughable. That's all he was interested in. Putting it behind him. Me, move on to what, retirement?" He sat back, wiped his mouth with the small paper serviette.

Jane sipped her coffee. "Your last case and one of the few not solved. You don't expect answers today, do you? Don't build up hope."

"No, no, not really. Not at all. I don't even know that this artist chap was in any way involved. Seems to fit the time frame. But there's hardly anything about him. It's difficult to imagine the man. And, okay, I certainly know anyone is capable of anything, it's hard to think an artist..."

"Caravaggio."

"Sorry? Caravaggio?"

"Yes. My new best friend Colin."

"Colin? Oh, Colin Wallace at the Gallery."

"Yes, dear Colin. He was telling me that artists can have a mean streak in them. Caravaggio, we've seen his work in Italy, John, was sentenced to death for murder. And do remember that Hitler was a would-be artist first, soldier second."

"Hitler? Oh come on. Edward Broughton was hardly…"

"I'm just making a point, darling." She smiled at him from behind her coffee cup.

"Back to Edward Broughton. Do we know anything more about him than when we started out?" John looked frustrated.

"Well, he was obviously famous in his day, but now no-one seems to remember him. I spoke to Connie last week and she's been here a couple of times gathering material for her art lessons at school and she said there's very little. Most of the stuff is about the restoration of the house and the gardens. But there is a portrait of the man, so you can look deep into his eyes and see if you can discover his secrets. Seek the truth, Mr Detective. I shall be in the garden."

"You'll get blown away."

"Not with all this toast in me. And its walled, sheltered. And don't go upsetting the staff at the house with your questions."

"Would I?"

"Yes."

They would also call on Mrs Johnson, whose house was damaged by the earthquake. Enquire if she was recovering and ask had she remembered anything of significance? She had been discharged from hospital to her daughter's and John had telephoned yesterday evening. Her daughter had promised they would be in all afternoon and happy to see him. They would put the kettle on. He promised to bring cake. Four eclairs were in the car. But first Broughton House.

The icy wind hurried them arm-in-arm to the iron gates in front of the building. They crossed the short paved courtyard to the front door, orange safety barriers to their left keeping visitors well away from the ruined gable. The door burst open with the power of the wind, leaves raced in with them. They struggled to close it.

"A bit of a breeze out there." The smiling, middle-aged woman was behind a desk in the entrance hall, glasses, straight blonde hair, blue jacket, arms stretched to hold down papers and brochures. "Are you members?" She re-arranged herself.

CHAPTER 17

ARTIST Edward Broughton sat at his polished writing desk in the library of his large house in Kirkcudbright. Sun slanted through the window alongside. Solway Hall dated back centuries and had been home to many of the town's distinguished worthies, including an earl and ministers. Easily the most imposing house in the town, and that appealed to the famous artist. Befitted his new status, though he cautioned against getting ahead of himself. But, he reassured himself, it was his talent, his genius alone that had brought him all the way from that dour croft to this splendour.

His builders had completed the renovation, moved on to the garden, and the interior designers had also been and gone. He hadn't realised it was possible to buy complete room furnishings, from curtains and carpets down to door handles and light shades, at select London stores and it would all be delivered and fitted as a package. Flora had organised it and he was extremely pleased with the result. Now his builders were working on the garden, shaping it to the Italian style he so admired.

Thankfully he had missed most of the disruption - the noise, dirt and general upheaval - during his days in Africa and the unfortunate stay in hospital on his return. Not only his wounded leg. The doctors called his other problem 'mental fatigue' and he was recovered. Fully recovered.

How excited he had been when Flora had written to his hotel in Cape Town, unbelievably almost a year ago, explaining that the large house next door to their end of terrace home and studio in Kirkcudbright was to be sold. Should they buy? He could easily afford the house which had been vacant for some years, and their friend, solicitor Hamish Robinson, had offered to 'sort things out'. He readily agreed to the purchase and the extensive renovation needed.

Edward leaned back from his desk, surveyed his library, light flooding in through a large bow window, his grandfather clock marking time to the side, a fire spitting in the grate. His books filled the shelves. A great sense of satisfaction. Flora had really come into her own, mixing the responsibility of visiting their aged and widowed mother and supervising the birth of their new home. His own letters of guidance sent from Cape Town would have been invaluable to her, of that he was sure.

His chief concern on returning to Scotland, had been to find that Flora had become close to their architect John McDonald. He hoped not too close. McDonald was a single man and charming, a pleasant enough fellow, though he was sure he had heard he was engaged to some woman in Edinburgh, and, if not, he ought to be. Though he had to concede his sister had developed into a stunning woman, tall, with chestnut hair, but perhaps too independent-minded and intelligent to make an ideal wife. He would have to ensure, somehow, that the relationship with McDonald did not develop. For McDonald's sake, of course. In many ways, Flora reminded him of his dear friend Emily Hobhouse.

Flora was away, yet again, helping their mother who refused to leave their family croft despite ill-health that was not being helped by the damp, cold darkness of the place. Here, there was more than enough room for mother to move in with them, but she ignored all talk of it. Turned her thin face. Mrs Puddle, their housekeeper, was in charge during Flora's absence. Her farm-hand husband had died suddenly on the very same day as Queen Victoria, leaving her with no prospects, a seven-year-old daughter and a demand they leave their cottage which was tied to the farm job. Flora had for years bought butter from Mary Puddle and moved quickly when she heard of their plight. Mary and her daughter had their own rooms in the attic and Edward was determined the girl, Dora, would have a good education in return for modelling for his paintings.

His new, purpose-built studio, a huge room, ran out from the rear of the house north towards the River Dee, designed with windows along the top to make the most of the light. The extensive garden with its own high walls giving privacy, extended around his studio and beyond. Stairs led up to the first floor where a series of rooms had been converted into a long gallery, opulently furnished, where he would display his work to wealthy clients.

He would now be painting large canvases, mainly of children in meadows and woodland, to meet the taste of his patrons. Some of the pictures were so large and heavy that the builders had installed a trapdoor into the gallery floor and a pulley-and-rope arrangement above so they could be hoisted from the studio into the gallery. He had also retained his studio in their old home next door, because, he told Flora, the light there was particularly good for portraiture.

He turned his attention to the letter he was writing to Emily Hobhouse, including photographs of his new home. They had not met since returning from Africa, and, he feared, would not again. Her own health was not good, illness picked up in Africa and the nervous strain of the quite unexpected censure she received on returning home. She had been branded a friend of the Boer and an enemy of the Empire. A traitor. Politicians and newspapers flatly refused to believe her accounts of conditions in the camps. Almost all the friends she had before sailing to Africa now refused to let her into their homes. Edward Broughton, privately, offered his support, but it appeared Miss Hobhouse was too ill to reply. He had escaped the furore engulfing her because his own accounts and sketches from the camps had not been published – in fact he had not sent them home, something he would never admit. His pictures of the heroic war fought by the British had enhanced his reputation. If anyone should ever ask, he would say his memory of the camps had been lost to fatigue and illness. He hoped no-one would make any such enquiry.

Tomorrow he would take the train to Glasgow. This would be his first journey since

The Painter Of Souls

the rail disaster two weeks previously when he had foolishly saved that damned woman from the inferno. That was not something he talked about. How he had slipped away, confused by his own actions, the risks he had taken. Then telegraphed Flora to warn he was delayed and had spent two miserable nights in a hotel in Carlisle, hoping no-one would recognise him, before feeling steady enough to resume his journey home. He had lost his hat, he could have lost his life, and it was only when he looked in mirror in his hotel room to check why his eyes felt sticky that he realised he had scorched his lashes, brows and his fine head of hair which he had noticed with concern some weeks earlier was starting to thin and recede. His late father had been quite bald.

He had rushed in like a fool amid the confusion and the shouts and the screams. What had he been thinking of? He was a veteran of war where good planning saved lives, and bad planning cost them. He had seen enough of that. He should have known better.

He had learned his lesson. He had been so foolish on the railway station, acting in hast, leaving his bag in the office where anyone could have looked inside. But would it have mattered? A bottle of chloroform from his doctor patron in Carlisle and a new surgical kit. His patron had refused to take money for them, believing it would help their mutual interest in the detailed study of butterflies and moths. The chloroform – "Only the tiniest drop, Edward" – would allow Broughton to overcome his delicate specimens without causing damage.

Why take the chance of someone looking in his bag and asking questions? "Are you a doctor, then?" If he'd answered yes he would have been expected to help with the injured. If not.....well, thankfully, it had not arisen. Now he was carefully prepared. There would be no more sudden rushes of blood. He would be methodical. Clinical. Ready. These things needed careful planning, which he had now done.

He required a woman for the painting he had in mind, one he hoped would be a breakthrough. Though would he ever want or even be able to show them? Of course he would. They would be the painting sensation of the age, of any age. There was no need for anyone to know how he had painted them. Just the genius of the work. He imagined the crowds: queueing, pushing, elbowing to see the canvas. Gasps of incredulity. Applause. Admiration.

He hoped to find her on the streets of Glasgow. Well, probably in the drinking houses. A new series of portraits painted in his old studio in the locked up and empty house next door. He had prepared well.

But, now to the matter in hand. He lifted his pen.

My Dearest Emily,

CHAPTER 18

"ON this very desk?" John Armstrong stood in the silver light from the large bow window in the library at Broughton House, formerly Solway Hall. Brown leaves blew against the glass, danced and scattered. His shadow fell across the heavily patterned carpet. He ran his fingers on the polished surface, the deep brown walnut as smooth as glass. Books filled the library and an old grandfather clock marked the time.

Jane, who had elected for the warmth of the house rather than the wild cold in the garden, perused the titles on the shelves. "Are these the man's actual books? May I?" The guide, looked past John, nodded to her. She ran along the spines: Walter Scott, Dickens, the usual stuff, a large section on taxidermy, anatomy and medical dictionaries. She eased out a heavy book - Henry Gray's 'Anatomy: Descriptive and Surgical'. It opened without effort to a section on the dissection of the human head, an illustration of the muscles

The Painter Of Souls

of the face. There appeared to be stains of old tea on the pages. She winced and replaced the book. Moved along. Botany. A deep red cover with golden writing and embossed golden butterflies. How could she resist? The book slid out. Edward Newman: 'Illustrated Natural History of British Butterflies'. In the index many of the butterfly names were not only obscure - she wondered at Acidalia - but had a line of blue ink carefully ruled under them. Books on butterflies and moths made up the bulk of the collection on this one shelf.

John asked again "On this desk?" The guide, who had been watching Jane, undecided whether she should have allowed her to look at the books, turned back to John.

"Yes. He would have sat there for his correspondence. Perhaps writing his diary. So would Flora, who shared his life here." The guide, a silver haired, middle-aged woman moved across to lift a photograph from above the mantelpiece. "This is Flora. A fine woman who never married. She devoted her life to Edward. Please, don't sit in the chair."

"Sorry. But none of his diaries and letters have survived?" He took the photograph. A striking woman with thick, dark hair. Jane moved across to glance over his shoulder.

"He was quite specific in his instructions to Flora to burn them after his death. His correspondence, his sketch books, his diaries, and quite a number of his own pictures which we believe he kept here. Gone. His entire archive on a bonfire in the garden here. And it seems Flora's are also lost, which is a pity because she was also active in the suffragette movement here in Scotland. I believe she was among the group of women who threw eggs at Winston Churchill. Imagine that."

"Surely the people receiving their letters kept them?"

"Yes, we have some records. But Edward never divulged much about himself or his life. Flora, we've managed to piece together a little more about her. But her brother was the famous one, and he fell out of fashion many years ago. So there was never a great deal of interest in researching his life. Or in keeping his correspondence. Now, of course, he's coming back. His, well, I think, genius is being recognised. Rightly so. I think he was one of the most influential artists of his time. Very gifted. A child prodigy."

"And they lived here from what, about 1910 until, well, until he died?"

"No, no. They moved here on his return from Africa, he was out in the Boer Wars, in well, I think 1901. I can check."

"Are you sure?" John did quick calculations in his head. He was sure Mrs Johnson had told him, when he saw her in hospital, that they had moved next door in 1910. Next door empty for ten years?

"I can check, as I say. But it was much earlier than 1910. And the family was here until the death of Flora in 1943."

"He died in 1912, I think."

"Yes. That's one of the reasons I know they moved here much earlier. He painted a great deal here, though little of it survived. After Flora's death a local trust was set up to look after the house and open it to visitors, but really they didn't have the money or resources to keep it going. The building began to fall into dis-repair so it passed to the National Trust about five years ago. We closed it down for a year to assess the work needed and spent three years and a small fortune doing it."

"So it re-opened a year ago. Your guide book doesn't tell us much about the Broughtons."

"John, it's not the lady's fault." Jane sidled across to him. Linked arms. Smiled at the guide. "He can be a little abrupt, but doesn't bite. Just barks."

"No, I'm sorry. I didn't mean that to sound critical. I apologise if it did. I was just surprised there's more about the house and the work on the garden than about the artist."

"We know more about the house. But a new guide book is being prepared. People have been looking into newspaper archives to find out more and I believe some material has been found in the Kennedy papers. Though they are notoriously difficult about allowing access. It might still not satisfy you because I understand we still know little about the life of Edward and Flora. But are you a gardener?"

"I'm interested. Certainly. Jane in particular. The Kennedys? I think I saw a piece on the internet about him being taken in by the family as a young land."

"That's right."

"Yes, I am."

"Pardon?"

"I am interested in gardening." Jane smiled at the guide.

"Well, a letter was found during the renovations that Edward sent to Flora from Italy outlining the changes he wanted to make to the garden. If she agreed. You see, it was set out as an Italian garden, but we know Edward was fascinated with Italy and all things Italian and he felt they hadn't got it quite right. The new guide will feature much about the garden."

"A letter? He travelled to Italy?"

"More than that. They apparently had a house

The Painter Of Souls

there. I don't know if they owned or rented. Or even where. I think the letter was the first we knew of it."

"Any chance of seeing the letter?"

"I think it was found in the summer house in the garden during the renovation work. I'm not sure where it is at the moment. I'm just a guide. You could ask in the shop."

"Downstairs?"

"Yes."

"Well thank you very much. " Another couple who had hovered on the edge of the conversation moved in quickly to ask which was the best fish and chip shop in the area.

Jane steered him away towards the stairs and down to the National Trust shop. A tea and coffee dispenser, a great many books on Robbie Burns and none on Edward Broughton.

"John, how far are you, or I suppose, we, going with this? What exactly are we hoping to find out? I'm enjoying it, but I'm wondering where we are going with this. We are, after all, supposed to be finding somewhere else to live. We're more or less squatters at the moment in our own house."

"I don't honestly know. I never felt we got to the bottom of that skeleton job. And the more we find out about Edward Broughton the more I realise we don't know anything about him at all. He's an enigma wrapped in a puzzle. It's most odd that someone so famous in his time is so anonymous now."

"But not unusual. Colin said…"

"Art expert Colin Wallace, your new best friend?"

"Indeed. He was telling me about an artist, Atkinson Grimshaw, who was incredibly popular in Victorian times, famous for his moonlit scenes, and he sank into obscurity. I looked at some of his work on the internet. Stunning. I'm getting a tea and if you are going to interrogate the woman at the shop counter please remember you are not a policeman anymore and she's not a suspect." She said it with a smile.

The young woman at the counter had a silver ring in her right nostril, another in her left eyebrow and bright purple hair. She wore black. John introduced himself, offered a hand to shake, which was ignored, and asked about Edward Broughton.

Her face lit up. "My favourite artist."

"Really? What can you tell me about him? He seems to be largely forgotten."

"The man himself? Not much. But his paintings are super-cool."

He discovered the letter was not at the house, but in archives at the Trust's headquarters in

Edinburgh.

"They're going to send us a copy of it to go with the garden exhibition that's being put together in the summer house. I haven't seen it, but there were a number of sketches in it by Mr Broughton so I imagine it will be quite valuable."

"And that's at the National Trust headquarters?"

"Yes. They have the archives where they can keep it safe, the summer house here isn't that secure. Unfortunately we've already lost one lot of gardening equipment to thieves and the police, as usual, were worse than useless. If you want to see the letter you should get in touch with our HQ. I'll give you the address and telephone number. Do you know Edinburgh?"

He returned to Jane and they left Broughton House to walk to Mrs Johnson's, picking up the eclairs from the car.

Mrs Johnson appeared fully recovered, sitting by an open fire, a rug around her legs and a stack of photograph albums to show to the Armstrongs. When they emerged two hours later, they were no clearer about who had lived in the house during the early 1900's. If anyone at all. It may have been a second studio for Broughton. It could have stood empty. Someone else may have lived there. Someone who could unravel the mystery of the skeleton.

CHAPTER 19

EDWARD Broughton, flustered and apprehensive, nervously stepped down from the crowded train into the dark chaos of Glasgow railway station. People hurrying, pushing, shouting, rushing. The steam from the hissing, throbbing engine filled the lunchtime air like fog. Madness. He was carried by the throng through the ticket barriers and out onto the sooty street where the masses dispersed and he was left, discarded like litter, propped against iron railings, gathering his breath. Drawing deep the sulphur stench of belching chimneys. He hated Glasgow. In fact any urban sprawl. He had believed it would be quieter at lunch time, the rush hour long past. How wrong. But, needs must. He adjusted his hat, fully buttoned his heavy overcoat against the wintry chill, and continued into the grey day. Glum.

His original plan was to hang around the railway station, find a suitable model, and head straight back on the next available train, but the bustle and then surging crowds had put paid to that. Far too public. How he hated this sordid business.

He knew the city well enough to continue out along central Hope Street. A rich irony, he thought, to name a street which was used by women, and shockingly and unbelievably, he had been told, by young men, with little, indeed absolutely no hope and no other option but to sell their bodies. If he was unsuccessful here, and, at first glance, it was too busy with shoppers and lunchtime office workers, he would continue the short walk to Bath Street. He had been in a public house on the street some months ago, the King's Arms, if he remembered correctly, taking refreshment before attending an evening theatre performance, when he had been approached by an obvious prostitute he had bluntly turned away. Good grief, Flora had only left his side moments earlier to powder her nose when the harlot had sought an opportunity and pounced. And she was ugly, rotten teeth and stinking breath. But now.

For ten minutes he strolled Hope Street, without a single person approaching him. Perhaps he looked a little too shifty, too preoccupied to be interrupted. He was muttering to himself, perhaps too loudly and wondered if he appeared deranged. This was

The Painter Of Souls

hopeless. But, spirits up. He walked on to Bath Street and to the King's Arms.

Noise, people shouting to be heard above the din, tobacco smoke, heat, the stench of human bodies and sour ale. All overwhelming. Edward Broughton moved hesitantly towards the crowded bar, paused, looked for an opening. Solid men shoulder to shoulder. But at least he would not be remembered among this crowd; should questions be asked later.

"You look lost." A woman. Husky.

Hell, he had only just stepped inside and halted for the briefest moment. The door hardly time to close. She was almost behind him, a hand on his arm, which he did not like. Had she followed him in?

"I was hoping to get a drink, but looking at that lot." He went to remove his hat, but thought better of it. No need for decency here. He half turned to take her in. Sallow and thin in the face, but a decent bone structure and a forced smile that struggled to crease her brown eyes. A white blouse with a high collar, creaming with age. Brown jacket, open to the waist where it was buttoned tight, and a long brown narrow skirt down to scuffed black boots. A chocolate brown hat, slightly cocked to the right, a straggle of hair curled beneath. Shabbiness trying to be stylish, and failing. A frayed cuff, missing button, a tired limpness to the hat, and perhaps the woman herself. He had an eye for such detail. Mid-thirties, probably younger, but aged by circumstance. Medium height. A scab on her upper lip, to the left.

"I know somewhere a little quieter." She pulled at his arm.

"I am sure you do." He had almost lost his voice, throat tight.

She tugged and he allowed her to lead back through the scrum of bodies to the street. He sucked in fresher air. His stomach gripped with tension. Could he go through with his plan? Doubt flooded through him and he shuddered. Could he? He came to a halt. They paused on the pavement, people jostling, moving around them. He felt panic rising. Just tell her, firmly: "No, but thank you". Head straight home. But the artist in him, he was sure it was the artist, wormed away in his ear: "She is worthless. You're a genius. A man of war. You have stared death in the face. Toughen up. It's now or never and if you choose 'never' you are a snivelling, weakling. Now or never? Get on with it."

"Well?" Her voice, harsh but weary. That false smile. Almost a pleading in her eyes.

Mouth dry, but growing in confidence, he felt himself becoming detached from the scene around him. Almost serene. "Not here." He

The Painter Of Souls

coughed to clear his throat. "Can I buy you a tea? You must know a café. I have a proposition for you. A suggestion. For both our benefit." That's better. Confident. The artist. He shrugged himself to stand erect. Found his true bearing.

She nodded. "A tea it is."

She walked slightly ahead, down a side alley to a run-down street and into a shambles of a café Broughton would not have graced in a thousand years, had he the choice.

The café was quiet, vacated by the lunchtime crowds, and he kept his hat pulled low. Sat on a wobbly chair, with his back to the counter. Condensation covered the windows and ran in small rivulets pooling on the flaking brown window sill. No-one was serving when they entered. Then he heard a noise behind him, his companion looked across to the counter and shouted: "Two teas, oh and a cold pork pie for me. You?"

"Just the tea." He put coins on the table.

"So, what's the game?" She leaned across the table, far too close, invading his space.

"You don't sound as though you come from Glasgow?"

"No."

"Right." He turned his face away as two mugs of tea and a pie were pushed over his shoulder. It was a woman serving, he could judge that.

"Take his coins and keep the change. You don't mind, do you? Well hard luck if you do. So?"

"I need a model for a painting and she must be able to stay at my studio for two or three days." He needed to assert himself. She was far too bold.

"Oh, aye. You a painter? Me a model? Hardly. What are you about?" She examined the round pie. "Pork?" she shouted at the women who had retreated towards the counter. "Pork? Has this ever seen a pig?"

"No, I'm serious. But you have to be able to stay. I suppose you have people who would miss you?" He studied her pie, not her face. Pale veering towards grey. Revolting.

"No. I don't have family." She avoided him, concentrated on wolfing down the pie.

"None?"

"None." She stopped chewing. Swallowed. "And it's nothing to do with you." Back to the pie.

Certainly not Glasgow, which gave him hope that she would not be missed.

"It certainly is something to do with me. I'll pay the piper, and I'll pay well, but you'll play the tune I want. Agreed?"

She nodded. Seemed to shrink a little. That was good. He felt better. Gaining control.

"I'm willing to pay £20 for two days of your time." He knew that was a fortune to her, more than she could earn in months of walking the streets. Certainly looking as she did.

"What's the catch?"

"None. None at all. I need you to come to my studio. It's a way from here."

"And you'll want me naked, I suppose. You'll be one of them."

"No. It's not like that. I'm not. Anyway, take it or leave it. I'm not here to discuss it. There's plenty of others."

"So why not one of them that models? If you are a real artist you'll have loads of them to go at. I'm no beauty and don't try to kid me. Show me the money?"

"Not here. I'm not foolish." He glanced behind from under his hat. The café woman had gone, presumably into the back room. Just the two of them. "We'll take the train to my studio. I already have the tickets. We'll travel in separate carriages."

"What, ashamed of me?"

"I'm a gentleman. Now, you follow me. I'll show you the money when we get to my studio. I'll also give you a return ticket, so if you don't want to stay you can catch the next train home."

"Home?" She spat it out, dry pastry crumbs across the table.

"Well, back here."

"Twenty pounds? Come on, why me?"

"Twenty and no haggling. I'm doing a series on the street women of Glasgow. I want real ones, not models. Call it your lucky day."

"Well I suppose I've nothing else. I'll follow you." She gulped her tea, stuffed the remaining pie crust into her mouth and stood, waiting for him. Chewing, mouth open, it seemed deliberate to offend him.

Edward Broughton left his tea untouched. He had expected it to be a little trickier convincing a woman to travel to his studio. He smiled. Money. The power of money. It was the difference between life and death. He walked the streets back to the railway station, euphoric. Erect. Determined. A man in charge. The journey could not pass quickly enough.

CHAPTER 20

THE congested traffic towards Edinburgh crawled. Halted. Crawled. Halted. Stopped. Started. The Armstrongs had set out in the darkness of a cold winter morning, damp and misted with drizzle, wanting to be sure of making their 11.30am appointment at the National Trust of Scotland headquarters. Their route took them east along the A702. In the past they would take a road further to the north to Edinburgh, by-passing the accident scene, but John had a point to prove. Jane offered to drive, but no, he had a point to prove. Privately, he wanted the distraction of driving. He had slowed as they passed the lay by and the tree. Jane had reached across, hand on his thigh. Squeezed. He had smiled at her. Swallowed hard. They drove on. Both fighting tears.

The AA route downloaded from the internet suggested a journey time to the archives of a little under two hours, joining the Edinburgh by-pass well west of the choked city centre and simply easing the final five miles to their destination. The HQ was a building seeming at odds with the historic nature of the National Trust. Google had shown them an unremarkable, ultra-modern black glass and white clad squat office development, quaintly named Hermiston Quay, on the side of the black Union Canal.

Three dreary miles from the junction with the ring road, the slab of cars and lorries ground to a halt.

Jane peered through the rain-smeared windscreen, dazzling red brake lights curved away as far as she could see. "We've loads of time. This is just the rush hour. Imagine doing this every day." They moved only yards. Stopped.

"What did it say on the AA map?" John, anxious.

"I think it was an hour and three quarters, or a couple of hours. It'll say on the print out." She looked down. "Two hours." A brief pulse of torrential rain hammered on the car roof.

"They must have been using a bloody helicopter to do it in that time. Why are we always stuck behind an idiot? This bloody car here. Look. He waits ages before moving up. There's cars shoving in." He blasted his horn.

The driver in front lifted a finger. Mouthed something in his rear view mirror.

The Painter Of Souls

"If I was still a copper I'd nick him. Ignorant sod."

Jane ignored him. Reached for the radio and Classic FM soothes the air.

It took them another thirty minutes to reach their destination, almost two hours early.

"We could just go in. Why not? They're hardly going to be overrun with visitors." He prepared to indicate.

"Wait." Jane reached behind for the road map book on the back seat. "Or we can carry on. This shows a shopping centre just down here, turn left, and I'm dying for a coffee and something to eat. And you need a break."

They arrived in rain at the National Trust at the appointed hour. A little more relaxed. Kevin, middle aged, bald, quietly met them at reception, signed them in, showed them silently where to leave their umbrella and led them through a hushed corridor to his silent, over-warm office decorated with two large photographs of National Trust sites. Familiar views - cliff top Culzean Castle and brooding Glen Coe.

"Filthy weather?" Almost a whisper. He grimaced as he noticed their anoraks dripping rainwater onto his polished wood floor.

Black and chrome desk and chairs. He asked

if he could see their hands. They held them out, like children before dinner. "You'd be surprised how many come here wanting to handle precious archive material with hands that are, well, I have to say, filthy. Yours are clean, but, ah, nail varnish. And a little damp. I'll have to ask you to wear gloves, madam."

"Jane, please."

"Jane."

John offered: "I'll put some on as well. I usually have them for things like this."

"Oh?"

John gave no explanation. "Do you know much about the artist? Edward Broughton."

"Me? Not a deal. I'm an archivist not an art specialist. We have the letters you were asking about."

"Letters?"

"I thought you wanted to see his letters?"

Jane who was leafing through a NT magazine looked up. "We thought there was only the fragment of one."

"Oh no. We have a small number and a couple from his sister. A very small number when you think how many there must have been. I seem to remember something being said about his correspondence, his diaries and the rest all being destroyed after he died. So I suppose it's only bits that we have and we're fortunate for that. Every little helps. What brings you both here? Are you researching the man?"

"Not in that sense." John was struggling with his gloves. "Do you have any larger sizes?"

"Sorry, no. I only ask because we have archive material on other artists here and I have the catalogue on material held at other sites. So that could be of help. They're just one size fits all."

"Really? At the moment we are looking at Broughton. He was my last case, if you like."

"Case?"

"Police. I came across Broughton when I was dealing with the aftermath of the earthquake that hit Dumfries and Galloway. I was surprised so little was known about him and thought I, well we'd, check him out."

"Oh yes. I was there a few days ago. It damaged the house next door quite badly from the looks. Our surveyor went over to check for damage to our own property and I tagged along to see how we could best show the letters we have, particularly the one about the garden. There'll be copies. We keep the originals here. Follow me and I'll show you."

"Can we have copies?"

"There's a small charge. But I don't see why not. If you wanted to publish them elsewhere you'd need permission, of course."

"Of course."

Kevin silently led the way to another hushed room. Bare white walls, a desk down the middle and chairs around. Black and chrome. Strip lights flickered, snapped on. He had arranged the letters along the desk. Five in all. Each in a clear plastic envelope.

"We found them during the renovation work. It's surprising what falls behind radiators, slips between floorboards. I believe the ones from Miss Broughton were found under a drawer in a kitchen dresser. They probably slipped there, I can't imagine from the contents that they were hidden. The one from Edward about the garden has rusty holes in the corners so we imagine it was stuck up with drawing pins, probably in the summer house where it was found. Remarkably poor handwriting for such an accomplished artist."

The first letter was from Flora Broughton to the housekeeper Mary. John supposed that would be Mary Puddle. It explained that she would be away at her mother's home for the next three weeks at least, not the one week first thought. More a note than a letter. No year. Just May 24. "Please ensure Edward eats regularly and takes his medication." Adding: "I hope young Dora's health is improving."

John asked for the letter. Held it. "Dora?"

Kevin was hovering. "We are piecing some information together to go with the display. It seems that Broughton's mother was a widow by the time they moved to Kirkcudbright and we believe Flora often travelled back to their home to care for her. Records show the mother died in 1903. Mary Puddle was the housekeeper. Young Dora was probably her daughter."

"So they were living at the Kirkcudbright house at that time?"

"Oh, I haven't properly researched this yet, but, yes, we think they moved shortly after Edward returned from the Boer war at the turn of the century. It's probably explained a little by the next letter also from Flora, this time to her builder."

This was dated, January 18, 1900, and was a reminder of a meeting the following week with the architect to discuss rooflights in the new studio.

The third was a single sheet of paper, headed with Edward Broughton's address on Hornel Street, to a Miss Emily Hobhouse, with a gap underneath, presumably for her address to be added.

"My Dearest Emily, We are now settled into our new home and my dear sister Flora has accomplished a remarkable job during my absence in Africa. You really must journey north to visit us. It would give us great pleasure."

The next paragraph was crossed out. Scratched and marked with ink blots. John tried to decipher the words. It seemed to be an apology for not writing earlier to offer support. It finished there. Presumably, Edward had started again. Certainly this letter had never been posted.

Jane turned to Kevin. "Emily Hobhouse?"

"She was a campaigner during the Boer Wars. There's quite a lot about her on the internet. A remarkable woman. She was seen as a supporter of the Boers and because she was British she was dismissed as a traitor back home. History now tells a different story, as it often does. He probably met her out there. We are currently collating the work Edward Broughton sent back from Africa to be published in newspapers here."

The fourth letter was an order for vegetable and flower seeds, written in one hand, and signed by Edward Broughton in another. They moved quickly to the fifth.

Kevin began: "This is a letter sent by Edward Broughton to Mr Taggart…from Italy."

"Mr Taggart?" Jane turned to Kevin.

"We believe he was their handyman and gardener. We are going through the census to identify who was living at the address."

He continued. "Mr Taggart, further to Miss Broughton's covering letter, I have finally managed to speak to our neighbour here. He and his family have come for the season to escape the heat of Verona. His garden, perhaps the finest in this locality, runs down to the Lake very much like ours to the river. My point is, we feel we have not quite captured the spirt of the Italian gardens that we admire so much. Our neighbour, a leading architect in the city and I believe a city councilman, is something of a plantsman and assures me that a number of the specimens he has growing here would survive our climate at home. Accordingly I attach plans and drawings of the alterations I propose. There is also a list of plants and trees you may enquire of

Robsons. We should return by the 18th of this month. I have read Miss Broughton's covering letter requesting a paler shade of green in the library. Let us not disappoint her or we'll both be in for it!"

Kevin put the letter down. "And that's it."

John picked up the letter to closely study it. Willing an address to appear as if by magic. In a separate clear envelope underneath was a sketch plan of the entire garden at Kirkcudbright with notations by Edward Broughton referring to more detailed drawings of sections of the plan, now presumably lost. One simply said: "North west corner refer to drawing C."

They both turned to Kevin.

John: "This is it? Do we know where in Italy he was writing from?"

"I'm afraid not. This is it. There's no envelope and he hasn't put his Italian address at the head of the letter which is unusual, although I imagine he thought it a waste of time when he was writing to one of his own employees. We've not really looked in detail, yet. Obviously Italy. Tantalising?"

John blunt: "No idea where? When?"

Jane interrupted: "But this suggests they perhaps owned or rented a house there. Wherever 'there' is."

"We are looking at it. My understanding is that we are probably on Lake Garda, which is close to Verona. I spoke to Mike Jones who's an expert on an artist friend of Broughtons - I've forgotten the artist's name, it's written down in my office - but whatever, he says there's sketches this artist friend has done which he's identified as a small town on the banks of Lake Garda. A place called Malcesine. So, who knows? Could be. He may have been staying with the Broughtons when he made the sketches. We just don't know."

John took a notebook from his anorak. "How are you spelling this place?"

Kevin looked startled. "I really don't know. As it sounds?" John tutted.

Kevin hurriedly slipped a photograph across to them. "And I found this. It might be of interest. It's taken in the very library referred to in the letter. On the left is Edward Broughton, the chap with the beard, Flora is next to him, an attractive woman who never married, and we think the girl at her side is the daughter of their housekeeper. That would be Dora. She'll be what fourteen, fifteen. Taken, we think, around 1910."

"The housekeeper Mrs Puddle? So this is the young Dora Puddle?"

"Perhaps. You can keep the photograph. It's a copy. I'll get you copies of the letters." He almost left the room, then paused to hold the door open for them. The door whispered closed behind them.

John turned to Jane. "Fancy a holiday on Lake Garda?"

"We are supposed to be house hunting in France. And," her voice dropped, "there's no need to be so awkward with our new friend Kevin. You're not a policeman now, though you let him believe you were, and he's not a suspect. He's trying his best to help." She smiled and patted him on the cheek. Knowing it would annoy.

"They have houses in Italy." He held open the door to Kevin's office where they had been asked to wait.

She punched him playfully on the shoulder as she pushed by. "Are you serious? House hunting in Italy?"

CHAPTER 21

NIGHTIME dark as tar when their train hauled into Kirkcudbright, the last station on the branch line. Moonless. Pale yellow light from the few gas lamps on the platform struggled to compete. Thankfully, and unusually, he had recognised no-one on the train earlier and now he was the only one to alight. Edward felt a surge of panic. Had she left the train earlier? A number of people had hurried from the station at Tarff and she could have slipped away with them. He stepped back into the shadows.

He assumed they were the last people on board, she a carriage below his. Perhaps he was the only person. He waited to see if she had stayed with him, or rather the money. A growing anxiety. He had braved it so far. All that planning gone to waste. Then the door of the second carriage opened and a woman stepped down, silhouetted against the jets of white steam from the engine. He waved to her. They were alone on the platform.

His mouth dry with tension and anticipation. "If you would just follow me, please. At a distance."

He walked hurriedly, head down, from the station into the darkened street and then into Old Gas Lane hoping to avoid any awkward encounters, although the town appeared deserted. He could hear her footsteps behind. Just a few minutes and we should be safe.

They emerged onto Broughton Street. Also quiet. Thankfully. Usually he would not have locked the front door, but he would have been foolish to leave it insecure this day. He was not concerned for the paintings in his studio next to the big house, valuable as some were, but other matters may have been difficult to explain. The table. Sacks. Heavy rubber sheets. Tools and equipment not obviously associated with an artist. His hand trembled, excitement or nervousness, probably both, as he fumbled the key into the lock. He could feel her standing at his shoulder. Urgent.

"This where you live, then?" She came close to him, leered into his face. Her breath stank. He hushed her.

The door swung open onto the dark, narrow entrance hall. He almost shoved her in, almost pushed her over. Shut the door. It

The Painter Of Souls

banged. He paused. Had anyone heard them?

"Steady on. How you going to paint me in this? It's dark as the Earl of Hell's waistcoat. It all seems a bit…" The air smelled of foul damp. Familiar.

He flicked a light switch.

"Bloody hell! You have electricity. Posh."

"And in my studio in particular. It gives me shadow I can use. The next train out isn't until the morning so you'll be fine sleeping here and I can work with the daylight tomorrow. I have a bed and food ready."

"I bet you have."

"No. No. I'm not like that. I've made that clear. I have a friend and no need for anyone else. I can work with my lights this evening, some preparatory sketches, and then you can go. If you don't want to stay I'll pay you half, ten pounds, and you'll find there's rooms at various public houses nearby."

"No. It's fine. Where do I go?"

"My studio is upstairs." He led the way.

The landing light was a thin yellow. "This door." He stepped into what had been a bedroom and turned on the lights. The already weak light on the landing, suddenly dimmed to a low glow that petered out in the gloom. She followed him into the room and had to shield her eyes. It was startling. She paused to let her eyes adjust. She had never before seen lights like these.

At the centre of the room was a large wooden chair, the lights, some on stands, seemed to focus on it, with arms, what looked like a rubbery cushion, and various gadgetry, including a headrest and straps which she hoped were all to do with his art. There was a low table behind it. An easel stood about six feet away and alongside it a long table with brushes, tubes of paint, jars, rags, sketch books. Empty, gilded picture frames were propped against the yellow walls and hanging here and there were a few paintings, one of a Red Setter, another of children in a sunlit meadow. Across the whole of one wall hung heavy, deep red curtains. Velvet? She glanced round. No other windows.

"I'll light the fire. Take the chill." A small fireplace was set into the wall on her left. "Please, your coat. Take it off. Your hat is fine. I'd like to include the hat. Take the chair. Could we start straight away? Just some sketches. I'll just need to fetch some things. The room next door." He was stiff with excitement and hoped she didn't notice the bulge in his trousers.

She hung her coat on the back of the door and sat in the chair, waiting. It had squelched when she sat down. She felt distinctly uneasy.

The Painter Of Souls

What was going on? The chair had wheels. She hadn't noticed until it shifted slightly as she sat. She stood and peered underneath. A white enamel bucket. Four wheels.

And what a strange man. One moment pleasant and the next, well, not. But it took all sorts, as she knew only too well. Some wanted straight sex, which was fine. Some disgustingly more than that. Not so good. And some were violent. It was not always easy to judge. But beggars could not be choosers. And this one was promising £20. A fortune. He said he only wanted her as a model. To look at her. He must be mad. She would do anything for money like that. Anything. There was no other work, no support for a widow. Perhaps she should ask for the money now.

She shared a damp, decaying cramped one-room tenement with Agnes Brown and her children in a rotting street in central Glasgow. Agnes, another widow, who had four children, was in the same profession as herself. What other choice was there? They got on. They had to. There was no room for disputes. Agnes, four younger Browns, and herself. She was becoming worn out by it all. The money would really change everything. She would share it with Agnes. That's how it was. If she got it. She would ask now.

He came in. Carrying a black bag. She smiled at him from behind the chair and all its contraptions. It was between them and made her feel a little more secure. "The money. The £20?"

"Yes. But first I need to prepare. Sit." He moved behind her. She heard him set the bag on the table. The painting of children in a sunlit meadow hung on the wall opposite her, two of the children sprawled among daisies and yellowing grass, a third in blue, kneeling and holding a bunch of she didn't know what, but flowers. Patches of sunlight.

"I said 'sit'." He pushed her to the chair. "I just need to hold your head steady in one position so I can catch you. Actually, I will remove your hat. Are there pins? Oh, it's off easily."

He forced her down into the chair. Then passed a strap of cold leather across her forehead. This she did not like and tensed.

"I don't want you moving." He moved to tighten the strap, feeding it through the buckle.

"I don't like this." She had that tense knot developing in her stomach. She pushed his hands away, stood before he could fasten the strap.

"Please. Obviously you haven't sat for a portrait before."

The Painter Of Souls

"Course not. But, I don't know about that" She looked at the chair and edged away from him. Moved to the door.

"It's only my artist chair. You can see that picture there." He turned one of the lights to a painting of a youth in full Scottish tartan, outdoors below a snowy Highland mountain and posed with his buckled foot on a hunted down stag. It had been hidden in shadow.

He moved across to her. Pleasant again. "Obviously that wasn't painted outside just as you see it. Please come and look. He was here, in this very chair. He had squirmed, wriggled, generally wouldn't sit still. All the time the light and the shadow were changing his face. I only need to hold a study for a few minutes to get the likeness down, find the tone, if you see. So it's fairly common practice for artists to use a chair like this. Mine has wheels so I can move it according to the light in the studio."

"Really?" She remained firm by the door, ready to run.

"Please." He opened his arms, beckoning her to move closer. "I've experimented a little myself with photography. But you don't get the spirit of things. Look at this."

He went to a shaded corner where there was a jumble of wooden frames, canvas bags, a tripod, a step ladder. He rummaged, lifted out a strange contraption, like a tall standard lamp but where a shade should have been there was a U-shaped clamp, and midway a wider one.

"A posing stand. Most portrait photographers have one of these. It takes only the slightest movement of a subject to ruin a picture because the exposure takes some moments. Their face can be a blur if they move. This helps them to remain still. The head fits here, it's quite comfortable and adjustable for height, and this lower one fits the waist. Again adjustable." He fitted himself into the frame. Fastened the straps. "There."

He looked ridiculous and she could easily flee. But she reckoned he knew that and in a way it eased her own fears. He unbuckled the straps, stepped forward and picked up a catalogue from the table.

"Look, it's in here." She came across. He held up the catalogue, open at a page showing all sorts of strange devices, including the stand.

"Naturally artists need their subject to be motionless a little longer. It will only be for a few minutes. Then I'll make tea. But I'd just like to get a first sketch done. Please."

"A few minutes? Why the straps on the arms?"

"The hands are the most difficult to capture. They need to be absolutely still. People fidget. A few minutes. If you are nervous I'll work as quickly as I can."

"And the rubber. What's that all about?"

"Oh, children. I have many commissions for children and they can have accidents because it can take quite some time to work on their portraits. All my paintings, that one in the meadow, all of them I like to paint the face here in my studio. I don't paint them outside."

"So, other artists have these?"

"Oh yes. There's nothing to be frightened of. It's perfectly normal. It won't be long. Look, I'll show you. Stay there." He walked across to the table and picked up a large sketch book and a stick of sharpened charcoal. "Hold steady."

"While I'm standing here?"

"Indeed"

She watched his hand moving quickly across the paper. In what seemed only seconds, he turned it to her. She was stunned. With only a few strokes he had caught her.

"You've already got me, so I don't need to get in that chair." She felt relief.

He gave a nervous laugh. Bowed his head to her. "Oh, thank you, but I need a little more. And see, you've already moved. You seem to think there's a danger, but I assure you there's none."

"Right." She moved slowly across to the chair.

Warily, sat down. He carefully placed the strap across her forehead, the metal buckle cold against her skin as he pulled it tight.

"Comfortable?"

"Not really."

"Then I shall hurry."

He fastened belts over her arms. Quite tight. He tugged again. Too tight. One more, thicker, across her waist and two around her ankles. Very tight. She was going to protest, but he spoke first.

"I'll be quick as I can to finish you. Please look towards the painting of the children in the meadow." He turned the bright lights onto her. Blinding.

The fear was rising again. She had known too many weirdos, none of them had the word tattooed on their forehead. There had been no way of knowing. Most had seemed perfectly normal. At first.

He was still behind her and she could hear him release a clasp, presumably on the bag he had brought in. She had seen doctors with them like that. Her senses were incredibly sharp. Then what sounded like a screw cap. Was it a screw cap?

"Won't be a second."

A strange smell, sickly sweet, was all around, and then she felt his hand on her shoulder, holding her quite firm. Too firm, fingers digging into her shoulder. She desperately tried to move forward but her head was held tight by the strap. Then his other hand on her face. The sickly stench. Cloth. Damp. Overpowering. Panicked. Heart thumping. Struggling for breath. She tried to twist away, but the lights caught her, blinding. She tried to stand, squirm. The leather straps bit into her. Call out, but she was suffocating. Blinded by the lights. The children in the meadow.

He had been warned by his doctor friend that chloroform took minutes to become effective. In humans - here the doctor had laughed because this would naturally not be relevant for Edward - it could be as long as five minutes before the subject became unconscious, and then they rapidly re-awakened unless a steady dose was applied. Butterflies, although quickly becoming insensible, took some time to die, perhaps minutes, depending on the dosage, not too much mind, and he would need to be patient, especially if he was tackling anything larger. They had talked of taxidermy. And to be careful not to let the chloroform come into direct contact with the specimen. Oh, and to be extra careful, because people had died handling the stuff. Always use a sealable bottle.

Edward Broughton did not want the chloroform to kill her. He had read those silly detective stories where the murderer used chloroform to quickly kill their victim. Rubbish. He thought the stories ill-researched and most distasteful. He thought of those books now as he pressed the cloth hard against her face, turning his own away to catch as much clear air as he could. It really was sickly stuff.

The five minutes were a painful eternity for him and he felt quite queasy by the end. At first the damned woman struggled, gave muffled cries. He feared she would break his chair. She lapsed. She convulsed. He couldn't help but shout at her to be quiet. Finally she slumped. "Thank God." He cursed her. He was offering immortality to this immoral woman. How ungrateful.

He felt drained and bilious and stepped out onto the landing where he paused to breathe deeply and clear his lungs and head. But, he could not delay, he needed to act speedily.

Edward had struggled when planning the next stage. He had finally decided, against his best judgement, to use a magnifying mirror. You see, he needed to be able to strangle her slowly when she came round and also be able to watch her eyes. Study them in depth. Capture that very moment when the soul escaped the body. When the light fled from her eyes.

He moved over to his work bench and selected a red scarf of fine silk. Its quality showed respect. He gagged her. It was quite a struggle to pass the cloth around the back of her head and he wondered about loosening the strap when she suddenly coughed and moved. There was no need for him to panic. It was as his doctor friend had described. He pushed the scarf through and tied it tight.

Quickly he wheeled a full-length dressing mirror in from his operating room next door and placed it so that it perfectly caught her reflection. He then clipped the round magnifying mirror to the top and adjusted it so that he could see her eyes from behind the chair. Perfect. She was moving, though he judged still slightly unconscious.

Satisfied, he took a length of rope and from the back of the chair looped it over her head until it passed across her neck. He then slotted a stick through its two looped ends. Not any old stick, but one he had fashioned as a candy twirl and carefully varnished. The care he had taken showed respect for his subject. He could see her in the mirror, clearly coming round.

He turned the stick to twist and bring the rope taut on her throat. He re-checked the mirror. Good. Her eyes were closed, but they would open wide, he hoped, when he further tightened the garrotte. He would see deep into them. His hands were shaking. He had anticipated this. He would not try to draw her until they had settled. He was confident that his finely tuned, artist's memory would recall every detail, no matter how small and fleeting.

Edward paused, the stick tight in his sweating hands. He took a moment to consider and, yes, accept the set-up was not perfect. He would have to work on this because he would prefer to be in front, looking directly into the face. A mirror flattened the image and would play tricks with light. But there would be room for adjustments in future. He regarded this as very much a test. An experiment in the name of his true art. A genius was the one who pushed the boundaries. That is what made them, him, so special.

It was taking longer than he expected for her to recover and his thoughts moved to the other problem which had troubled him. The bits and pieces he dissected in the adapted bedroom across the landing could be put into sacks and thrown into the river. No problem. Tissue, fats, muscle. If found, it could all be dismissed as animal remains. A thoughtless butcher. But not the bones. If they were found they would be easily identifiable as human.

He was sure of this and dismissed the idea of throwing the bones into the river. Body parts easily identifiable as human would be burned in the kitchen stove.

Yet his art demanded he had to know exactly what was underneath, like Stubbs with horses. He had to get to the essence of the human form. No guessing. He had flayed animals up to, and including, the size of a stag, carefully removing the skin down to individual muscles and then down to the bone. At first he had felt sickened by the whole process, but had, over time, become used to the gore. And skilful with sharpened blades. After all, he was not a killer, not a murderer, he was an artist. This woman had no value in life, but was invaluable at the point of death.

His studies had already considerably improved his painting. No-one had produced a finer stag. Now his art had moved him to explore the soul. Surely, capturing the spirit, the very essence of life, would scale the pinnacle of portrait painting. His would be acclaimed the finest ever.

For the time being he decided to keep the stripped bones in a storage space behind the bedroom wall and then cover over the small door that led into it. No problem. At some future date he could move them, if necessary.

The bones of future sitters, brought from the

Glasgow streets to his special studio, would be disposed of in the long garden being built next door, the wild area where it dipped down to the river would not be landscaped. Currently the garden was not the place to go dancing with a skeleton. He smiled at this thought, the image it created.

She was coming round. He re-checked the mirrors and the lighting. He took the carved stick in his right hand, a slight tremor, ready to turn. Clockwise. Ever so slowly.

He leaned forward, not too close because he didn't want to fog the mirrors with his breath. But close enough. Yes. He could feel her hair on his chin. Her eyes blinked and then suddenly opened wide.

Slowly he turned the stick.

CHAPTER 22

THEY could have flown. They were driving. It was early spring and could have been sunny. It was raining. Light rain. The sky could have been clear and blue. It was heavy, dark and pressed down low. But they were finally, once again heading south, re-joining the European north-south highway E25 after a two night stop-over in Liege. Jane's price for agreeing to the journey. She had studied author Georges Simenon at Edinburgh University when a student a lifetime ago and wanted to visit his home town and museum. Four days ago they had driven across country from their Scottish home, now sold, to Hull where they took an overnight ferry to Rotterdam.

John Armstrong had taken the wheel for the first leg of today's drive. "I cannot believe it. 10,000 women in 61 years? I had a look on my calculator and that works out at three a week. Different ones?" He shot a glance across to Jane. "10,000?" The car wipers swept intermittently.

"Apparently." She was studying their map book, a large scale spread across her lap, although the car sat nav confirmed they were on the correct road. It was 8.30 in the morning, but could have been evening considering the lack of light. Traffic was heavy and the spray was increasing.

John switched the wipers to full. "He wrote hundreds of books. How did he find the time? In fact, the energy? What was he on?"

"We know what he was on, or who. It was his claim. Since the age of thirteen he claimed to have had 10,000 women in the following sixty-one years. I hope our sat nav is right. It looks to be a different road in here." She was pointing at the map book. Switched on her overhead light and adjusted her reading glasses.

"I can't look. I'm sure the sat nav is spot on. But surely he was boasting? And he's not French?"

"No. Well, no to him not being French. Whether he was boasting is another matter. The sat nav says continue, but it seems to show here that we go right."

"No offense, but we'll trust to the sat nav for the time being. So why did I think he was French. I've seen it on television that detective stuff. Maigret. All French. Are you sure?"

The Painter Of Souls

"Sure we carry straight on or sure about him being French? I think this map's out of date." She closed the book and tossed it onto the back seat. Turned off the overhead light. "Maigret was a French detective, most of the books were set in Paris, but Georges Simenon was famously Belgian. In fact I can't think of any other famous Belgians."

"Audrey Hepburn."

"The actress? Rubbish. Have you got the headlights on?"

"Yes. The actress. She was born in Brussels. I read about her in the hotel last night. I couldn't begin to remember her original name. It went on forever. But, Belgian."

"She was a Hollywood actress. American. Hardly counts."

"Your man wrote French detective dramas. So?"

"You went to the museum with me. You saw how they'd recreated his office there. You were told off for sitting in his chair. You read the same things as me. Concentrate on the road."

"We're hardly moving in all this traffic. It could all be a fiction. A myth to drag in the tourists. Liege hasn't got much else. Perhaps they stole him from the French. Do you think his secret was oysters?"

"We need to concentrate on the road."

Heavy black clouds had closed in and the rain intensified, puddling across the dual carriageway and reducing visibility to zero when they passed heavy lorries. John felt the steering lighten whenever they hit standing water so he slowed further, pulled into the line of trucks, almost crawling.

Their original plan was to stop for lunch and sightseeing in Strasbourg, but the weather had spoiled that. Instead they agreed to push on to Basel hoping the rain would ease as they climbed out of France to Switzerland, perhaps allowing them at least a glimpse of the Black Forest away towards Germany, the Vosges mountains to the east and views of quaint villages and ruined castles promised by their guide book. Instead they struggled to keep the windows clear enough to see the road ahead. Heater on full, all vents open. Clouds so low it was like driving in fog.

At home they had drawn up a schedule allowing three days to travel south from Liege to the medieval town of Malcesine on the eastern shore of Italy's Lake Garda. A planned detour into the Alps might also have to be abandoned to the grim murk and rain.

Jane had opened her laptop. "I'm just reading the Basel travel guide we downloaded at the hotel last night. Says here: 'Frequent rain, year round'. I don't want to put a damper on things, but..." She wiped at her side window, dribbles of condensation ran down.

John took a cloth to the windscreen. "We should have known that to track down someone with the name Puddle would result in this bloody weather. I thought we only had rain like this in Scotland. A summer's day in Glasgow. Put the air-con on. It'll clear the windows."

Jane closed the laptop. "But we found no trace of them. Hardly any Puddles at all, unlike today. The road's full of them, like driving through a swimming pool. No Puddles with connections to Dumfries or the Broughtons. I think it's raining harder if that's possible. Are the headlights on? I know there are a small number in Australia. I know we tried there, but found no Scottish connection whatsoever. They all seemed to come from an area around Hereford. Okay, it could be that their daughter, the one we want, went out there in search of a new life, married, family name lost." Jane again wiped her side window. "Still can't see a thing. This could all be another dead end. Perhaps we should have gone to Australia, at least the weather would be better than this."

"Lost in the mists of time. I know we found no records of a Puddle marriage in the area.

They seem to have vanished. I asked Mike to check on the police system, as far as he could without getting a bollocking, but there was nothing. But then, I was always amazed how many people disappear into thin air. Missing persons was a nightmare job. To be avoided. Around 250,000 people reported missing in the UK every year, according to a briefing note I read just before packing it all in, and although the majority soon turn up, many don't. Hang on, we're slowing even more. We'll soon be at a standstill at this rate."

A car in front was showing emergency flashers, smearing orange into the grey light. They were down to 15 mph. Slowing. John turned on their hazard lights, pumping at the brake pedal to add to the warning for the driver of huge Waberer truck behind, its large yellow sun logo had already inspired comment from John.

He leaned forward, peering over the steering wheel into the gloom. "Jesus, this visibility is appalling. Anyway, it's bad enough when people don't want to be found – and there's plenty of them – but when people simply disappear, they do just that. Murdered, alien abduction, suicide, sit on the street begging, give themselves a new name, which, let's be frank, if your name's Puddle, it's hardly surprising."

The Painter Of Souls

Jane suggested she take over the driving after the next stop, which she hoped, from a toilet point of view, would be soon. "It must be terrible for the families left behind. Hoping for years. I can imagine them setting a place at the table, not changing the bedroom, jumping every time the doorbell rings. Terrible for them. What's that - is it rain?"

It was coming down so hard they could hear it thrumming on the car roof. Brake lights struggled to show through the dense spray. Many cars had hazard lights flashing. Rear fog lights smeared. Traffic slowed again almost to a standstill, even the lorries whose driver's must have thought they had second vision and were earlier careering through fog in the overtaking lane, were now crawling in convoy. Headlights blazing. Two lanes almost at a halt.

John had the windscreen wipers on full and furious, but they struggled to clear the way ahead. "It's bouncing off the road. This is becoming unsafe. It's as dark as bloody night. Anyway, we need fuel and the sat nav shows a petrol station ahead. We'll pull over, hope for a coffee. I know you said you'd drive the next leg, but let's see how we feel. If there's the chance of a decent motel we can stay over."

Jane pulled her map book from the rear seat and flicked on her overhead light. "We aren't far from Basel. Let's stop for petrol and coffee and then see if we can make it on to Basel for tonight. I don't fancy a motel in the middle of nowhere in a storm like this. Surely it can't last. Can it?"

In the steamed-up café, packed with travellers sheltering from the torrential rain, they used their laptop to search out a Basel hotel. Outside, the storm was easing, black sky turning gun-metal grey.

The Hotel Wettstein promised to be easy to find off the E25, and had free internet, basement car parking, free travel passes for public transport around the city and rooms available for the night. Or two nights.

John agreed. "Book it. We can do two. Give us chance to dry out and we can easily make Malcesine. I should be able to contact Professor Cuthbertson, Frank, from there. He's out of hospital now, or he should be."

"How is he? Did they arrest that idiot driver?" Jane stood and was putting on her coat. The café was emptying – the storm had brought an unexpected windfall of customers.

"On the mend. I texted him just before leaving home. His leg has mended and, as I said the other day, he says he has some interesting information for us. He wanted to do some further investigation of the bones once he's back at work and suggested we call him first thing tomorrow."

"I dread to think what he'll say. And the driver?"

"No. Apparently no action. You can see why people are pissed off with the police. They don't seem to realise that Frank managed to take away a couple of bones."

He drank the rest of his coffee and pushed away his chair to stand and don his coat. "It will be interesting to hear what he's found; or not found. Officially, let's hope he found nothing to contradict the idea this was an unfortunate death a hundred years ago. Over and done with. But I suspect it's going to show the whole thing was closed down too quickly. These things always come back to bite. Act in haste and repent at leisure. It could be embarrassing for some."

Jane straightened his collar. "Well, as Shakespeare said: 'Truth will out'. Merchant of Venice. Let's go." They walked through the packed café. "I think it's getting lighter outside."

"Hope so. Here we are in the middle of rain-soaked bloody Europe, have a mystery with a woman called Puddle in it and are now heading for a ruddy hotel called Wetsomething. Perhaps we should've come by boat."

"Sea plane would have been interesting. It's Wettstein."

They emerged into a light drizzle, a cold wind blowing huge black clouds away to the east, dragging heavy curtains of rain.

In the car, before setting off, Jane, who would drive, went through the instructions to find the hotel as John loaded the co-ordinates into the sat nav.

The screen glowed on his face. "I don't trust this thing. It's likely to take us to Geneva and back. Here it says we keep on the E25 until, until, err Schwarzwaldstrasse, take exit 3 for Basel-Wettstein, keep to the middle lane towards Grenzach and Wyhlen. Then we turn right at traffic lights onto Grenzacherstrasse, drive past the Roche Tower."

"The what?" Jane started the engine.

"Hang on, don't set off yet. Roche Tower. It's the tallest building in Switzerland, there was a picture on the internet of it, a huge glass wedge, so we shouldn't miss it."

"Wanna bet?"

"We follow, I thinks its pronounced Grenzacherstrasse, to just before, ah, you'll like this, Wettsteingplatz and, marvellous, we have the hotel on the left. I can talk you through it if you like."

Jane swung the car out from its parking space. "I think I'll rely on the nice lady in the sat nav. Just this once." She advised them to turn left and they exited the service station into a weak yellow sun. "Continue following this road."

CHAPTER 23

SPOTLAMPS perfectly positioned, not reflecting from the mirrors directly into her face. He did not want her squinting or her features flattened. He had carefully adjusted them to show her contours, her nose with its slight bump midway, cheekbones heightened by hunger, brown eyes and rather thick, perhaps masculine, eyebrows. She was, he decided, or could have been, an attractive woman.

The red silk gag was doing its job. Her eyes opened and he could see the panic. She strained, eyes bulging, the muscles on her neck taut, but the restraints held. He was offering her immortality, why fight it? Slowly he turned the carved, polished stick, tightening the rope around her neck. His one reservation had been whether a prostitute would have a soul, but he quickly dismissed that as the sort of foolish prudery uttered by puritan fools. Slowly he turned the stick.

He stopped. Held her just there. Gurgling and

rigid. He moved round to study her eyes directly, closely. Right arm outstretched to hold the stick. Peered deep into her. They were misted by tears. Should he wipe them? Then, that sharp stench of urine. She was staring deep into his own eyes. He was transfixed. Mesmerized. They had a union. A meeting. She understood. Finally. He felt a great sense of calm.

He moved back around the chair and turned the stick a little more. Moved to look again. Her eyes were now wide, wide open, bulging. She was on the brink. He was sure. Perhaps he wouldn't need to watch this through the mirror. Excited. He pushed the stick down into the chair behind her back where it was held and could not unwind. He grabbed his sketch book. Tears rolled down her cheeks, stained the red gag almost black where they touched and soaked in. Perhaps another slight adjustment. He pulled out the stick, no more than a quarter turn, and pushed it back between her and the chair.

Quickly he sketched. Glancing from face to paper. Face to paper. Her deep gurgling was tiresome. Then suddenly it stopped. Replaced by a long sigh. He paused. Searched her face. Her eyes. Leaned in up close. Almost lips on her cheek. Her eyes steaked with red veins, rolled.

"My God, no." He shouted. Not realising. Dropped his pencil and reached to pull the eye balls back down so he could see the pupils. It was no good. He searched her face for the sign of a rising soul escaping, but was hit by the rising smell of shit. "Damn. Damn."

But then, then. Had he caught one of the lamps? Had he? There was a shift in the light on her face. From the mouth? He pulled the gag down and her mouth sagged wide open. A loud belch and horrible stench. He moved back, hurriedly turned the lamps away from her face, and yes, there around her eyes, he saw a yellow sheen, like a heat haze, caressing and moving. And then it went. She belched loudly again.

He had seen it. He had seen it. He put his hand to his brow. This was unbelievable. He had seen the soul. He would now need to capture it, adjust his technique, get that pale glow. Cadmium yellow and a soft white deep under the final layers of paint.

He bent forward, hands on knees. Sweat dripped from his face. He breathed deep. The stench of shit. He stood.

"First things first," he said to no-one.

Edward tilted the chair, almost dropped it, heaved and slowly wheeled the body through to the adjoining room, surprised by the weight. He had prepared the long table with rubber sheeting which he also spread across the floor. He had numerous buckets, sacks and a ready supply of water. Alongside a waitress trolley now equipped with an array of surgical instruments.

He struggled to hold her in the chair as he undid the restraining straps. She seemed determined in death to slide out onto the floor. Her arms sagged. Her head dropped forward and butted him in the face. Almost collapsed with her as he tried to lift her onto the table. Impossible. Finally he edged her on, head first, bending to lever her upwards, hoisting her legs, all very undignified, and then arranging her flat on her back. The smell was awful. He staggered to an easy chair by a white sink in the darkened corner of the room and fell into it. Exhausted.

Next time he would do something about the smell. Perhaps wear his own scented mask.

CHAPTER 24

SUN out, slanting low into the car, sometimes blinding. The view across snowy mountains spectacular as the road wound through a green, wooded valley, climbing higher.

"I'm finding all this rather difficult to take in." Jane was driving them to the Mont Blanc tunnel deep under the Alps, on their final leg from France into Italy. They would stop in the car park by the entrance and John would take on the seven mile haul through the tunnel under the mountains. Both had been silent for the last few miles. John deep in thought. Jane, also troubled but trying to concentrate on the road.

He squinted at the sun. Adjusted the visor. "The phone call with Frank? I agree. I've been thinking over the implications. I must admit my first reaction was to turn round and head straight home. But, even if what Frank believes to be true is actually the case, then there's no rush. It's hardly a race against time.

We aren't chasing Dr Crippen across the Atlantic, though they now reckon he was no murderer at all and was wrongly executed. No rush."

Professor Francis Cuthbertson's opening remark on answering the early morning call had been unnerving.

"Dissection. The marks on the right humerus are without doubt caused by a sharp blade. Not an animal. I would say it shows careful dissection by someone with some, shall I say, finesse. Not hacked at, but the flesh, the tendons have been carefully removed down to the bone."

"Butchered?"

"Not at all, John. Butchers would take offence as they are very skilled. I would say this was also performed by someone with skill. You said before that the remainder of the skeleton had been lost?"

"If not incinerated then 'lost'. I asked before setting out and no-one had any record."

"Sloppy."

"Not sloppy, I suspect deliberate. No bones, no comeback."

"Such a pity. As I said this was done by a person who knew what they were doing. Let me explain. The joints to the shoulder and the elbow were intact. No marks of hacking at the bone or chopping at the joint to separate it. You would expect an amateur to have damaged the humeral epicondyle or the humeral head, sorry those are the bony bits at the end of the, well, let's call it the arm bone. There are some tough tendons. But no, this was neatly done."

"Dissection?" John looked across to Jane, who was sitting on the opposite side of the bed in their hotel room in Basel. "Hang on Frank. I need to speak to Jane. Frank is saying that it looks like our mystery woman was carefully dissected." She grimaced.

Frank continued. "Yes, John, I would say so. Reflecting on our time with the fuller skeleton I would say the body had been carefully taken apart, and most probably millimetre by millimetre. Skin, flesh, muscle, tendon, organs. It would be so beneficial to see the skeleton again. Have they found the photographs?"

"Also missing. Pathology reckon the police have them. My disinterested former colleagues say they never arrived. Typical. There's no enthusiasm either end to find them. They'll be a bit livelier if this turns out to be murder. Any idea when it was done?"

"Just when is hard for me to tell, John. You mentioned that it could be around a century ago taking account of who was living at the house and when it was built and all that. I wouldn't disagree. If I had the remainder of the skeleton I could do so much more to pin it down. But this was not necessarily murder. It could be body snatching. It went on for years. Remember Burke and Hare? I know, I know, they didn't snatch bodies from graves like many of their colleagues to sell for experimentation and dissection, but murdered their victims to sell on to anatomy classes. There's always been a demand for corpses to, shall we say, study? I remember it from my own student days. Even today. So your original idea that this was connected to an artists may still be spot on."

"I don't believe there's an innocent explanation. This was no medical school, Frank. It's an end of terrace house in Kirkcudbright. We did wonder about strangulation at the time we looked at the bones."

"True, John. And it could remain the case."

"So we were looking at a woman, well the remains of a young woman, who had been carefully taken to pieces, bit by bit. Could have been murdered, could have been dug up, could, I suppose, have even been donated to science? Could be a crime, could be an innocent explanation, though, as I say, I very much doubt it."

"Could. All are could be's. If I may add a few

more, John. Could we find the photographs? Could we find the skeleton? Could we get your former colleagues interested?"

"Don't hold out much hope. They reckon they have enough on without adding an unsolvable, possible murder, of an unknown woman, by an unknown killer, at an unknown time though probably a hundred years ago. They were keen to remind me they have six current murder investigations on the go."

"Let sleeping bones lie, so to speak. Sorry"

"Indeed. I'm convinced she was murdered and I've heard nothing to change that. She had to have been murdered."

"John. I'm going to a conference in London today. It could be interesting for you. I'll let you know the hotel."

"I found most conferences quite boring."

"Ah, well, this is all about decomposition. There'll be lots of body parts around in various stages of decay…..hopefully all of them sourced legitimately."

"Sounds gruesome. Surely you know more than enough already?"

"Hardly. You can always learn more. We have a key note speaker from the body farm in Texas where they study cadavers as they rot down under various circumstances. Gruesome, you say, I say fascinating. Must go. Train to catch. Happy hunting."

The sky cleared to an intense steel blue as they followed the E25 away from Basel for the four hour drive to the Alps. Much of the journey, skirting Bern and Montreux, had been on flat plains, but now their route wound up through forest to a roundabout on the outskirts of the ski town of Chamonix, its high pitched houses huddled beneath the towering, snow-capped peak of Mont Blanc.

They continued through Chamonix, mountains closing in all around, jagged black and ice white against the sky. Jane followed signs for the tunnel which had been drilled for over seven miles through the Alps to Italy.

They climbed higher on a switch-back double carriageway through trees that filtered the sun into flashing red bands. Progress was slow. An unbroken line of huge lorries and tankers hugged the inside lane, spewing out a fog of exhaust fumes. They became sandwiched in a convoy of cars and motorcycles that finally emerged from a long blind bend onto a straight road that, with a feeling of relief, led to a jumble of toll booths and the tunnel entrance. To their left, on a grassy mound cleared of trees, stood a large monument of gold and black; like a giant, twisted, broken flower bud spearing the clear sky.

John had a detailed map and notes they'd downloaded from the internet the night before. "If we keep left we can cross to a car park. Take a break."

"In some ways I wish we hadn't found out about this. It just adds to the sadness of it all." She signalled, pulled out of her line of traffic, squinted into the bright sun. The turn off road led them across the carriageway carrying traffic from Italy into France, and towards a car park in front of the memorial. Jane waited for a break in the traffic. "I would be happier seeing this after we've done the tunnel. Not before. It's a bit unnerving considering the next part of our journey. To think we could have flown." She pulled across the carriageway.

"Flying is dangerous."

A deceptive sun. They bent from the warmth of their car into the freezing Alpine air, trying to catch their breath. Pulled on coats. Arms about each other. No-one else had ventured from their cars.

"So, John, what does it tell us?" She pulled away so he could read his printout.

"Right. It was 1999. A truck caught fire in the tunnel which quickly spread to other lorries and cars and thirty-eight people died in the inferno. Apparently no-one could get near to help. Temperatures reached 1,000c and it burned for over two days. There was nothing left but ash. One Italian security guard tried to help and repeatedly rode his motorcycle into the tunnel to bring people out. He finally paid for it with his life. His motorcycle was later found melted into the road. Quite a hero."

"It's strange, but I don't remember anything of it. Some holiday this. We're surrounded by death."

"There was George Simenon's sexual appetite. That was very different."

"Indeed. Very. It's freezing here."

They hurried back to the car. John took the driver's seat. Jane ran around to the passenger door and in one deft move opened it, slid towards the seat and picked up the instructions and map.

"Seven miles through the tunnel and we're into Italy. We stick with the E25, skirt Milan and we should be at Malcesine in about six hours. Book in and find somewhere decent to eat. I'm keeping my coat on." The tunnel opening gaped like a mouth waiting to swallow them.

Five hours and twenty minutes later they finally left the motorways, dropping down through a confusion of slip roads and roundabouts onto the SR249 promising a relatively short journey along the side of Lake Garda direct to Malcesine. First they had to navigate the could-be-anywhere modern streets of Peschiera del Garda, seeing with dismay a McDonald's restaurant.

They pulled into a petrol station, topped up and stretched their legs.

John returned from the small shop with bottles of orange juice. "I thought this was supposed to be the gateway to Lake Garda. It's more like the gateway to a shopping park in Glasgow. Can't even see any water."

"We saw plenty of water yesterday. Enough rain for a lifetime. Now, swap over. I'll drive."

CHAPTER 25

THEIR train, on schedule out of Leeds, strained slowly north towards Carlisle sending plumes of steam and soot across the northern dales as it approached the massive limestone and brick Ribblesheaf viaduct striding high across the Pennine Hills. Sunlight shafted between high white clouds onto the tinder-dry, beige moorland, here and there smeared purple with the last of the brittle heather. Yet another stifling hot day burned its way into September.

Flora's daily newspapers had been full of the deadly heatwave. Yesterday, in baking, stinking London, thermometers had peaked at a summertime record, claiming 100f. The stench of sickly sweet sewage had been unbearable and sleep in their stifling hotel rooms impossible. Although sleep, in the circumstances, would have been difficult whatever the weather. Factories had begun to start early and close at midday because it was simply too hot to work in the afternoon. Dockers had walked out, complaining of the heat. Across the country trees and gardens were dying. Crops ruined. Wells and reservoirs dry. Roads melted. People were dying. She had read the last fact to her brother, Edward, while they waited their train departure in Euston Station and immediately regretted how inappropriate it was. How anyone who knew would have condemned her as unfeeling. She flinched at the memory. Edward had gruffly shot back: "People are always dying, it's the nature of things. You, as well as anyone, must know that." His look had been fierce. She deserved the rebuke.

Grey steam billowed from the engine over the carriages misting the view out for Edward and Flora in their first class compartment. His London exhibition had been successful, not as popular as earlier ones, no sensations now, fashions had changed, and this, given the gravity of the news, would probably be the last he would attend.

While in London they had visited Edward's doctor in Harley Street for the final verdict. It was not good. Not at all. They had previously travelled down in July, shortly after the coronation of George V and Queen Mary, for exploratory tests. The following weeks had been agony. Edward had hardly worked, rarely emerging from his library at their home in Kirkcudbright. He had left the organisation of his London summer exhibition entirely in the hands of the prestigious Sefton Gallery which acted as his agent in the capital. Then the letter had arrived urging them to return to London.

"I think they call them retrospectives."

Flora looked up from the book she was pretending to read. On the seat opposite, her brother, thin and sallow, was leaning towards her. She fanned herself with the open book. "Pardon?" He had been silent, deep in thought for almost the entire journey. She had understood. The news from the doctor had been devastating. And she had then stupidly read the newspaper story to him.

She wore a light jacket of amethyst velvet, unbuttoned to reveal a white cotton blouse, and a hat from simple straw held in place by a silver thistle pin, studded with a purple crystal. Edward was weighed down by his heavy dark winter coat, collar up, scarf tucked in despite the weather. Always a contradiction. Anyone else wrapped in such a coat would have been red in the face with the heat, but Edward's skin was an alarming mix of yellow and grey.

"I think they call them retrospective exhibitions. Usually when an artist dies they throw loads of their work at a wall and call it a retrospective. The last bits and pieces, see if they can sell. You should try it, the money would be useful.""

"Edward, please, you sound so bitter. "

"Bitter?" He leaned back into his seat, let out a long sigh. "Bitter, indeed. My eyes are failing, my hands shake, the damned leg hurts like hell and now I have this bloody thing growing inside me and they can't get rid. Flora, I can hardly work. I'm a damned wreck. It's the price I'm paying."

"Africa was a long time ago. Years. Your health...."

"Not Africa. No. Not Africa." He almost shouted. His anger shocked. He fell back into thick silence and Flora returned to her book, looking, though not reading. She fought back the tears she did not want him to see. Turned slightly away towards the window, then felt guilty, as though she was removing herself when he most needed her. Turned back and sighed. They were silent for minutes. She glanced out as the train clattered over the viaduct, the moors a hundred feet below. Sunlight gold on parched brown grass and heather. Hills of shimmering gold.

"Flora?" Edward squinted against the sun streaming in through the window.

"Yes?" She placed the book on her lap. He

reached across, winced at the stabbing pain in his side, flopped back.

"When we get home I'm going to burn the women." He had kept them in the house, passed them every day. A reminder of places he did not want to visit ever again. He had seen the light in their eyes, how it intensified at that moment, and then went, like an electric bulb switched off. He had captured that moment. But a soul? He had doubted it, but now, as his own death neared, he again questioned. He looked at his unsteady hands, they trembled like leaves in a gentle spring breeze, hands that had brought flowers to life, and women to their finest moment of beauty.

"What?" She was shocked. The carriage rocked. "You want to burn them? Whatever for?"

"I don't really know. Although, no, I do. It could be my last chance. Salvation."

"Salvation?" Flora, puzzled. Their carriage lurched again as the train struggled on a tight curve. Wheels screeched hot metal on metal. Their doctor had warned the cancer could spread to his brain. Bring on madness. She was used to his moods, but she had been warned to prepare for worse. Could it be so sudden? Was he mad?

He did not reply, appeared shrunken into his heavy coat, surely he was boiling hot, though he said he was chilled.

Again they fell into an awkward silence broken only by the metallic, repetitive beat of the train on the rail, the creak of their carriage, the distant pulse of the engine. She reached for his hand, but he moved away. The train whistle pierced the silence as they approached a lonely road. A man with his sheepdog stood by the crossing and waved as the train thundered by.

Sometimes she felt she hardly knew the man curled tight opposite. She had devoted her life to his genius, but there were times when he had shut her out. Many times. He hardly spoke of Africa. Made her a stranger. As children they had travelled with the Kennedy's out to the coast on summer weekends and while everyone played on the sands, Edward would sit alone, staring out to sea, claiming he was listening to the voices carried to him by wind and waves from countries far away. She would ask: 'What are they saying? Tell me'. He would turn and scowl. And silence.

Days ago, in their sitting room, during a rare moment of togetherness, windows wide to catch the vague breeze from the shrunken River Dee, they had read aloud to each other. The Strange Case of Dr Jekyll and Mr Hyde. Robert Louis Stevenson was one of her favourite authors. Edward had read the pas-

The Painter Of Souls

sage containing the letter from Jekyll to his friend, lawyer Gabriel Utterson. "You must suffer me to go my own dark way. I have brought on myself a punishment and a danger that I cannot name. If I am the chief of sinners, I am the chief of sufferers also. I could not think that this earth contained a place for sufferings and terrors so unmanning; and you can do but one thing, Flora, to lighten this destiny, and that is to respect my silence."

He had looked at her as he read that final line. He had substituted her name for that of Mr Utterson. And then he had fallen silent. Placed the book onto the small table at the side of his chair and sank back. Eyes closed. She had sipped from a glass of fresh lemonade, waiting for him to start again. But he did not move. She watched him. She knew.

Now as the train continued to descend, picking up speed, she realised he was wrestling with something he wanted to say.

Finally, without looking at her, his gaze far off: "I have thought long, dear sister, in all seriousness about what should happen. And in this I am serious, deadly serious. I would ask that you burn all my paintings that are left, my sketch books, my letters, the whole damned lot. Well, the paintings that might sell, sell them. But not the women, they must burn. My diaries, unread. They must be unread."

She moved forward, to interrupt.

"No, Flora, please, I want you to promise that you will burn it all. I want nothing left of me. Nothing. Build a bonfire, get rid of it all. It's my wish. I would do it myself, but I fear I just don't have the strength, neither of body or mind. You must promise me. A solemn promise."

"Edward, you know I would do anything for you. Have done anything for you. But to destroy everything, it's impossible. I couldn't. It would be like destroying you. Everything about you. Why?"

He had always been intensely private. Refusing to speak about some of his pictures. His diaries and correspondence locked in his safe. Secretive, not sly. Irrational, yes. Charming one moment, hurtful the next. They had all got used to him. Had put it down to his artistic temperament. But this?

"I could explain, but I can't. I won't. It is my wish. You might think it mad, that I'm mad, but I'm not. I know it puts a heavy burden on you, but it all needs to go. Every vestige of me. Here and Casa Sul Lago. Send a letter. Tell them to burn all that's mine. In fact I'll write when we get home."

"No." She was sharp. He turned from the window to her. "Let me think about this, Edward.

Let me think."

"It's not a request I'm making. Not a choice I'm giving. It has to happen and I'm entrusting you to do it. That's final."

"I understand, Edward. But I need to think. Please." She put her hand up to silence him. He shrank deeper into his coat. So often she had bitterly chastised herself for not doing more to stop him going out to Africa. Her beloved, talented brother had sailed away, and a haunted man had returned. She could not remember when she had last heard him laugh.

"Flora." Calm now, he broke into the silence. "There's a darkness greater than night at the edge of my vision. Always there. And it's spreading. I can barely see."

She reached across to take his hand. He tried to pull away, but she held him. He looked away, His long stare into nothingness.

"Edward." He turned to her, tears on his sunken cheek.

CHAPTER 26

JOHN, on lookout from the passenger seat, missed the sharp right turn on the first pass, blaming the lowering sun and deepening dusk. Jane managed to swing round at a tight roundabout near Malcesine's small bus station and headed back along the SR249 to the Strada Panoramica, a narrow lane that led steeply up from the main road, away from the lake, towards the huge mass of Mount Baldo. A view back over the medieval town and lake opening as they climbed between high garden walls, waving thank you to the few pedestrians who moved to the side to let them pass.

Suddenly they spotted a sign. Pulled into the driveway. Hotel Casa Oliva. A stunning building of glass, stone and chrome set into olive groves and green gardens with panoramic views across the jumbled red tiled roofs and narrow cobbled lanes of Malcesine towards Castle Scaligero, high on a lakeside promontory, its mighty, square tower turning from white to pink in the late sun. The cobalt blue of Lake Garda was slipping to black as night fell across distant jagged mountains.

"Think we've dropped on here." Jane used the key fob to lock the car. "We'll take the luggage up after we've checked in. John?" He had already walked across to a grove of olive trees, easing his back. He turned to Jane: "Paradise."

The hotel looked immaculate, with an outdoor swimming pool across the front, glass canopies, balconies catching the late sun. Lights were flickering on. A tall, dark, lean man in narrow black trousers and blinding white shirt who could only be Italian came from the entrance, arm outstretched.

"Mr and Mrs Armstrong? Welcome. My name is Paolo and let me settle you in, as you say."

"Please, Jane and John." She extended her hand and they shook. John was now by the pool, breathing deep air scented by rosemary. "John!"

They walked through to the reception area, all pale beech, dark glass, blue lights and chromium. Spotless.

"Have you been with us before? Your first time Malcesine?"

Jane glanced across at John who was now inspecting a large black and white poster showing sailing boats on the lake.

"No and no," She said. There was the soft smell of citrus. Silent luxury. "Our first time. It all looks quite stunning. Beautiful. Your English is very good."

"English, French, German. All needed. And I lived in York for some months where my brother has a restaurant. You know York?"

"A little. We are a good few miles from there in Scotland."

"Edinburgh. Been there. Grand city. Well, welcome to Malcesine and Casa Oliva. I will show you to your room and arrange a bottle of prosecco and light snacks in the lounge area just behind you once you're settled. Half an hour? What brings you? It's fairly early in the year for English."

"We're researching an artist called Broughton, Edward Broughton. We believe he had a home here for holidays many years ago."

"Many artists do come here."

"I'm not surprised it's spectacular. Beautiful."

"But Edward Broughton. Not a name. How long?"

"About 100 years."

"Phew. Beyond me. Not even, as you say, a twinkle in my father's eyes. Yes?"

John joined them. "We think he had a house

by the lakeside, perhaps with friends. But that's really all we know."

"I will ask mia madre. My mother. She is Malcesine born and may know something. You will be looking for somewhere to eat tonight? My sister Patrizia has a restaurant on the waterfront and she is open tonight. I can phone for you. 8pm? It's very good. Ten minutes walk away. Here is a map and there" - he marked with a blue pen - "is her restaurant. Her English not bad too. But first, your room. Let me help with luggage."

They had slept heavily after eating at Patrizia's lovely restaurant. Both had agreed they did not fancy breakfast after such a meal, but when they stepped into the dining room the following morning they were met by the smell of fresh bread and rich coffee. A cold glass of prosecco awakened an appetite and they moved to plunder the buffet of fresh breads, jams, cheeses, cold meats, cereals, fresh fruit and unlimited coffee and tea.

"I didn't think I would manage anything after last night. That meal was superb. The seafood risotto was the best ever. I'm going to be piling on the pounds." Jane opted for fresh fruit, breads and cheese, thick yoghurt and a deep golden honey.

Paolo had been good to his word and last

night they had arrived at his sister's restaurant in time to be warmly greeted by her.

An outside table lakeside had been reserved, looking over a small harbour where a board showed boat cruises departed every half hour during the day. They declined the offer of lap blankets, feeling it was a mild evening with hardly a breath of wind, the stars bright in the sky. To their side stood an old, faded house, which had once been grand but now looked as if it would crumble and fall into the lake at any moment. Its walls, presumably once pale yellow, were dirty cream, the rendering cracked, crazed and missing in parts revealing soft red brick. Once handsome wrought iron balconies, some with broken railings, extended over the top three stories. The whole place hung precariously over the water. On the very top balcony sat an elderly woman, silver haired and dressed in black, quietly watching the diners below. Across the water, on the far lakeside, lights in homes and restaurants flickered yellow.

Their waiter appeared. Saw them gazing across the lake. "Away to your right, those lights are Limone. My home. You must visit. A good place of interest. Are you ready to order?"

The only sound was the soft lapping of water and the hush of conversation from other

The Painter Of Souls

diners. They ate too well, walked slowly back to their hotel, promising not to eat again for twenty four hours, but here they were, in the plush dining room.

"I spoke last night with numero people and no-one remembers an artist of the name Broughton. Do you mind?" Paolo indicated a chair and lifted it to their breakfast table. He sat. "There have been and still are lots of artists. And some do not mix so we don't always get to know them. Some also have places away and come here to paint and draw because our Malcesine is the finest place. Have you any more information?"

John put down his coffee. "Your sister's restaurant was superb. Or should I say 'Superbo'? As for Mr Broughton we know very little. He was a very private man. He may have come here with his sister, Flora. And he may have had his housekeeper with him and perhaps her daughter. His sister and housekeeper may have been known here because they would have done the shopping. Perhaps."

"His sister. She was?"

"Flora. Flora Broughton. But she died many years ago. He died ninety years ago or so. He was quite young."

"Even so, I will ask. And the housekeeper? Is there a name?" He turned to Jane.

She hurriedly swallowed a piece of fresh

pineapple, making her cough. "Excuse me. She was a Mrs Puddle. Her name was Mary. But she was elderly and would have died a long time ago. Her daughter was called Dora and she would have been a teenager at the time they were here. So she is also unlikely to be alive now. She would be over a hundred. But, we think, but aren't sure, that Dora also had a baby, a daughter. Although she would have been very young to be a mother. We couldn't find her daughter's name, though it was common to pass on names so, if she did have a baby girl, she could have been Mary. All a little confusing, I know. So it was Mary Puddle, her daughter Dora Puddle and her daughter, perhaps Mary."

"And how old would this last Puddle be now, do you think?"

Jane reached for a glass of clear, cool water. "Very. Perhaps ninety. Or more. We don't expect to find anything, really. It's more an excuse for a holiday. But, you never know."

"Novanta! Very old. I will ask. Today you are going anywhere special?"

"Thank you. We thought we'd explore the town. We saw very little of it yesterday and we have travelled so much in the car. John, are you ready?"

They walked out into warm sunshine and on through the olive grove, again that smell

The Painter Of Souls

of rosemary, to a narrow lane leading down to the town. At the bottom they crossed Via Gardesana to where a shuttered, crumbling villa stood behind overgrown shrubs and high, spiked rusting railings. Red tiles had slipped to expose the wooden bones of the roof.

"Now there's a renovation project for you, John." The air was still and warm, suffused with the aroma of baking. The road quiet. They peered through rusted iron gates.

John pushed at the gates. A chain and padlock held them secure. "Some project. Somebody must own it. But they've just let it go to ruin. Scandalous. The other side must look clear out over the lake. What a waste. I wonder who owns it. Our new friend at the hotel might know. Perhaps our man Broughton lived here."

"You aren't serious? I mean the place is a wreck. But Broughton? That would be more than a coincidence."

"We passed a very nice looking cake and coffee shop when we walked down to the restaurant last night. Reckon I can find it again." He set off across the paved square by the Town Hall.

"John, you've only just had breakfast." She patted his stomach. "That's getting a little large of late."

They headed back to the hotel late afternoon, tired, full of the history of Malcesine and coffee and pastries. But of Edward Broughton? Nothing. The day had grown very warm and they were keen for a shower and rest before heading out to eat. Malcesine had many fine looking restaurants. They reckoned they could stay a month and not eat in the same one twice; and from the looks of them, not have a single poor meal.

Immaculate Paolo was in reception dealing with a middle aged couple, who sounded German, John and Jane smiled and waved as they strolled passed.

"No. No." Paolo excused himself to the German couple. He called across to John and Jane. "Please wait. I have news."

They stopped dead. Turned. Paolo smiled, held up a finger. "One momento." They took seats at a gleaming glass table where stylish magazines had been carefully fanned out. Jane picked up an English magazine with her favourite gardener Carol Klein on the cover.

"News?" Jane looked across at John, a puzzled expression. He laughed. "He's probably booked us in at another restaurant run by a sister or brother. Which, if it's anything like last night, is more than fine by me. And you?"

"Perfectly fine."

The glass door swished open automatically as the German couple made their way outside, presumably to collect their suitcases, and Paolo came out from reception. "They were asking for directions to my brother's bakery. I have time. Can I get you a coffee? Cold drink?"

John held up his hands in surrender. Jane asked for a fruit juice, with ice.

He placed her glass on a paper mat and drew up his own chair. "Do you speak Italian at all?"

John explained they could get by in shops and restaurants. And they had a translator downloaded on the phone.

"Pozzanghera?" Paolo raised his eyebrows in question.

"Sorry," John smiled at him, turned to Jane "Pozzanghera?" She shook her head.

"Pozzanghera. It's an Italian word. Not one I expect you to know. But an interesting one for you. Just as your name last night Puddle meant nothing to me. A new word."

"Really? In what way?" Jane. Puzzled.

There was a long silence. Paolo was obviously enjoying the word game. He beamed.

"Pozzanghera translates as a pool with soil, err, you would say, what, mud. A muddy pool. Or as you would say a puddle. The English puddle."

Jane put down her drink. John leaned forward. "And?"

"Well, here we would have pozzanghera in the road after rain. You have puddles. A new word for me. There is a lady here in Malcesine, a Miss Pozzanghera. You would say Miss Puddle. And she is very old. You would say ancient. My mother and my sister, Patrizia, the sister you met last night, they know her well. She is not hearing too well, but Patrizia says she will help."

"An English woman?"

"I am not sure. She has lived here as long as I know. I'm sorry, I should have asked. I will ring Patrizia. One moment." He returned to his reception desk.

Jane took hold of John's hand. "This is too good to be true. Surely it can't be."

John exhaled long and hard. "Bloody hell. If there's one thing being a policeman taught me it's never be surprised at…." He didn't finish. Paolo called across. "Is six good for you? There's a table free and afterwards Patrizia can take you to Miss Pozzanghera. She'll see to it. Yes, she says she's English, or was."

"John, don't build up your hopes."

They were greeted warmly by their waiter

from the evening before and shown to the same table, but neither had an appetite. Both silent, unable to express their hopes, expecting disappointment. Patrizia was not there to greet them and had left word they should be welcomed with wine on the house.

The restaurant was heavy with the smell of tomatoes and herbs. Rosemary and basil hung in the still air as evening gathered itself turning the mountains across the lake a darker shade of purple, almost black. They passed on starters and dawdled over their pasta.

Finally, Patrizia came across to their table.

"I am sorry I missed you. A late emergency with my youngest. She is six. You enjoyed the meal?"

John stood to thank her. "It was very good. And thank you so much for the wine. But, Miss Puddle, or should it be Miss Pozzanghera?"

"I have seen her. She is happy to meet. She's a little deaf and so please speak slow and loud. The door there is open. Go on up. Two heights, stairs, whatever."

John and Jane turned to the shabby building dipping into the lake they had noticed last night. Patrizia pointed up. "Miss Pozzanghera." They followed her gaze to the balcony where the elderly woman, clad in black, had sat last night looking out across the lake and occasionally glancing down at diners. She was there now, in the yellow light spilling from the room behind her, and raised a hand to them.

The ancient door with its flaking paint led them into a lit corridor lined to waist height with art nouveau tiles in electric blue and acid green. An open door on their right showed a large square room becoming dark with shadow, the black lake beyond its far window. They could smell lavender. A stair lift had been installed on a staircase and they climbed to the first floor landing, surprisingly long and wide, where electric lights without shades revealed a ceiling plastered with intricate patterns, the walls covered with a warm red paper and paintings of what looked to be Malcesine and other lakeside scenes. Here, off this landing, all the doors of a heavy, dark, polished wood with brass fittings, were closed.

Jane turned to John. In a hushed voice: "It's incredible in here. Fabulous. You'd never guess from the outside. Never. And anyone could have walked in."

"I suspect the door was left open and the lights on to spare the old lady the difficulty of getting down to let us in. You don't think these paintings could be by Broughton?" He stood in front of one of lemon groves.

Jane joined him. "They look different to his work we saw back home. Watercolours and sketches. We shouldn't get ahead of ourselves, John."

"True. Patrizia said the second height. I assume she meant to go up one more. There's no-one here. All very odd."

They climbed the stairs, again lined with paintings, to the next landing where Miss Pozzanghera was there to greet them, slightly bent under the weight of a heavy shawl around her shoulders. Bright eyes. A smile.

"Please come through." Her English had an Italian accent. She led them into a cosy snug. "Patrizia said you have travelled from England and are staying with her brother. She is a very kind woman and helps me a lot." John moved to help her sit in an old, winged chair. "Thank you, but I'm fine and can manage. But, thank you."

Jane walked across to the open windows. "It's very kind of you to see us. We've actually come from Scotland. And yes, Patrizia has been very good to us, too. She seems to be a lovely lady. I'm Jane and this is my husband John." She looked down on the diners below, could smell seafood and hear hushed voices.

Despite the warm evening, a two bar electric fire glowed red in a brightly tiled hearth enclosed by a delicately carved wooden fire surround with a polished brass canopy. It looked to Jane to be a classic piece of Arts and Craft work. Books lined the walls. A settee and more winged chairs around a coffee table with glasses of cut crystal and a carafe of red wine. Large windows opened onto the balcony letting the distant chatter and clatter from Patrizia's restaurant below. And that aroma.

"Please sit and pour us all a glass of wine. How can I help you young people?" They took the settee opposite.

Jane poured and John turned to Miss Pozzanghera. Loud and deliberate. She leaned forward, towards him. "We came to Malcesine hoping to find out more about an artist called Edward Broughton. We believe he may have had a house here. He was Scottish."

"And how do you think I can help?" She sat back. Sipped the wine. Her eyes never left his.

"We know very little about him. But we believe he had a housekeeper called Puddle and we wondered if you had any connection." She did not change her expression. "We know it was many years ago."

"And if I said 'No'?"

"Then it would be a grave disappointment, but not a surprise." He laughed. He had interviewed hundreds, if not thousands of people, some very, and had not felt so nervous. Was he losing his touch?

"Why would you want to know about this man? This Edward Broughton?"

"Oh, that's a long story." John knew to be cautious. She knew of him, he was sure. "I was a policeman in Dumfries and was investigating an incident and Mr Broughton's name and work came up. Remarkably, for someone who was apparently so famous in his lifetime, we could find very little about him. It made me curious. And I came with my wife to see if we could find out any more. I'm retired. Jane was a teacher and we've developed a bit of a passion for him. His work is remarkable. Well, the little we've seen of it."

"I see. And my name you thought might be a connection."

"Yes. We wondered if there could be a connection. Although we know it's highly unlikely you knew him. It's so long ago."

"That is true and I'm afraid I never did meet an artist called Edward Broughton. Are you trying to get his pictures? Make money from this?"

John replied: "Not at all. Money has absolutely nothing to do with it. We only wanted to find out more about Mr Broughton and his life and work. He's an artist, an important one, who is in danger of being completely forgotten. There's a mystery about him we would like to try to solve."

"A mystery? Indeed. I'm afraid that as well as never meeting him, I have to confess I also never knew him. I can honestly say I never knew him, nor met him."

John and Jane shrank back. Together: "Never."

She put down her wine and continued: "I'm sorry. Though, yes, I have sat many nights, many years on my balcony, watching people come and go, listening to their conversations in Patrizia's restaurant below and wondered always if anyone would ever look up here and know.

"You see, I have lived in Malcesine almost all my life. My mother Dora was Scottish and we came here when I was young, well a lot younger than I am now, so I speak English and Italian. She and then myself worked in the restaurant below, more to fill our time than, well, anyway. This was a long time before Patrizia. I was engaged to a lovely Italian man who died in the Second War, a man from here. His parents, he was their only child and my only true love, owned the Hotel Touring and when they died it fell into ruin. You probably saw it as you walked here, at the bottom of the lane from Casa Oliva. Such a shame. But Malcesine is my home. Here."

"So, Edward Broughton, you never knew him."

"No, I never knew him. I have mixed feelings about that. Even now. You see Edward Broughton was my father. He died before I was born."

"But your mother…"

"My mother was fifteen when she became pregnant. Edward Broughton died and…."

Jane interrupted: "His work and everything was all destroyed so you have nothing to remember him by. Nothing to know him by."

"No. And everything was passed to his dear sister and as you say his instructions were explicit. Burn it all. So terrible. But she didn't. She couldn't. She was devoted to her brother, even though she knew. She must have known. She passed it all to my mother who had cared for her during her last years. They were painful and difficult years for Miss Broughton. Flora. Very painful. She asked my mother to destroy it all and…." She paused.

Restaurant chatter and lake water slapping against the house wall drifted though the warm air. A glass shattered, somewhere below. The old lady sipped her wine. Studied the couple opposite.

"Instead we gave up the house in Kirkcudbright and we brought everything here. Flora had already moved most of the paintings here. Safely out of the way. I've waited a long time for someone to come. Oh, I knew someone would, I knew it, and so I've had a long time to consider what I should do."

John leaned in towards her. "So his diaries, his sketch books, his work. They survive?"

"Some of his paintings we sold. We needed to live. There is a dealer in Verona who has been a very good friend. Very discrete."

John: "So, are those his paintings here? We have seen his paintings back in Scotland. Magnificent."

"No, no, the ones on the stairs and landing are mainly by me, some by my mother. Not accomplished. And by other artists who stayed here mainly as friends of Miss Broughton, not my father. No, my father's work is in the rooms below. They may be, as you say, magnificent, but, well there was a price paid for some of them, a terrible price, as you will see."

She drifted away. John and Jane exchanged questioning looks. Moments passed. Had she gone to sleep? Suddenly she sat forward. Said something in Italian. Apologised.

"Sorry, English. I think I was saying that I have often wondered what I should do. Now I am old. No, no, very old, and there's no other family. We don't need to hide the truth away.

Not any longer. But not now. I need to think a little longer."

Jane broke the silence. "You must take your time. We wouldn't want you to do anything you may regret." John nudged her knee. She gave him a warning look and turned back to Miss Pozzanghera.

"Perhaps you could return tomorrow, if it's not too much trouble. Around mid-afternoon. I would like Patrizia to be here."

"Of course," John. "But could I just ask? In Edinburgh we saw a superb painting, full size, of a beautiful woman. Stunning. We were told it was the only known one, but there could be more. Do you know if…"

"There are seven here. The diaries tell the terrible story of each one. But tomorrow. Oh, and there is my one strict condition that no-one should make money from this. It will be my one strict condition. I insist. If it's decided to exhibit his work and keep his diaries and the rest then so be it." She sat back. "Perhaps after all this they'll be burned anyway. Perhaps they should be."

Patrizia knocked and entered. "Is everything good?"

Jane stood, turned to her. "We're just leaving. Thank you so much for your help." She looked back at Miss Pozzanghera. "Tomorrow?" But the lady appeared to be asleep.

"Please, this way." Patrizia led them through the corridors and out into the flavoured night air. "Tomorrow will be fine. I'm sure."

POSTSCRIPT

A STINGING hot breeze moved across the parkland, searing their bare arms, despite the lateness of the evening. They followed a blood-red path which cut an arrow-straight line through the carefully cropped, surprisingly green lawns towards a startling white obelisk rising over 100 feet into the blue African sky. At its base, cast in bronze, a pair of women cradled a skeletal, limp child. A low stone wall, turning gold in the late sun, embraced the monument. Beyond the wall, young trees lined the crest of a hill and rustled into the silence like gentle sea water swishing and sucking on a pebble beach. This was a long way from any ocean. Hundreds of miles.

"I always thought in my old job that some people were simply born evil and that explained why they did what they did." John Armstrong drank from bottled water. At his side, Jane held an umbrella against the sun, welcoming the thin shade. She had heard this conversation he had largely with himself numerous times in the last weeks. They continued walking towards the memorial, ever so slowly. They were the only ones.

"And the internet has certainly demonstrated just how evil some people can be. And how many are out there. But Broughton? I believe we all have the capacity to kill. Do or die. Kill or be killed. For most of us it remains deeply hidden. But our friend Mr Broughton shows how easily it can be out. I suppose today it would be put down to post traumatic stress disorder. But, by Christ, he's an extreme example. God, it's bloody hot."

John Armstrong, squinted into the sun as it set over Bloemfontein and the memorial to the women and children who had died in concentration camps set up by the British during the Boer War. Many more had died on death trains transporting them to a so-called new life, but going no further than the camp gates. The terminus. The end.

"Not everyone, John. Emily Hobhouse's ashes are buried here, at the base. Some people, a few, weren't corrupted by it. They tried to stop it. They tried to help."

"They, well, we, tried to wipe out an entire race of people. No better than the Nazis. No better. It's no wonder that Edward Broughton went mad amid that lot. And it's no wonder our own history has tried to cover all this up. I knew nothing about it."

"Nor I." They arrived at the base of the obelisk. Hugged.

In the weeks since leaving Malcesine and on their return home they had researched the Second Boer War.

In eighteen months of war, 26,370 women and children died from disease and starvation in the concentration camps. Of them, 24,000 were children under 16. Dying at the rate of 50 a day. Deliberately starved to death.

At least 20,000 black people had also died in special camps set up for them and even now much less has been written about them.

Another 6,000 Boer men and boys died trying to defend their homeland from the British.

Six weeks ago they had returned to Miss Pozzanghera's house for the 'tomorrow' meeting with Patrizia. Rooms opened for what seemed the first time in many years. In one, a library-cum-study, they found a complete archive of diaries, notes and sketch books. Some showing the detailed, stage by stage dissection of human bodies. All female. Carefully described. Beautifully illustrated.

Others held dozens of sketches and watercolours by Edward Broughton.

In what had been the lounge during the Broughton's life in Italy, along three walls clad in red damask paper, hung seven life-size, full-length paintings of women framed in gold. Each was standing, and each had the same glow on their faces revealed when dusty, heavy curtains had been drawn back to allow in silver light from the lake. Stunning, but horrifying. Each similar to the one in Edinburgh's National Gallery. All rich with symbolism.

It was hard to understand how Flora had lived with it all. Mrs Puddle had explained that the paintings of the women had been brought across from Scotland after Edward Broughton had died. One painting had gone missing and that was the one hanging now in the Scottish National Gallery. The remainder were hung, the room locked and never re-opened during Flora's remaining years. But, even so.

The diaries revealed the names of the women, or at least the names given to Edward Broughton when he picked them up from the streets of Glasgow.

They had contacted Frank and had met at a restaurant in Dumfries to discuss their findings. Later they brought in journalist Tony Jewson who had first enquired about the bone found in Kirkcudbright after the earthquake which now felt a lifetime ago. John had always felt some guilt about the way he had misled Jewson. The journalist had agreed not to publish anything until everyone agreed.

Jewson's research found newspaper clippings about the murders which became known as the Glasgow Ripper Killings. One from the The Glasgow Herald featured an interview with a retiring city detective in 1920 lamenting they had never solved the mystery of Glasgow's missing prostitutes. He had disputed the Ripper tag, saying none of the women had been found, so they were very much unlike the London Ripper who left mutilated corpses as a mark of his trade. But he suspected the women had been murdered and that one man was responsible, though not a clue as to the identity of the culprit.

A week ago, John, Jane, Frank and Tony Jewson had travelled to Malcesine for the funeral of Mary Pozzanghera. It marked the end of one life, and the beginning of the truth about the life of Edward Broughton.

John and Jane continued their travels on to South Africa. Yesterday, they had driven south on the N1 from Johannesburg past Kroonstad and Winburg to Bloemfontein, City of Roses.

On the car radio they had been surprised to hear Teal's re-released hit from the 1970's. John had finally given permission for the band's music to be used and the track had become an instant hit after featuring in a TV advertising campaign for a famous brand of jeans.

Jane had turned to him. "Don't you think the drummer's crap?"

AUTHOR'S NOTE

THE main characters in this story are all mostly fictional. Edward Broughton did not exist. Some, such as Winston Churchill and Arthur Conan Doyle, obviously did and were involved in the Boer War, but their roles in this book are fiction.

One character is real, even though she is largely forgotten, perhaps deliberately forgotten by the Establishment. These are the words of campaigner Emily Hobhouse on her experiences during the Boer War:

"Some people in town still assert that the camp is a haven of bliss. I was at the camp to-day, and just in one little corner this is the sort of thing I found. The nurse, underfed and overworked, just sinking on to her bed, hardly able to hold herself up, after coping with some thirty typhoid and other patients, with only the untrained help of two Boer girls.

"Next tent, a six months' baby gasping its life out on its mother's knee. Two or three others drooping sick in that tent. Next, a girl of twenty-one lay dying on a stretcher. The father, a big, gentle Boer kneeling beside her; while, next tent, his wife was watching a child of six, also dying, and one of about five drooping. Already this couple had lost three children in the hospital and so would not let these go, though I begged hard to take them out of the hot tent. I can't describe what it is to see these children lying about in a state of collapse. It's just exactly like faded flowers thrown away. And one has to stand and look on at such misery, and be able to do almost nothing.

"It was a splendid child and it dwindled to skin and bone. The baby had got so weak it was past recovery. We tried what we could but today it died. It was only three months but such a sweet little thing it was still alive this morning; when I called in the afternoon they beckoned me in to see the tiny thing laid out, with a white flower in its wee hand. To me it seemed a "murdered innocent". And an hour or two after another child died. Another child had died in the night, and I found all three little corpses being photographed for the absent fathers to see some day. Two little wee white coffins at the gate waiting, and a third wanted. I was glad to see them, for atSpringfontein, a young woman had to be buried in a sack, and it hurt their feelings woefully.

"It is such a curious position, hollow and rotten to the heart's core, to have made all over the State large uncomfortable communities of people whom you call refugeesand say you are protecting, but who call themselves prisoners of war, compulsorily detained, and detesting your protection. They are tired of being told by officers that they are refugees under "the kind and beneficient protection of the British". In most cases there is no pretence that there was treachery, or ammunition concealed, or food given or anything. It was just that an order was given to empty the country.

"My work in the concentration camps in South Africa made almost all my people look down upon me with scorn and derision. The press abused me, branded me a rebel, a liar, an enemy of my people, called me hysterical and even worse. One or two newspapers, for example the Manchester Guardian, tried to defend me, but it was an unequal struggle with the result that the mass of the people was brought under an impression about me that was entirely false. I was ostracized. When my name was mentioned, people turned their backs on me. This has now continued for many years and I had to forfeit many a friend of my youth."

When Emily Hobhouse travelled back to

South Africa, having returned to the UK to deliver her report to the Government on conditions in the camps, she was refused permission to land and de-ported. She died in 1926 largely ignored in the UK – a national heroine in South Africa.

Oh, and Lizzie Van Zyl, if you remember her, and few do, the seven-year-old daughter of a Boer who refused to surrender? She too was a real person, until she was deliberately starved to death in the Bloemfontein murder camp.

END